P9-DLZ-118

BAD NEWS

BY

pseudonymous bosch

THE BAD BOOKS

Bad Magic

Bad Luck

Bad News

THE SECRET SERIES

The Name of This Book Is Secret

If You're Reading This, It's Too Late

This Book Is Not Good for You

This Isn't What It Looks Like

You Have to Stop This

Write This Book: A Do-It-Yourself Mystery

pseudonymous bosch

Illustrations by Juan Manuel Moreno

LITTLE, BROWN AND COMPANY
New York Boston

This book is a work of fiction. Names, characters, places, and incidents are the product of the author's imagination or are used fictitiously. Any resemblance to actual events, locales, or persons, living or dead, is coincidental. *Any resemblance to actual dragons is a different story—a story that the author of this book would very much like to hear.*

Little, Brown and Company
Hachette Book Group
1290 Avenue of the Americas, New York, NY 10104
Visit us at lb-kids.com

First Edition: March 2017

Little, Brown and Company is a division of Hachette Book Group, Inc. The Little, Brown name and logo are trademarks of Hachette Book Group, Inc.

The publisher is not responsible for websites (or their content) that are not owned by the publisher.

ISBNs: 978-0-316-32048-1 (hardcover), 978-0-316-32049-8 (ebook)

Printed in the United States of America

LSC-C

10 9 8 7 6 5 4 3 2 1

For Asa and Cyrus
(eventually)

From *Secrets of the Occulta Draco; or, The Memoirs of a Dragon Tamer*

When people meet a Dragon Tamer, they ask many irritating questions, but the most irritating of all is: *What is it like to ride a dragon—is it like riding a horse?*

Usually, my answer is to stare at my questioners until they nervously excuse themselves and go away. (Word of advice: Do not try this at the palace.) But if I am feeling charitable, I may say something like this:

"No, riding a dragon is nothing like riding a horse. Unless the horse is a wild horse, galloping as fast as the wind. And you are riding without saddle or reins, your seat no more comfortable than a cactus. And there is every reason to believe that you are about to fall off and plummet to an early and painful death. Then, yes, in that case, riding a horse might be a little like riding a dragon. But even then, you'd have the horse's mane to hold on to. Dragons do not have manes. Some have horns, true, but I dare you to hold on to a dragon's horn. By which I mean never hold on to a dragon's horn. They don't like it."

Here I pause, allowing my audience to imagine what a dragon might do to them if they dare touch the dragon's horn. Then I continue in a mocking tone:

"*If not a horse, then what?* you ask. *A rhinoceros has a horn. Perhaps a dragon is a flying rhinoceros?* Here's a test: Would you be afraid to make the comparison in front of a dragon? If the answer is yes, better to stay silent."

Now my voice turns to a growl. "In other words, to heck with horses! It is an insult to dragons. A dragon is not a mindless animal—a dragon's mind is wiser and impossibly more complex than yours."

When I get to this last bit, I narrow my eyes into my most intimidating glare, which, if I may say so, is very intimidating indeed.

"You really want to know what riding a dragon is like? First of all, you don't ride a dragon; the dragon rides you. As soon as you climb onto a dragon's back, you let go of the idea that you are in control. The dragon is the pilot; you are a passenger—no, a barely tolerated stowaway.

"A dragon is so strong that even the slightest flap of a wing will raise a wind forceful enough to throw you back to the dragon's tail. When the dragon flies, your face feels as though it is being torn apart. Your hair whips behind you, or is shorn from your head altogether. Clouds blur as you pass them. Birds seem to rocket backward, so much faster are you going than they.

"Exhilarating? Certainly. If you are able to hold on. Oh, did I say you had to let go when you ride a dragon? It was a metaphor, a figure of speech, you nitwit."

Here I've been known to jab my finger into someone's chest. (Note: This also is not a good thing to try at the palace.)

"You can't *really* let go, obviously. You have to hug the dragon's mighty neck, dig your nails into the dragon's scaly skin, squeeze your legs into the dragon's massive sides. And don't let go for a single second. Or else.

"And when, as sometimes happens, the dragon makes one of its fabled leaps, then it is not only the dragon you must hold on to, but also your head. As the old ones tell us, *Let not a dragon leap when you're astride, lest you lose your mind on the other side.*"

That much of the saying is well known, and it is true that a dragon's leap is not for the faint of heart. But there is more, known only to the followers of the Occulta Draco. Of course, I do not repeat the rest to strangers, but to you, dear apprentice Dragon Tamer, I will impart the whole:

Let not a dragon leap when you're astride,
Lest you lose your mind on the other side.
Yet if you must this dizzy journey make,
Three things will keep you woozy but awake:
First, your enemy's sword will point the way.
Next, the shield you made will keep ghosts at bay.
Last, if you'd not return your brain half-dead,
Please, a helmet from home put on your head.

CHAPTER ONE

THE SECRET IN THE CRATER

There wasn't supposed to be a moon.

It was just a sliver, barely a crescent. Still, it cast more light than she would have liked. Even in her black clothes, her face smeared with soot, she stood out against the rocks that spilled down the sides of the giant crater.

Pausing in the shadow of a boulder, she pulled her night-vision goggles off her head—she wouldn't be needing them after all—and considered how best to move forward. In a few moments, she would reach the top of the ridge. And she had no idea what or whom she would find waiting for her. Rather, she had several ideas, none of them cause for optimism.

If only she'd gotten there two days earlier, she would have been making her ascent in perfect darkness, as planned. The problem was that instead of the anticipated four days to cross the Kalahari on foot, it had taken six. Or six nights, to be more precise. Traveling by night was cooler. Also safer.

Supposedly.

Of course, she'd met with her fair share of mishaps anyway, hadn't she? The scorpion that fell out of her hat. The herd of Cape buffalo that forced her to walk three miles out of her way. The "water hole" that was really a mud hole. (Luckily, she'd spent a good portion of her childhood reading about quicksand.)

And then there were the humans—nomadic San people. They couldn't believe she was traveling alone. No guide. No camel. No cell phone. Her cover story about being an ultra-marathoner did not convince them. Running a hundred miles in the hot desert *just because*? So instead she told them she was a student from the university, studying the effects of drought on local animal populations. This they could believe. Although they still had a big laugh over her experimental sweat-conserving jumpsuit. They were right about the jumpsuit; it made her so hot that she sweated out more water than she saved. (Her experiments with urine were another story. A story better left untold.*) In the end, she'd spent an entire eve-

---

* Note: The woman herself did not feel squeamish about the subject. It is this author who prefers not to go into the intricacies of how to preserve and treat urine in such a way as to make it potable. (And, yes, if you must know, *potable*

ning listening to their observations about the Namib Desert beetle—a fascinating creature, to be sure, but she lost precious time.**

Never mind. Survivalist rule number one: Don't dwell on what can't be fixed.

She felt around in a side pocket of her backpack, where she kept her energy bars—she'd packed a few as a special treat, despite the excessive sugar and nonbiodegradable packaging. There was only a half bar left.

"Well, you wanted to travel light," she muttered to herself, breaking the half in half.

She popped one piece into her mouth and then stowed the rest for later.

Hoisting her backpack onto her back, she resumed her climb.

She would just have to summit as fast as she could and hope to find cover on the other side.

She breathed a sigh of relief when she got to the top. There were no sentries pointing guns at her, just a

---

MEANS "DRINKABLE.") IN HER MOISTURE-CONSERVATION EFFORTS, OUR INTREPID DESERT CROSSER WAS INSPIRED, I BELIEVE, BY THE FAMOUS SCIENCE-FICTION NOVEL *DUNE*. HER JUMPSUIT BORE A DISTINCT RESEMBLANCE TO THE STILLSUITS WORN BY NATIVES OF *DUNE*'S DESERT PLANET, ARRAKIS. UNFORTUNATELY, HER SUIT DIDN'T WORK NEARLY AS WELL AS THE ORIGINAL FICTIONAL VERSIONS.

** THE NAMIB DESERT BEETLE IS NOTABLE FOR AN ODD BUT INGENIOUS ADAPTATION TO ITS ARID ENVIRONMENT. THE SHELL OF A NAMIB COLLECTS MOISTURE FROM THE AIR, WHICH THEN CONDENSES AND DRIPS INTO THE BEETLE'S MOUTH.

narrow plateau surrounded by jagged rocks. She was exposed for only a moment before she was able to crouch behind a ledge and look around. No sign of cameras or motion detectors, she noted. Maybe they assumed that nobody would be foolhardy enough to come up there.

Below her was the crater proper, a three-mile-wide bowl protected on all sides by walls of rock and miles of desert. An impressive sight, even in the dim light of the moon. What bribes or tricks the enemy had employed to lay hold of this vast natural fortress in the middle of nowhere she did not care to know. What concerned her was why they wanted it in the first place. They claimed in public documents to be building a "nature preserve and resort hotel," but there was very little nature to preserve. All life at this location had been destroyed by a meteorite thousands of years ago. As for a hotel, the crater would be nearly impossible for most tourists to reach.

Why, then, were they there? What nefarious activity required such an enormous and remote location?

She'd been trying to answer that question for months when she heard a rumor about a secret and very technologically advanced breeding program. The rumor sounded far-fetched, yes. But when it came to *them*, nothing was truly far-fetched. Her colleagues had urged caution, but she felt there was no choice: She had to investigate.

She put a scope to her eye and peered down into the distance. The satellite photos that she'd studied before her trip must have been older than she thought. Or else construction was proceeding very fast. Twinkling lights revealed at least three more buildings than she remembered. And she was nearly certain that the lake hadn't been there before. Not to mention all those trees. Tens of thousands of them, it looked like. Where are they getting the water? she wondered. Talk about environmental irresponsibility. It was as though they were trying to create their own tropical ecosystem in the middle of a desert.

She glanced at her watch. She had to get down there, survey the site, plant the hidden cameras and chemical-emissions sensors, and then climb out—all before daybreak. Less than three hours...

EEEYAHYRR! A terrible screech pierced the silence.

What on earth—?

She stood still for a moment, then heard it again. *EEEYAHYRR!* It was not a human cry; nor was it like any animal cry she'd ever heard. Nevertheless, it was a cry of distress—of that she was certain.

It sounded quite close, but she couldn't tell where it was coming from.

Cautiously, she made a circle, looking above and below and in the surrounding rocks. She saw no signs of life, not even a weed. Perhaps the creature was farther away than she thought.

She was on the verge of giving up the search when a new sound caught her attention. It was a softer, hissing sound this time. And it was coming from directly beneath her.

Suddenly very nervous, she turned on her flashlight.

And then she saw it. About four feet down. Stuck in a crevice. Its yellow eyes staring, unblinking, into the flashlight's beam.

It was about the size of a small dog or maybe a very large owl. And its wings and tail were twisted together so that it looked like nothing so much as a bat being attacked by a snake.

And yet there was no mistaking it for anything other than what it was.

She studied the creature in mute astonishment.

So the rumors were true; she had suspected as much, but it was another matter entirely to see the evidence in real life.

How could anything be at once so fierce and so fragile, so earthly and so unearthly?

EEEYAHYRR!

It screeched again, its mouth opening to reveal several rows of sharp teeth. She took a step backward.

She couldn't tell whether the screech was an angry warning or a desperate plea, but either way, the creature was likely very dangerous.

Moving slowly, she leaned in again. One of its wings was torn. There were almost certainly some broken bones.

It couldn't have been very old. It looked like it was still a baby.

Without assistance, it would probably die where it was. But how to help?

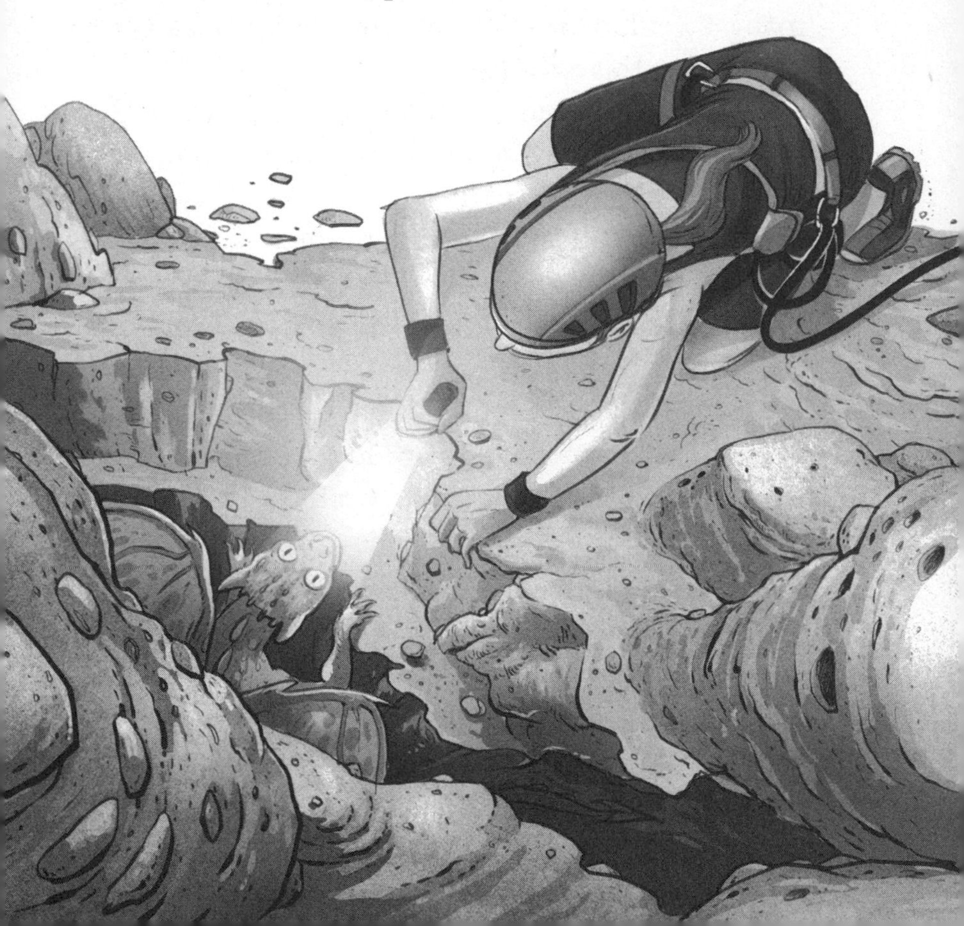

She had a first-aid kit, of course, but she wasn't sure whether human medical supplies would work on fairy-tale animals. Or even whether she could pull the creature out of the crevice without it scratching her eyes out.

She had to earn its trust. But there was hardly time for that.

"Are you hungry? No nut allergies, I hope," she whispered, reaching around to her backpack and pulling out the remaining bit of energy bar. "Normally, I wouldn't feed machine-made food to a wild animal, but this isn't really a normal situ—"

Her words were interrupted by a decidedly machine-made roar. She looked up to see a helicopter heading straight toward her.

She swore under her breath.

How could she have been so careless? In her concern for the injured creature, she'd forgotten to stay out of sight.

By now the helicopter was hovering low in front of her. It looked slick and new, like a helicopter one would expect to see ferrying executives to an office tower rather than patrolling a desert. Except, that is, for the extensive weaponry jutting out from either side. If it was a helicopter for executives, they were executives in a war zone.

She hesitated. The ledge where she'd taken cover before would hardly protect her from cannons like those. Maybe she should jump over the side of the crater and scramble down the rocks, hoping she could lose her pursuers. In her mind, she went over the supplies in her backpack. She had ropes and grappling hooks. Flares that might provide a moment's diversion...

No, it was too late. Only a magician could disappear fast enough. She had many skills; vanishing into thin air was not one of them.

Besides, if they shot at her and accidentally hit the baby dragon, she would never forgive herself.

The helicopter's floodlight hit her eyes, temporarily blinding her. The pilot's voice boomed over the sound of the spinning blades:

"Put your hands over your head and don't move."

Cornered, she did as ordered.

She thought about the various cover stories she'd used before. None seemed to explain why she was infiltrating their half-constructed nature preserve in the middle of the night, dressed like a ninja.

As her eyes adjusted to the light, the helicopter landed in front of her on the small plateau, blowing sand in all directions.

A woman leaned out of the passenger side, her platinum hair gleaming in the darkness.

"*Mon dieu.* Is that who I think it is?"

Her pale face registered only the slightest surprise.

"It's been ages, darling, but I would know those pointy ears anywhere. How kind of you to visit, Cassandra...."

Cass's pointy ears tingled in alarm at the sound of her name. It had been well over a decade since she last heard that chilling voice; and yet suddenly she felt as if she were a young girl again, forever caught in the clutches of Ms. Mauvais.

CHAPTER TWO

THE VIEW FROM NOSE PEAK

Although located on an island, and thus by definition surrounded by water, Clay's summer camp, Earth Ranch, was tucked inside a valley, with mountains separating it from the ocean on all sides. If you wanted a glimpse of the ocean, the closest vantage point was a rocky hill called Nose Peak in honor of the unique geological formation on top. Nose Peak was steep and slippery, and, strictly speaking, campers weren't supposed to climb it (or "peak the nose") without special permission. But it was an open secret that Clay made the twenty-minute climb every day at dawn, usually returning only after the sun had risen well into the sky.

This morning, like most mornings, he sat with his legs straddling the big rock proboscis, staring at the horizon. Price Island was home to a volcano, Mount Forge, which regularly belched smoke into the air and blanketed the island with a hazy layer of vog (volcanic smog). The volcano had been especially active lately. As a result, it was difficult for Clay to see very much.

Still, every so often, something would catch his eye—a dark cloud, a large seabird, a shadow on the ocean—and he would get to his feet, an expectant expression on his face, only to sit down again a moment later, evidently disappointed.

Nearby, a llama sat with his legs tucked underneath his body so that he looked almost like a second, smaller rock formation. The llama never moved

from this position, but whenever Clay stood, the llama would shake his head, as if disgusted by the behavior of his human companion.

"I know, Como, you think I'm totally loco," said Clay, after the llama had shaken his head especially vigorously. "But I swear, Ariella's coming back. *El dragon viene aqui.*"

The llama, whose full name was Como C. Llama and whose first language was Spanish, regarded Clay with undisguised skepticism.

"So what if it's been over a year—that's just like *uno minuto* for a dragon," continued Clay in his broken middle-school Spanish.

The llama snorted dismissively.

"*Es verdad,*" Clay insisted. "They have this whole other idea of time."

The llama yawned and nibbled on a stray wildflower.

"Admit it: You don't want Ariella to come back." Clay looked at Como, daring the llama to contradict him.

The llama looked back meaningfully.

"What?! Dragons don't eat llamas," Clay protested. "And, uh, okay, even if they do, Ariella knows you're *mi amigo*. Ariella would never eat you."

Como sniffed and turned away.

"Come on, bro. You know that's not what I meant. You probably taste awesome.... Oh, whatever. I'm not *hablo*-ing with you anymore."

An old book lay beside Clay, weighed down by a small rock. Covered with a tough, scaly hide that had yellowed with age, the book was called *Secrets of the Occulta Draco; or, The Memoirs of a Dragon Tamer.*

Sighing, Clay removed the rock; immediately, the book opened, then closed, then opened again, pages fluttering noisily. Before the book could fly away, Clay gripped it firmly, and the pages settled into place.

He'd read the whole book three times already, but there was one passage in particular that he kept going back to:

Let not a dragon leap when you're astride, lest you lose your mind on the other side.

What kind of leap? Just a jump, or something else? And what "other side"—the other side of what? The counselors at Earth Ranch spoke often of some mysterious and powerful Other Side—an Other Side with capital letters—by which, as far as Clay could make out, they meant the magical side of the world. A fourth, magical dimension. But it seemed doubtful that a guy who was writing more than four hundred years ago would be swallowing the same mystical hogwash as the counselors at Clay's hippie summer camp. And even if the two Other Sides were one and the same, what did it have to do with dragons?

Clay's reflections were interrupted by a loud spitting sound; Como was trying to get his attention.

Standing, and not looking particularly happy about it, the llama nodded toward the horizon.

Clay squinted. The wind had changed direction, blowing most of the vog away from this side of the island, and now the morning sun reflected dazzlingly on the water. The view was almost impossibly bright, but in the middle, directly below the sun, was a small dark spot. It was not much more than a dot, but the shape of wings was unmistakable. Far out over the ocean, something—something big—was flying toward them.

"No way!" Clay's heart thumped with excitement. "I mean, do you really think . . . ?"

Not responding, the llama sat down again, duty done.

With his hand to his forehead, Clay strained his eyes, waiting to see if the unknown flying object really was Ariella.

A moment later, he looked down, shoulders slumped. It wasn't a dragon; it was an airplane.

Figures, Clay thought bitterly.

The truth was, Clay had no real confidence he would ever see Ariella again, only a desperate hope. Sure, he'd rescued Ariella the previous summer when the dragon was chained inside a storage container and about to be shipped away like a circus animal. But the proud creature had made it clear that this brief episode did not mean they were friends in any sense that a mere human would understand. Afterward, Ariella had barely said good-bye, let alone anything about returning to Price Island. And yet, for a few precious minutes, Clay had been allowed to fly on the dragon's back—by far the best, most electrifying (and also most terrifying) experience of his life. Joined with the dragon, he'd felt at one with himself for the first time. He couldn't bear the thought of never having that experience again.

"Boo."

Clay looked over his shoulder. His friend Leira, who had an annoying talent for treading softly, had crept up behind him.

"Do you *always* have to do that?" Clay griped.

"Hmm. Let me see. . . ." Leira took off her cap and scratched her short red hair, pretending to ponder the question. "Yes."

She looked up at the sky. The airplane—a seaplane—was circling the island, getting ready to land in the shallow water. They could hear the whir of propellers in the distance.

"So I guess you figured out that Owen's on his way."

Clay nodded grumpily. "I thought he wasn't back for another three days."

Owen, the seaplane's pilot, ferried campers to and from the mainland, and he made biweekly trips to deliver supplies.

"I know, it's weird. You're supposed to go meet him."

"Me? Why?" said Clay, surprised.

Leira shrugged. "No idea. Buzz sent me to get you. . . . Well, not *me*, exactly. I just tagged along for fun."

She gestured behind her, where a small hive's worth of bees were hovering in the air. They spelled out these words:

CLAY TEEPEE
NOW

As Clay watched, the bees flew out of formation, making one big, buzzy, blurry cloud. Then they divided once more, forming three very emphatic exclamation marks:

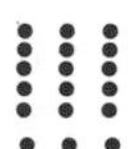

"Okay, okay, I'm coming—chill!" Clay shouted at them.

"Hey, can I ask you something?" he said to Leira as they started walking down the hill.

Leira smirked. "No, I won't be your girlfriend."

"Seriously . . ."

"What?"

"Do *you* think Ariella will ever come back?" He nodded toward Como, who was plodding along the trail ahead of them. "That guy thinks I'm crazy."

"I don't know, Mowgli. Some people might say it's crazy to talk to a llama."*

"Don't call me that. And you're not answering the question."

"What question? That reminds me. Missing anything?"

"Why, what did you take this time?" Clay asked suspiciously.

Leira, who was an incredibly skilled pickpocket and thief, frequently stole things from Clay—for sport. She smiled innocently. And held up the *Occulta Draco*.

"That book is, like, four hundred years old and maybe the only one in the world!" Clay complained, irate. "Do you know what Mr. B would do to me if anything happened to it?"

---

* Mowgli, as you may know, is the hero of *The Jungle Book*—a collection of stories written more than a hundred years ago by Rudyard Kipling and made famous in our time by a certain cartoon kingdom familiarly known as the Mouse House. Mowgli is a feral, i.e. wild, boy who grows up in the jungle, talking to animals. I'm sure your behavior is always perfectly civilized, but if you were ever to lapse—momentarily—into bad manners, you might find a stern adult asking if you were "raised by wolves"—a common Mowgli reference that wolves no doubt find very insulting.

"If it's so priceless, why'd you leave it on that rock?" said Leira, handing it over.

"Oh, I did?" said Clay, grimacing. "Sorry—"

"Or maybe I lifted it from your backpack." Leira grinned. "Can't remember."

Clay laughed. "Why am I friends with you . . . ?"

Ahead of them, two old garbage-pail lids with rope handles had been left leaning against a rock. Wordlessly, they placed the garbage-pail lids side by side and sat down on them.

"Ready?" asked Leira.

"You know it," said Clay. "Eat my volcanic dust."

Together, they pushed off and started sledding down the scree-covered slope, spinning and bouncing as they went, the llama trotting behind.

CHAPTER THREE

THE MEETING IN THE TEEPEE

Have you ever been called to the principal's office without knowing why? (Or perhaps knowing why but not knowing what your fate will be?) Clay, I am somewhat reluctant to report, had been called to the principal's office more than once. At Earth Ranch, the director's teepee was the closest thing to a principal's office; so it was with a familiar sense of dread that Clay landed at the bottom of Nose Peak.

As Clay handed over his garbage-lid sled for Leira to return to his cabin, she made him promise that he would tell her what the meeting with the director was about. "Maybe they're finally kicking you out!" she said brightly.

Then she ran off, the two sleds on her back clanking against each other.

What had he done wrong lately? Clay played

back the past few days in his head.... The previous morning, he got caught skipping out on weeding, but everybody was expected to skip once in a while, right? And then he was busted for putting chocolate chips in his oatmeal, but again, nobody could exist entirely on the camp diet of seeds and sprouts. The day before, he had skateboarded on top of the picnic tables—a more serious offense, no doubt. But serious enough to get him sent home? Not when everyone, including the counselors, had laughed and applauded. And anyway, Pablo, not Clay, had made the skateboard.

It seemed far likelier that an emergency of some sort had brought Owen back to the island. Had something happened to Clay's parents? Or to his brother? Yes, Clay decided, it had to be his brother. His brother the hypercautious hypochondriac.* Despite (or because of) his excessive efforts to stay safe, Max-Ernest had always been accident-prone. Images of hospital beds and funeral parlors swam around in Clay's mind.

The atmosphere at camp did nothing to reassure him.

Earth Ranch was built on the shores of Lava Lake,

---

* It goes without saying that I, er, rather, Max-Ernest, might not agree that he is a hypercautious hypochondriac. (He would more likely consider himself a judicious medical expert.) However, I have to say I like the alliteration.

a long, crescent-shaped lake that was normally a brilliant tropical turquoise; today, though, the surface was dark and moody, and swirling like an oil slick. At the far end of the lake, smoke rose in a steady stream from Mount Forge, roiling the sky with ominous gray clouds. Vast lava flows, black except where the edges burned orange, slowly advanced down the sides of the volcano.

Meanwhile, the camp's ever-changing but previously omnipresent rainbow kept flickering in and out, sometimes vanishing for minutes at a time, only to come back brighter than ever. According to the counselors, the rainbow acted as a sort of supernatural "barometer," measuring the level of magic in the island's atmosphere.* At the moment, this level appeared to be extremely unstable.

As Clay led Como into the barnyard, a random assortment of chickens and turkeys and goats and sheep crowded around Clay. Nudging him in the leg and other less comfortable places, they snorted and bleated and honked and squawked.

"Don't bust a gut, guys," said Clay. "I fed you already, remember?"

---

* A *BAROMETER* MEASURES ATMOSPHERIC PRESSURE, MUCH LIKE YOUR GRANDPA'S KNEE, WHICH SHOUTS "HEY, A STORM'S COMING!" EVERY TIME A STORM IS COMING. GRANDPA'S NOT KIDDING—OR NOT COMPLETELY. CHANGES IN ATMOSPHERIC PRESSURE AND AGING JOINTS OFTEN HERALD SHIFTS IN THE WEATHER. CHANGES IN MAGICAL PRESSURE, ON THE OTHER HAND, CAN HERALD JUST ABOUT ANYTHING: VOLCANIC ACTIVITY, DRAGONS, PLOT TWISTS....

A man in a beekeeper suit—Buzz—addressed Clay from outside the gate. "Did you get my message?"

"Yeah, I'm on my way. . . . Do you know why I'm supposed to see Mr. B?"

Buzz shook his head. "No idea. But it sounds urgent."

Clay swallowed. He didn't like the sound of *sounds urgent.*

Around him, the animals continued to complain noisily, scratching the fences and pawing the ground. "What are they saying?" asked Buzz.

"I can't tell—they're all talking at once," said Clay.

"Then tell them to speak one at a time," said Buzz, as if this were a perfectly obvious solution.

Buzz was the only person at camp who could relate to animals in the way that Clay could, although Buzz's particular gift was an ability to communicate with bees. Clay, on the other hand, seemed to be able to talk to most species, at least to some degree. He simply spoke and animals understood him—not his words exactly, but the intent behind them. It was the same when they spoke to him. He couldn't have done a word-for-word translation of barks or neighs, but he always seemed to understand what the dog or horse was trying to say.

"Um, guys, quiet, please," said Clay, in what he hoped was a stern but not unkind tone. "You." He looked at one of the goats. "What's going on?"

As the goat bleated heatedly, Clay tried to focus on her and ignore the other animals.

"It's the smoke in the sky; they're not digging it," he said to Buzz, after a moment. "But the volcano's always acting up, and I've never seen them behave like this."

"They must sense something different this time."

With great effort, Clay managed to slip out the gate without letting any animal inmates escape.

"Like what?"

"Oh, maybe a disturbance in the Force."

Clay looked at Buzz's face, which was partly hidden under his beekeeper hat. Was he joking? Buzz was Earth Ranch's resident yogi-wizard-Yoda type, and he often invoked *Star Wars* in perfect seriousness.

"You mean the Other Side?" said Clay tentatively.

"Maybe," said Buzz. "Randolph Price chose this island years ago because he was certain it was a power spot. It's only a guess, but this latest eruption may not be simple geophysics."*

---

* As diligent readers will remember, Randolph Price was a poor street urchin who stumbled on the lost secrets of the alchemists. When he got older, he used his knowledge of magic to speculate on the stock market, eventually amassing enough wealth to buy his own private island. His story is told in *Bad Magic*, in which novel all his secrets are revealed. If you read it, you will become as rich as he was. (Maybe.)

Clay struggled to understand. "So then the Other Side is underground? The way you guys talk about it, I always thought of it as behind the sky."

"Who says it can't be both? The Other Side is everywhere and nowhere." Buzz smiled and pointed upward. "Speaking of the sky, looks like your meeting is coming to you."

It was the second time that morning that Clay had seen something big flying toward him, but this time there was no mistaking it for a dragon.

As the teepee sped over the lake, heading toward camp, it spun this way and that, looking as though it were about to tip over at any moment. Yet somehow, whether because of Mr. B's expert steering or some mysterious balancing spell cast years ago, the teepee managed to descend from the sky without any passengers falling out.

When Clay finally caught up with it, the teepee was floating at the far end of the lake's long but narrow beach. The teepee kept skirting the shoreline, as if debating whether to land or go for a swim.

Owen stuck his head out the flap door. "Hi, Clay. Right on time... Eli, how do I stop this thing?" he shouted over his shoulder.

"You don't!" came a voice from inside. "You pilot your plane; I pilot my teepee!"

At these words, the teepee lowered itself almost

but not quite to the ground and then stopped moving. Even so, Clay nearly fell over as he entered; stepping into the teepee was like stepping into a rowboat on a choppy sea.

"Sit down, Clay, before you knock over the teapot!"

The teepee pilot—Eli, aka Mr. Bailey, aka Mr. B—a small, round man with big mutton-chop sideburns, put a hand on the tall glass teapot resting on the brass tray in front of him. Flowers and herbs and other less identifiable botanicals steeped inside the pot.

On the other side of the teepee, Owen, the seaplane pilot, was settling back on a pile of cushions, a teacup in hand. Younger, taller, and slimmer than Mr. Bailey, he had a shaved head and a scruffy chin. A master of disguise, Owen was usually to be found playing one role or another—whether a ponytailed airplane mechanic or a cantankerous old janitor—but for the moment he seemed not to be playing anyone but himself.

Clay chose an empty spot to sit down, whereupon he discovered he had an unwelcome view of Mr. B's naked hairy feet.

"Is it my brother?" he asked Mr. B, unable to hide his anxiety. "Is he okay?"

"Your brother's fine," the camp director reassured him.

Owen laughed. "Or as fine as he ever is. You

know Max-Ernest. . . . Actually, I've got a message from him. Well, a mission, really."

"A mission?"

The knot of tension in Clay's stomach relaxed (his brother was alive, at least), but it was soon replaced by a bilious ball of indignation.

In the year that had passed since his first summer at Earth Ranch, Clay had seen his older brother exactly once. Max-Ernest had promised to come home sometime in the spring to visit, and indeed he did come—for all of one day. A day that Max-Ernest spent arguing on the phone with his old friend Cass while Clay skateboarded around the block over and over, waiting for Max-Ernest to pay some attention to him.

When the attention finally came, it consisted mostly of Max-Ernest criticizing him for not wearing a helmet. . . . To which Clay responded that he was almost fourteen years old and he would do what he wanted. . . . To which Max-Ernest responded that you could crack your head open at any age. . . . To which Clay responded, you're never around anyway, so what do you care if I crack my head open? . . . To which Max-Ernest responded, depends, is that like cracking a joke? . . . To which Clay responded, huh? That isn't even funny. . . . To which Max-Ernest responded, you're right, it's not. Cracking your head open is never funny.... And that was pretty much that.

And now Max-Ernest had the nerve to send Clay on a *mission*?

"That's right, a mission," said Owen. "For the Terces Society."

The Terces Society. That was the secret organization to which Max-Ernest and Cass had belonged since childhood. Max-Ernest had always kept Clay away from his Terces Society activities. He wouldn't even confirm that Terces was *secret* spelled backward. Clay had had to figure that out for himself.

"And for the SOS," Mr. Bailey added. "It's a joint operation, you might say."

SOS. Society of the Other Side. That was them. That is, Mr. Bailey, and the counselors and campers at Earth Ranch. Last year, by agreeing to stay at camp, Clay had agreed to join the SOS, but he hadn't thought of the SOS as the kind of group that sent you on missions. It wasn't like it was the CIA. Or the Terces Society, for that matter.

"Here—" said Owen.

He handed Clay a glossy black brochure. There was no picture on the front, only words:

> You've gone on safari in Kenya and ice fishing in Sweden.

You've ridden camels in Egypt and elephants in India.

You've been swimming with dolphins in Mexico and sharks in the Bahamas.

Now it's time for the ultimate thrill....

Frowning, Clay opened the brochure. Inside was a photograph of rippling sand dunes. In the center: the unmistakable shadow of a dragon flying above.

"So they're saying you get to... fly on a dragon?" asked Clay slowly.

Owen nodded. "It's some sort of wild animal park–style resort. Hasn't officially opened yet. Still supersecret. The brochure is supposed to attract investors. We had to bribe a very exclusive travel agent to get it."

"Is it for real?" said Clay, confused. "I mean, there aren't any dragons left, are there? I thought Ariella was the only one in the world."

"As far as we know, Ariella *is* the only one..." said Mr. Bailey. "But, yes, it's for real."

Clay looked at Mr. Bailey in alarm. "Wait, you don't mean they've got Ariella?"

"We can only assume so," said Mr. Bailey gently. Everyone at camp knew how attached Clay was to the dragon. "I'm sorry. I know this is bad news."

His mind reeling, Clay looked down at the brochure again. "The Keep—this is the place the Midnight Sun said they were building, isn't it? The dragon sanctuary or whatever?"

"That would be the one," said Owen.

Clay clenched his teeth. After all he and his friends had gone through to rescue Ariella, the Midnight Sun had captured the dragon again! It was too terrible to contemplate. And yet at the same time, squirming inside him, barely acknowledged, there was another feeling: relief. Maybe Ariella hadn't abandoned him after all; maybe the dragon had simply been unable to come back.

"At first none of us believed the Keep was real," said Owen. "Except for Cass. She was convinced that the Midnight Sun was using Ariella to breed more dragons, and she wanted to know why."

"I can think of a few reasons." Clay thought of a line from the *Occulta Draco*: *He who has power over dragons has power over us all.*

"I'm sure you can," said Owen. "Anyhow, she went to the Kalahari Desert to investigate."

"So what did she find out?"

"We don't know," said Mr. Bailey. "She disappeared."

"Disappeared?" Clay repeated.

Mr. Bailey nodded gravely. "We think she's been taken hostage, and we want you to help Owen bring her back."

Clay blinked. Cass, a hostage? It seemed impossible. She was the most kick-butt person he knew.

Cass had been a constant presence in his life. When Clay was little, the young survivalist was always with Clay's brother, and she always took the time to give Clay a key tip or two: like how to make a compass with duct tape and a cork, or how to use cayenne pepper to stop himself from bleeding.* Later, after Max-Ernest went away, she'd been the one to let Clay know that his brother was okay.

Now *he* was supposed to rescue *her*.

---

* In retrospect, it wasn't such a good idea to get lost in the park or cut his pinkie finger "just for practice," but how was Cass to know he would attempt those things? She was only trying to help.

"Why me?"

Owen smiled. "Know anybody else who can talk to a dragon?"

"So you want to get Ariella out at the same time?" In the back of Clay's mind, he'd already begun planning to do exactly that.

"I was going to go by myself," said Owen. "Then we thought, we can't rescue Cass and not rescue the dragon as well. Too dangerous—leaving it in the hands of the Midnight Sun. And who knows? A dragon might just come in handy when we're all trying to get the heck out of there."

"And my brother's really okay with this? He doesn't even like me to ride my skateboard."

"I told him you're the only person in the world that Ariella trusts," said Mr. Bailey. "You're the only man for the job."

"Why isn't he going? Wait—don't tell me: He's allergic to dragons," Clay scoffed.

Owen laughed. "That *would* be his reaction, wouldn't it? No, it's because we're going undercover, and Ms. Mauvais is there, and she would recognize Max-Ernest in a second. That a good enough reason for you?"

Clay shrugged, but he had to acknowledge it was a good reason. Ms. Mauvais was the notoriously cruel, and famously ageless, leader of the Midnight

Sun. Clay didn't know much about her, but he knew that his brother had had more than one unpleasant encounter with her over the years.

The camp director poured a cup of tea and handed it to Clay. "Here, have a sip of courage. Nurse Cora made this tea specially."

Clay sipped cautiously. Knowing Nurse Cora, *sip of courage* was not just an expression. Sure enough, the drink filled Clay with a pleasant tingling feeling that couldn't be attributed simply to the tea's temperature. He suddenly felt he was ready for anything.

"Well, what do you say?" asked Mr. Bailey. "Of course, we would never make you do something like this if you didn't want to. It is an incredibly dangerous mission for someone your age to undertake. The Midnight Sun members are practically vampires, and for a day or two you will be entirely in their hands."

"It's okay," said Clay firmly. "I'll do it."

But not for Max-Ernest, he said to himself. For Ariella. And Cass.

"Great," said Owen. "I knew we could count on you." He reached behind his back. "Your brother asked me to give you this."

"Er, thanks," said Clay, taking the gift.

It was a Day-Glo green skateboard helmet, decorated with graffiti-style words in various other Day-Glo colors: exclamations like RADICAL! GNARLY! awesome! mixed with skateboard terms like OLLIE and FAKIE and grind. Did his brother really think Clay would like this helmet? Just because he liked graffiti?

"There's another surprise waiting for you outside," said Mr. Bailey.

Oh great, thought Clay. Kneepads. Or would it be wrist guards? Bracing himself, he opened the teepee's flap door.

CHAPTER FOUR

THE DRAGON IN THE YURT

"Brett! You're the surprise?"

Brett grinned as Clay stepped out of the teepee. "About time! I've been waiting here forever."

"I thought you were still on that ship," said Clay. "With what's her name—Captain Abad."

"I am. I mean, not right this second, obviously, but most of the time, yeah. Can you believe she has me mopping decks and washing dishes? *Moi?* Brett Perry?" Brett shook his head, seemingly aghast and delighted at the same time. "It's like I joined the navy. Except I don't even get to wear a sailor suit."

Clay laughed. "She's toughening you up."

The previous summer, when Clay had found him washed up on the beach, Brett was half-drowned, dehydrated, and scared for his life, so maybe it wasn't the best basis for comparison, but he certainly looked a lot better now. He still wore a bow tie—his "signature accessory," he called it—but the tie was no longer black; it was purple.

"So you never made up with your dad?" Clay asked.

"You kidding?"

It was Brett's father who had pushed Brett overboard. It was also Brett's father who had led the Midnight Sun's expedition to capture Ariella the first time around. Needless to say, Brett didn't like him much. Neither did Clay.

"So your dad's still hanging with those Midnight Sun types?"

Brett shook his head. "No. They ditched him when he wasn't useful anymore. Serves him right. I think he's in Mexico now. . . ." Brett trailed off as Mr. Bailey and Owen exited the teepee. "Anyway, these guys said you needed help. And it was a good excuse to take a break."

"You're not here to take a break," Mr. Bailey corrected.

"Brett is here to coach you," said Owen to Clay.

"He is?" Clay couldn't hide his surprise.

"What? You don't think I'm the coach type?" Brett laughed. "You haven't heard what the plan is."

The plan, it turned out, was deceptively simple:

Clay and Owen would enter the Keep as guests, rescue Cass and Ariella, and then escape on Ariella's back and in Owen's plane, respectively.

Clay's role: a rich kid eager to be the first guy he knew to see a real live dragon.

Owen would play the billionaire father taking Clay on the trip of a lifetime. To secure their place at the Keep, he had made a sizable financial contribution toward "dragon research and conservation efforts."

Brett, who'd grown up as the real son of a real billionaire, had the rest of the day to prepare Clay for his part; at six p.m., Owen's plane would be leaving for Namibia.

"... So I think you should say you go to boarding school," Brett said later, over breakfast by the lake. "St. Matthew's, maybe. That's kind of like Andover or Choate, but a little less well known, so it'll sound more realistic."

"Uh, okay..." said Clay, not completely following.

Brett gestured toward the nuts and berries in front of him. "I can't believe they call this breakfast—you eat like rodents here. Luckily, I brought provisions." Grinning, he pulled a fistful of candy bars out of his pocket.

Clay laughed; this was the Brett he knew.

"Remember, it's not just knowing names and

places," said Brett, munching chocolate. "It's knowing what to think about them. Like, Saint Bart's is okay, but you'd rather go to Tulum. For skiing, your family has a house in Aspen, but it's such a scene, and anyway you prefer Gstaad. . . ."

"*Gistot?*"

"*Gstaad.* G-S-T-A-A-D. It's in Switzerland. . . . The most important thing is that you be blasé about everything."

"Blasé, got it," said Clay. "Wait, what does *blasé* mean again?"

Brett gave him a look. "*Blasé* means blasé. It's like bored, but with an attitude."

"So basically I should be a jerk?"

"Basically."

"But you're not like that," said Clay. "Well, you're a snob, for sure, but not a jerk exactly."

"Maybe not, but I'm different. I'm, well . . ."

Clay grinned. "A dork?"

"I prefer *nerd*," said Brett, raising himself up. "But, yes, if you insist. The point is, I'm thinking of how *you* would be if *you* were rich."

"And I'd be a jerk?"

"Let's just say you'd think you were pretty cool. Or at least that everyone else was really *un*cool."

"Everybody *is* uncool."

"See what I mean?"

Before Clay could respond, Leira came up to

them and whispered something in Brett's ear. He nodded; smiling, and she ran off.

"What was that about?" asked Clay suspiciously.

"A surprise," said Brett.

"Another one?"

"I'm supposed to take you to Big Hurt, I think she said?"

"Big *Yurt*. That's what we call the big . . . yurt."

"Original," said Brett drily.

There were three yurts that formed a triangle in the middle of Earth Ranch: Art Yurt, the arts and crafts studio; Little Yurt, the infirmary, more often known as Puke Yurt; and Big Yurt, the camp's multipurpose space and dining hall.

Above the entry to Big Yurt, a handwritten cardboard sign read:

WELCOME TO THE KEEP
Here be dragons!

When they reached it, Clay heard somebody shout, "He's here!" and suddenly a strange mechanical creature made from wood and tin cans jumped out, clawing at the air and waving its tire-rubber tail. It let out a gear-rattling roar, and flames—mostly just sparks—came out of its mouth. It was a robot dragon.

Clay immediately recognized it as the work of his friend Pablo.

"SURPRISE!" Clay's campmates yelled from inside.

"Is this somebody's idea of a going-away party?" Clay asked skeptically as he tried to edge past the dragon without getting pawed or singed.

"No, it's your training room, you dope," said Leira, who was waiting inside.

A girl who looked remarkably like Leira, but with long hair and a dress, stepped up to them. "Hello, monsieur, welcome to ze Keep," said Leira's twin sister, Mira, in a chilly French accent. "May I have somebody to take your luggage?"

"Uh, I'm good, thanks, Mira," said Clay, not quite ready to play along.

"Who eez zis Mira? I am Ms. Mauvais, leader of ze Midnight Sun," said Mira imperiously, and indeed, as she spoke, she seemed to be inhabited by the spirit of the ancient French villainess. (In reality, Ms. Mauvais's accent was not nearly so strong, but let's not quibble.)

Clay looked around. Pablo had just brought in the dragon and was moving it onto a high shelf, from which it would be able to pounce at will.

More hand-painted signs were hung around the inside of the yurt, arbitrarily identifying parts of the room as RESTAURANT, HOTEL ROOM, and DRAGON ZOO.

"Sorry, but isn't this kinda, um... ridiculous?" said Clay.

"Mr. B told us to train you, and that's what we're going to do," said Leira stiffly.

"Please, 'ave a seat," said Mira in her Mauvais voice. "You must be very 'ungry after your journey."

She motioned him to a table in the "restaurant" that looked as though it had been set for a fancy dinner—or a very makeshift, summer-camp version of a fancy dinner. Another one of Clay's cabinmates, Kwan, grinned up at him from behind the table. Reluctantly, Clay sat down opposite Kwan, propping up his backpack in the corner.

"So, you gotta know which fork to pick up first, right?" said Kwan, gesturing to the array of mismatched cutlery on the table.

"Okay," said Clay, resigned. "Which fork do I pick up?"

"Like I know?" Kwan laughed. "I can show you how to pocket a knife, though, if you want."

"You go from the outside in," interrupted Brett, who was watching from behind Clay's shoulder. He pointed to the fork a person should use first.

"Does it really matter?" Clay complained.

"Yes!" Brett insisted. "The Midnight Sun members are very formal. And it would seem weird if you didn't know this stuff, being who you are—even if you're playing the rebel and you think manners are lame."

"Rebel? I thought I was blasé," said Clay.

"Blasé rebel."

"A blasé rebel. Got it." Clay folded his arms, trying to look like a blasé rebel.

"Well, blasé this, my friend—" Kwan started tossing pieces of cutlery into the air. They spun in flashing circles and then, one by one, vanished up his sleeves, behind his ear, or seemingly into thin air.

"And last but not least..." A single knife was left on the table. With a flick of a finger, Kwan sent it spinning into the air. It landed between his teeth. "Always handy to have a weapon on you, right?" he said, teeth clenched.

Clay laughed. "I'm not sure a butter knife is going to be much help against the Midnight Sun."

Leira glared at Kwan. "He's supposed to learn how to act rich, not how to entertain kids on street corners."

She gripped Clay's arm and pulled him to his feet. "Let's say you've gotten through dinner. Now you find where they're keeping Cass." Leira pointed to an old door that was leaning against the wall of the yurt. A sign on it read:

HOLDING CELL—KASS INSIDE

Clay shook his head. "Why don't I think they'll have a sign like that?...And by the way, it's *Cass* with a C."

Leira scowled. "That's just for concept. Now, here is my most prized possession," she said, opening her hand.

"A paper clip?"

She gave him an I'm-not-joking look. "With this, you can pick almost any lock in the world."

"Isn't that Owen's job? I'm the dragon guy."

"It's going to be all hands on deck."

She pointed to the keyhole in the door. Clay tried inserting the clip in various ways while Leira gave him suggestions about angles and wrist movements and how much pressure to exert. Nothing seemed to work.

"Hmm, maybe you'd be better off stealing the actual key," said Leira fretfully. "Let's work on your pickpocketing skills. It all comes down to the three Ds: *divert, detach, disappear.*"

After Leira made him pick her pocket five or six times, never very successfully, Pablo took over the training session. He reached inside his mouth and pulled out a wad of chewing gum. "Here—"

Clay made a face. (Pablo's green hair and pimples made the gum even less appetizing.) "No, thanks, man. I'm good."

"Better take it. It's exploding chewing gum. If it stays unchewed for longer than thirty seconds, it ignites."

"Really?" Disgusted, Clay took the gum and put it in his mouth.

Pablo smiled. "Actually, that piece is just a stand-in. But I'll have the real thing ready before you go, I promise."

Clay hastily spit the gum from his mouth. "What do you think this is—a James Bond movie? I'm not going to have to explode anything."

"You never know," said Pablo earnestly. "For one thing, explosions work a lot faster than paper clips." He looked with disdain at Leira's prized clip.

"Did somebody say something about an explosion? I like explosions."

An older teenage boy entered the yurt, an unpleasant smirk on his face. It was Flint, Clay's least favorite person at camp—possibly his least favorite person anywhere.

He took Pablo's dragon robot off the shelf and started playing with it. "Is this thing the dragon I heard about? Not very impressive, is it? Now, if you guys want to see some real fire-breathing..."

As the younger campers watched anxiously, he put his finger to his mouth and blew on it; a flame suddenly burned from his fingertip like a candle.

He held the flame up to the dragon, and for a second the dragon breathed fire again. Then it exploded into pieces.

Flint grinned. "Oops."

"You little..." Swearing, Pablo clenched his fists and—

Clay's friend Jonah, who'd been watching from the side of the yurt, grabbed Pablo. "Let it go. He's a counselor now, remember?"

"That's right, don't forget it!" Laughing, Flint walked over to Clay. "You make about as convincing a rich kid as you do a Dragon Tamer."

"I'll take that as a compliment."

"Don't," Flint sneered. "You think all this is going to prepare you for the Midnight Sun? They're going to eat you alive."

"You would know," said Clay angrily. "You were the Midnight Sun's spy. Or did you think we all forgot?"

Clay stared hard at Flint. He still couldn't believe that Mr. Bailey hadn't kicked Flint out of camp after learning about his betrayal. ("If I expelled everyone with a criminal record, there'd be nobody left," Mr. B had explained, only half joking. "This camp is all about second chances.")

Flint stared back at Clay. For a moment it looked as though he might slug Clay. Or shoot a fireball at him. But he appeared to think better of it.

Flint eyed Clay's open backpack. "*Secrets of the Occulta Draco*, huh? You steal that from the library again?"

Clay shrugged. "So? You should talk." Flint had stolen the very same volume from the library the year before.

"Yeah, I should, shouldn't I?" Flint walked out, chuckling.

"Bye," said Kwan to his departing back. "Tool."

Brett looked at Clay clinically. "Why would you admit that? Your problem is you're too honest."

"It's one of his worst qualities," Mira agreed. "He's a terrible actor."

Leira nodded somberly. "This is going to be a disaster."

"He can't handle this mission alone," said Brett. "If only we could go with him."

"Thanks for the votes of confidence, guys," said Clay, not sure whether he wanted to laugh or cry.

Pablo looked from Clay to the others. A smile spread across his face. "I think I have an idea...."

After his long training session, Clay barely had time to pack—in a trendy duffel bag borrowed from Brett—before it was time to go.

As his friends gathered by the ocean to see him off, he watched Owen transfer boxes to his dingy old seaplane via a small rowboat. Clay remembered the first time he saw Owen's plane, more than a year before; he'd wondered then whether such a rusty piece of machinery could actually fly. If anything, the plane looked more beat up now. And this flight was going to be a lot longer than the flight to camp!

"Not a very swanky ride, is it?" said Kwan, standing beside him. "I mean, considering you're supposed to be billionaires."

Clay smiled thinly. His sense of humor had started to fade hours ago—just around the time he learned he was going to visit the Midnight Sun.

Pablo walked up to them, hiding something behind his back. "I've got one more thing for you to take."

Clay eyed him warily. "What does a guy need besides exploding chewing gum?"

"This!" said Pablo, revealing what he was hiding: a black ski cap. Pablo tugged it over Clay's head, messing up his hair and covering his eyes.

"Hey!" Clay protested. "Did you forget I'm going to the desert? It's going to be, like, a thousand degrees."

"It's for your character," said Brett, before Clay could remove the hat. "You know, the hipster rich kid trying to look street. Don't ever take it off."

"Great," Clay grumbled. The hat was already making his scalp itch.

"*Well, it's better than that helmet your brother gave you, anyway,*" came a voice in his ear.

"What the—?" Clay reeled around.

The voice in his ear laughed. It was Leira, but Clay didn't see her anywhere.

"Look behind you."

He glanced around and saw her heading up the beach toward them. She waved, revealing a large conch shell in her hand.

"*Pablo made this rad long-range two-way radio with some hanger wire and this old shell,*" she continued, talking into the conch. *"So we can keep helping you when you're out there playing dragon whisperer."*

"You mean, so you can keep making fun of me," Clay said, imagining the long hours ahead, with Brett and Leira laughing at him in his ear.

"That too."

He shook his itchy head. "Thanks. You guys think of everything."

"Seriously, this way I can talk you through your first act of grand theft," said Leira when she reached him. Her voice echoed in his ears. "When you want us, all you have to do is talk. If you don't hear us right away, it means we put down the shell for a minute. Tap the side of your ski hat, and we'll know to get on the line."

"Okay, got it," said Clay. "But can you stop talking into that shell? You're giving me a headache."

"Fine," said Leira, reluctantly lowering the conch shell. "What else are you taking with you? What about the book?"

"The *Occulta Draco*? Yeah. I got it."

Leira nodded slowly. "So you're not worried about it getting into the wrong hands? Not that it would. I mean, unless . . ."

"Unless they catch me," Clay completed her sentence.

"Right. But that's not going to happen," added Leira, a beat too late.

Clay hesitated, thinking about all the secrets revealed in the *Occulta Draco*. Besides, he'd read the book so many times, he practically knew it word for word.

"No, no, you're right," he said finally. "That would be bad. You'd better put it back in the library for me." Clay reached into his backpack and felt around. "Wait, where is it . . . ?" He gave Leira a look.

She shook her head. "I swear I didn't take it this time."

Clay stared at her. She looked so serious he almost believed her.

"Who, then?" Clay demanded, panic churning his stomach. He didn't want to think about what losing the book might mean.

"I dunno. You sure you didn't drop it somewhere?"

Clay thought back, trying to remember the last time he saw the *Occulta Draco.*

"Flint," he said suddenly.

"What?"

"Flint took it. I'm sure he did. When he was in Big Yurt, my bag was open." Clay looked up and down the beach. Flint was nowhere to be seen.

"C'mon, get in, Clay!" Owen shouted from the rowboat that would take them to the plane.

"Okay—just a sec!" Clay replied.

"Get it back from him," he said quietly to Leira. "Please."

She nodded. "I'll try. And, hey, give me a shout when you need me." She pointed to the ski hat on his head. "Any problem—I'll be there."

"Thanks," said Clay, meaning it. "But don't get all nice on me all of a sudden. You're scaring me."

Glancing around one last time, Clay started walking toward the water. With or without the *Occulta Draco*, it was time to go.

CHAPTER FIVE

THE NEWS FROM CAMP

Clay started feeling grateful for the ski hat almost as soon as they were in the air: It muffled the roar of the engine, as well as the alarming clanking sounds that rattled the plane at frequent but jarringly irregular intervals.

Almost muffled them, that is.

He glanced over at the pilot. "Hey, Owen . . . ?"

Owen looked back at his young passenger. There was sweat on Clay's brow. "Not to worry, pal—it's going to take more than a little turbulence to knock this baby out of the sky. But if you have to puke, there's a bucket behind your seat."

He smiled reassuringly, but Clay noticed that Owen's knuckles were white. He had a very tight grip on the seaplane's steering wheel.

"Actually, it's about the Midnight Sun," said Clay. "This is going to sound totally crazy, but they're not *actually* vampires, are they? That was just an expression, right?"

Owen hesitated, as though Clay's question wasn't crazy at all. "Well, some of them are pretty old—hundreds and hundreds of years old—but they're not vampires exactly. They're alchemists. The Midnight Sun is on a never-ending search for a potion that will make them live forever."

"Okay..." Their being hundreds of years old was not the same as their being vampires, but it was hardly any better. "And what's with the white gloves? They really never take them off?"

"Never," said Owen. "Because no matter how young their faces look, their hands always show their age."

Clay shuddered, imagining their secretly withering hands.

"But do yourself a favor and act like you don't notice the gloves. Asking about them is the quickest way to get your head bitten off."

"They do that, too?" asked Clay, joking (mostly).

Owen laughed. "Well, maybe not literally." He reached over and patted Clay on the shoulder. "Whatever you're worrying about, don't. It's all going to be fine. You saved Ariella once before, didn't you?"

Clay tried to smile back, but then they hit the worst bit of turbulence yet, and he focused on sitting still and not losing his lunch.

Clay jerked awake to find that he had drooled all over his chin and the sun was peeking over the horizon. Below them, the dark ocean had been replaced by sunbaked desert.

"Morning, welcome to Africa," Owen said. "We're already over the Kalahari. About twenty minutes now."

They passed over deep jagged ravines and wide desert plateaus. Past one particularly impressive canyon, a flock of birds appeared beside the plane. Clay watched them for a moment. Rather than flying in one direction, in a V formation, the birds swooped and dove, circling erratically.

"Is that... normal?" Clay asked.

Owen frowned. "I don't think so."

"They look lost."

"Maybe their brains got scrambled by airplane sonar? Or a change in the magnetic fields?"

They're scared, Clay thought as the flailing birds disappeared from view.

Owen pointed out the windshield. "There—that's where we're going."

Clay peered out into the desert. He could just make out the crater near the horizon; from this distance, the giant ring of rock looked like an upside-down bottle cap lying on the ground.

There was a crackling in Clay's ear. As he

clutched his ski hat, he heard Leira's voice, shouting at him.

"Clay! Clay! Come in, Clay!"

"I hear you," he said, wincing. "You don't have to yell so loud."

"It's Mount Forge," she said, slightly out of breath. *"It's erupting."*

"When is it NOT erupting?"

"Not like this." Leira sounded uncharacteristically serious. *"You should see it—like a geyser. And the lava's heading right toward camp. I mean, you know how lava flows are—not exactly fast. But still, looks like we're going to have to evacuate."*

"Evacuate?"

"Mr. B says you have to abort the mission and come back. Right now. We need the plane."

"What about the teepee?"

"You think that thing can fly all the way across the ocean?"

Owen grabbed Clay's shoulder. "What's going on?"

"They want us to turn around." Clay told Owen what Leira had said.

Owen let loose a string of swear words that I won't repeat here, then abruptly cut it off. "Well, I guess we don't have a choice, do we?"

Clay looked down at the crater, which was looming larger and larger in front of them. A moment ago, he'd been terrified at the prospect of staying with the Midnight Sun. Now he found himself unexpectedly disappointed to be aborting his mission.

More than disappointed. Devastated.

"Do we *both* have to turn around?" he asked.

"Huh?" Owen said.

"*Huh?*" Leira said in his ear.

Clay clenched his fists and sat up straight. "I want to stay at the Keep, even if I have to do it alone."

"You're asking me to leave you there by yourself?" said Owen, incredulous.

Clay nodded. "But I won't be by myself—that's the point. Cass and Ariella are there. And if I don't get them out, who will?"

"No way," Owen said. "Your brother would kill me. Never mind Mr. B."

"Say I jumped out of the plane before you could stop me. Besides, if they really need to evacuate camp, I'll just be taking up more space."

"Did you think I was just kidding about the Midnight Sun? These people...well, this isn't like an overnight at your grandma's house."

"I know. Don't worry—all I have to do is get to Ariella and I'll be fine," said Clay, hoping he sounded more confident than he felt. "Once that dragon is free, nobody can hurt me."

"But how would you get back?" Owen said.

"On Ariella's back. Wasn't that the plan?"

Owen looked out over the desert, which was growing lighter all the time.

"Cass could die there otherwise," Clay persisted. "Ariella, too."

"All right," Owen said finally. "I know I'm going to regret this, but okay."

"Really?" Clay blurted. "I mean, good! I can do it—I know I can."

"Are you sure?" said Leira in Clay's ear. *"Shouldn't we ask Mr. B first?"*

"NO!" said Clay. "I mean, please don't. This is my decision."

There was a pause at the other end. *"Okay, but Brett and I are going to stay in your ear twenty-four/seven. We're not letting you do this alone."*

"Don't you have some lava to worry about?" Clay muttered.

"What?"

"Nothing."

Clay glanced over at the pilot's seat to see if Owen was having second thoughts. Owen stared out the windshield, grim but determined.

Directly ahead of them, the crater rose like a massive fortress out of the desert landscape. By the looks of it, the only thing harder than getting in would be getting out.

A moment later, the plane began its final descent.

"What's that?" Clay asked. "Not a jet stream, right? Aren't they usually white and puffy?"

Something had appeared in front of them: a bright silvery line, just above the crater. It looked like a cut or slit in the sky, as if someone had sliced into the sky with a gigantic knife, revealing some secret light source behind the blue. Clay almost thought he could see lightning inside. Or maybe blinking stars. The air around the line shimmered strangely.

"Dunno," said Owen. "But you should probably be more concerned about what's waiting on the ground."

"Yeah, guess so," said Clay, his whole body tense.

More birds flew around the plane, pinwheeling haphazardly. There was only one consistent thing about their movements: All the birds were heading *away* from the exact spot Clay was headed *toward*.

From *Secrets of the Occulta Draco; or, The Memoirs of a Dragon Tamer*

I've said it before, and I'll say it again: You cannot train a dragon. It cannot be made to hunt like a dog or to fly on command like a hawk or a falcon. Many are the falconers who have tried to train a dragon with hoods and ropes, as they train their birds; they have paid for their hubris with their lives.*

In short, a dragon is not your servant.

Still less is a dragon your friend. Friendship as such has no meaning to a dragon.

And yet, between our species and theirs, a relationship of mutual trust and respect is possible. In the Occulta Draco, we call this relationship an *alliance*. Like an alliance between nations, the alliance between dragon and Dragon Tamer must never be broken, else death and destruction will surely result.

How is the alliance made? Alas, there is no surefire method of allying with a dragon, any more than there is for allying with a person.

---

* *Hubris*, or exceeding pride, usually leading to a fall, is often exhibited by the villains in narratives for young readers. These gloved ne'er-do-wells will underestimate the sleuthing prowess of, say, a young spiky-haired magician, a pointy-eared survivalist, or a skateboarding graffiti artist, and so be thwarted book after book, series after series.

Less so, in fact. Two people may at least have interests in common. There are no commonalities between dragons and people, and do not forget it.

However, broadly speaking, most alliances are forged in one of three ways:

1. The bestowing of a gift, such as food or gold. Be warned: Many gifts are interpreted by dragons as insults. Do nothing that will suggest that a dragon is needy or greedy.
2. The performance of a favor, such as the retrieval of an object from a place that a dragon cannot reach. Again, one must be careful not to insult a dragon by emphasizing any inability on its part.
3. A song. Though dragons cannot themselves make music, they are sometimes entranced by it. However, be sure that it is the right song and that you sing it well. There is nothing harsher than the criticism of a dragon.

CHAPTER SIX

THE AIRSTRIP IN THE DESERT

As Owen lowered the seaplane onto the Keep's narrow landing strip, Clay kept looking up at the strange line in the sky. It seemed like a warning, like one of those marks hoboes leave on farmhouse walls: *Danger! Evil people here—stay away!*

He was on the verge of telling Owen not to land after all when the plane hit the ground with such a jolt that Clay was certain it would break into pieces on the spot.

"Does this thing even have wheels?" Clay asked, his face pale.

"Sure, but, well, she prefers the water, no question," admitted Owen.

As the plane taxied to a halt, Owen kept one hand on the steering wheel and pulled his shirt off with the other. By the time the propeller stopped spinning, he was transformed: He wore a navy-blue suit and dark sunglasses, his bald head was as shiny as a billiard ball, and he looked ready to guest star as a villainous billionaire on a crime show.

"Here, you'll be needing this more than I will." Owen removed a diving watch from his wrist and handed it to Clay.

"What does it do?" asked Clay, his throat dry. "Explode?"

"No. Just tells time." Owen smiled. "Ready for nothing?"

"Yeah...definitely." Forcing himself to move, Clay hoisted his backpack onto his shoulders and tugged the ski cap down around his head. He could feel a bead of sweat rolling down his back.

Owen nodded. "Let's rock."

With that, he opened the door, and they both jumped from the seaplane to the airstrip.

Someone had rolled out a red carpet for them, but the plane had stopped just shy of it, so they had to make the awkward walk over to where the carpet began. The asphalt was so hot it made the air wavy, and Clay could feel the bottoms of his sneakers melting.*

---

* Air looks wavy over hot surfaces because of a phenomenon called *refraction*. Hot air is less dense than cool air, so light speeds up when it reaches a hot surface and then curves upward. As a result, we see waves. This happens over hot asphalt or a barbecue grill, or around a dragon's fiery breath.

At the end of the red carpet stood a jaunty blue-and-white-striped tent that might have been more at home at a Renaissance fair than on a landing strip. It was furnished with a couch and a ceiling fan. Parked nearby were several gleaming Cessnas, private jets that made the seaplane look like a broken sandbox toy.

As Owen and Clay approached, a young woman in a yellow sundress and an enormous hat emerged from the tent. When she tipped her hat, Clay saw that it was Amber, Brett's father's ex-girlfriend and Clay's brother's childhood nemesis. Clay had only ever seen her in passing, and he was pretty sure she wouldn't recognize him; now was the test.

"Hello, friends!" Amber stepped onto the red carpet and spread her arms wide like a cheerleader's. "Welcome to the Kalahari!"

Owen walked ahead of Clay and stuck his hand out to shake Amber's. "Max Bergman," he said in a brusque, confident voice that suggested he was used to giving orders. Clay was reminded momentarily of Brett's father. "And this is my son, Austin. Thank you for having us."

"Thank *you* for coming! And for that generous contribution to our work! I'm Amber, your, oh, let's say, activity coordinator?"

Amber gave a self-deprecating laugh. Her brilliant

white teeth looked straight out of a toothpaste commercial.

Clay exhaled. Evidently, she didn't recognize him after all.

Before he could really relax, however, a large swarthy man stepped out from behind the tent. He had a big bushy beard and wild curly hair barely contained by a safari hat, and he was covered in dust and sand from head to toe. He looked like some monstrous creature risen out of the desert, the Kalahari cousin of the Abominable Snowman: the Abominable Sandman.*

"Sorry about my inelegant appearance," he said gruffly, brushing sand off his shoulder. "The Land Rover's radiator was acting up again."

Amber smiled a little less enthusiastically. "Allow me to introduce the most important member of our staff: namely, our resident animal handler, and of course"—Amber lowered her voice for effect—"dragon wrangler, Vicente."

---

* The Himalayan cousin of the American Bigfoot, the Abominable Snowman, or yeti, is a creature out of cryptozoology, the study of ~~mythical~~ **unconfirmed** animals such as Bigfoot, the Loch Ness monster, chupacabras, and even dragons. Sightings of this massive, white-furred ape-like beast go back hundreds of years, but as of yet, there is no firm scientific explanation for the mountainous monster of the snow. There's even less peer-reviewed research on the Abominable Sandman, which is wholly made up.

The hairy sandman tipped his hat. He motioned past the row of shiny Cessnas to Owen's plane, now covered with a layer of dust and sand almost as thick as the layer covering Vicente. "I usually fly hawks or falcons, not airplanes, but isn't that a seaplane?"

Uh-oh. Clay tried to avoid looking at anyone.

Owen laughed. "You're not insulting my trusty old *Tempest*, are you?! Actually"—he winked slyly—"don't tell my office, but we came straight from Fiji. She may not look like much, but that old girl really knows her way around an island. Besides, my Gulfstream has the carbon footprint of a 747."

Clay was pretty impressed with Owen's acting job, but Vicente seemed less so. "Sure," he said, looking between Owen and Clay with inscrutable dark eyes.

What was it the *Occulta Draco* said about hawks and falcons? Clay wondered whether Vicente's experience with birds was the reason he was hired as a dragon wrangler.

Owen coughed. "So, I hate to cut this party short, but I got a really... badly timed phone call just before we landed."

"Not an emergency, I hope?" said Amber, her eyes wide with concern.

"It appears I am being accused of insider trading." Owen shook his head dismissively. "These days, everyone thinks you're a thief if you run a hedge fund."

"How awful!" Amber clucked sympathetically. "Believe me, we're not so closed-minded here. Right, Vicente?"

She turned to Vicente for support, but the falconer-turned-dragon-keeper said nothing. He looked like he thought it very probable that Owen belonged in jail.

"Unfortunately, I have to turn right around to give a deposition," Owen continued. "But Austin here, well, he's been looking forward to this trip for weeks, and he's heartbroken at the thought of having to leave. Is there any way...I hate to ask, but since we're already here..."

"Of course he should stay," said Amber. "We'll give him the trip of a lifetime!"

"Now wait a second." Vicente stepped forward, scowling. "I already have a kid to look out for. Not to mention a dragon or two."

A dragon *or two*? Clay thought. Was that just an expression?

"Don't be silly, Vicente," Amber said. "He's not going to be any trouble at all. Anyway, it's not your decision to make, is it?"

Vicente didn't say anything more, but his glowering stare only became more intimidating. Clay swallowed nervously. He was going to have to watch out for this guy.

Amber turned back to Owen. "Well, Mr. Bergman, I wish you could stay with us and avoid that yucky deposition, but don't worry about Austin. We're gonna have a *super* time."

"*Yeah, real super,*" mocked Brett in Clay's ear.

"Terrific." Owen turned to go. "I'll be back as soon as I can." Then he said casually to Clay, over his shoulder, "Be good. And try not to run up too crazy a bill."

He gave Clay a subtle thumbs-up.

Clay's very strong instinct was to run after Owen, yelling to his "dad" that he had changed his mind. Nonetheless, he returned the thumbs-up—weakly—and remained rooted to the spot.

Amber sidled up alongside Clay. "Well, we had planned to have a drink in the tent, but with your dad on his way out, why wait? Let's get to the dragons!"

Clay was barely paying attention, but he forced a smile. "Yeah, sure, okay," he said with as much enthusiasm as he could muster.

"That's the spirit," said Amber.

"*Wait, did she say* dragons, *plural?!*" asked Leira, startling Clay by saying exactly what he'd been thinking.

"So that means they got Ariella to reproduce?" Brett marveled.

In the distance, Clay could already hear the seaplane's engine revving. He turned and saw the propellers starting to spin. There was no backing out now.

On the other side of the tent, a classic sand-colored Land Rover jeep awaited them. The Keep's name was stenciled on the door—along with a slick logo that looked like it might be the emblem of a high-tech weapons manufacturer or multinational security firm.

As Clay climbed into the back, Amber hopped into the passenger seat, holding on to her hat. "To the Keep, Vicente," she shouted (obviously for Clay's benefit, since there didn't seem to be any other place to go).

Vicente kicked the Land Rover into life. Clay

scrambled to buckle himself in as they left the smooth asphalt of the landing strip and made straight for a dirt road that snaked up the side of the crater.

"So how many dragons are there?" he asked, leaning toward Amber.

She looked over her shoulder. "All together?" Amber counted on her fingers. "Nine."

"*Nine?*" repeated Clay, unable to hide his astonishment.

Amber nodded delightedly. "Yep. We've had four babies hatch just this week! You're going to love them."

"Wow... that's... awesome," said Clay.

Nine dragons. Nine Ariellas. It was a thrilling prospect. And a daunting one.

CHAPTER SEVEN

THE ROAD TO THE KEEP

The narrow, rocky road twisted back on itself time and again, each turn more treacherous than the last, until Clay had to shut his eyes. This was worse than riding in Owen's seaplane; the only question in Clay's mind was whether he would throw up before or after the Land Rover went tumbling down to the desert below.

In the front seat, Amber spoke quietly into a walkie-talkie. Then she clicked it off and smiled back at Clay. "Sorry! I know the ride's a little rugged, but I promise it's worth it!"

Eventually, they crested the crater's rim. Behind them was the seemingly endless desert, but within the crater Clay could see what looked like miles of green jungle. A few buildings stuck out of the greenery, and he could see a row of tents. In the center was a long, sparkling lake.

If he squinted, it could almost be Earth Ranch, Clay thought. There was some similarity to the layout. Although here there was no rainbow, of course. It was as if he were entering a darker, eerier version of his summer camp.

The Land Rover made a steep descent, crossed over a small creek, and then wound its way under a canopy of trees dripping with vines. It looked like a tropical rain forest.

Amber gestured to the foliage around them. "We just planted all of this in the past year, but you wouldn't know it, would you?"

Clay shook his head. It was true. Had she not said anything, he would have thought that the greenery had been there forever. The Keep was already weirder than any place Clay had ever been—but then how many other desert craters had been turned into jungles?*

"The idea was to create an island in the middle of the desert," Amber explained.

Clay nodded, wondering if Price Island had inspired the design of the Keep. After all, it was the one dragon habitat they knew.

---

* The answer is very likely none, though scientists once built something called Biosphere 2, a vivarium, or ecologically closed system (everything inside was recycled and reused), where eight people lived together for two years. The experiment fell apart when the inhabitants started squabbling—not a surprise to anyone who has ever lived with other human beings. But Biosphere 2 was a giant greenhouse, not a crater, so let's give the Midnight Sun credit for trying something new. Never mind the dragons.

In any case, Ariella must feel at home here, Clay thought. Who knows, maybe Ariella had sensed Clay's presence already. He tried reaching out in his mind but felt nothing.

"Getting close now," said Amber.

Finally, the vines and ferns and bamboo trees cleared, and they drove under an arch-shaped sign decorated with the now-familiar logo. It was considerably larger, and considerably less welcoming, than the sign Clay's friends had painted for him at camp:

How would any unauthorized visitors get here anyway? Clay wondered. Then again, Cass had been an unauthorized visitor, hadn't she? For that matter, he was an unauthorized visitor, too; they just didn't know it. Yet.

A little ways past the sign, the Land·Rover pulled into the courtyard of a large U-shaped building with a sheer glass facade, sides of stone, and half-zipper-style crenellations on top.* It looked like a medieval castle that had been split in two to make way for a slick modern hotel.

In the center of the courtyard, two huge dragons rose out of a fountain, frothing at their mouths. They looked ready to kill each other. Clay held his breath—

Then he realized that the dragons were statues—very *lifelike* statues—and the froth was only water.

Amber giggled. "I know, they fool me every time."

---

* *CRENELS* ARE OPENINGS CUT INTO THE WALL-TOPS OF CASTLES, KEEPS, TURRETS, AND SNOW FORTS. CRENELLATION ALLOWS THE DEFENDERS OF THESE IMPORTANT BUILDINGS TO SHOOT ARROWS, POUR BOILING OIL, OR THROW SNOWBALLS AT THEIR ENEMIES, BE THEY DRAGONS, VISIGOTHS, OR OLDER BROTHERS, AND THEN TO HIDE FROM THEIR PREDICTABLY ANGRY RESPONSE.

They parked next to the fountain, and Amber beckoned for Clay to follow her out.

"What about my bag?" he asked.

"What? Oh, don't worry. Gyorg will get it."

She gestured behind them: a squat, muscular bulldog of a man—Gyorg, presumably—had already grabbed Clay's duffel bag and was now carrying it out of sight.

Brett complained in Clay's ear. *"Didn't I tell you? You never carry your own luggage in a place like that."*

Clay jumped out of the jeep before he realized that the courtyard was still under construction and there were mud puddles everywhere. Several feet ahead, Amber picked her away expertly across the ground. He tried to follow suit, but his shoes sank in the mud, and his pant legs got splattered. Terrific, he thought. He would be tracking dirt everywhere.

"Oops!" said Amber, looking back at him. "Forgot to warn you."

"No worries—I'm fine," said Clay, feeling anything but.

And there, waiting in the castle entryway, holding binoculars that were mounted like opera glasses on a long stick, was a woman whom Clay immediately recognized as Ms. Mauvais, though he had never seen her before.

Her perfect blond, blond hair was pulled back from her perfect pale, pale face with its perfect red,

red lips, and she was dressed all in white, except for gold stiletto heels that were totally unsuited to the environment but that on her looked exactly right. She was the most beautiful woman Clay had ever seen. Or she would have been were it not for something in her expression—or maybe in her expressionlessness—that caused him to shiver. An inhuman cruelty he could sense even at a distance.

Or was he just imagining it because of everything he'd heard?

She nodded curtly to the new arrivals like a queen acknowledging the return of her soldiers. And then a very unexpected thing happened—she broke into a smile. At least, her lips curled upward in what appeared to be a friendly fashion; the rest of her face didn't move.

"Austin Bergman, Esquire, I presume?" She looked reprovingly at Amber. "You didn't tell me our new ward was so handsome, dear. Did you intend to keep him all to yourself?"

Ms. Mauvais turned to Clay. "Don't worry, darling. Whatever Amber has said, we are delighted to have you, father or no father."

"That's just what I—" protested Amber.

Ms. Mauvais waved Amber away. "Go be a good girl and find Satya for me, will you?"

Reddening, Amber scurried off as ordered.

"Please do pardon the construction," Ms. Mauvais

continued graciously. “I hope you agree that you are lucky to be among the first to see the Keep, but it does mean facing an exposed wire or two. *Très désolée.*”

“That means she’s very sorry,” Brett whispered in Clay’s ear. *“Tell her, er,* de rien.*”*

“Day ree-en,” Clay hazarded.

His attempt at French seemed to delight Ms. Mauvais. “You speak French—wonderful! I daresay you’ll fit right in.”

She gestured for him to follow her into the Keep’s gleaming marble foyer. As they entered, Ms. Mauvais snapped gloved fingers over her head, and instantly two sweaty uniformed attendants appeared with glasses of sparkling lemon water on a tray.

“Er, thanks,” said Clay, taking one.

“So, what do you think of our little castle?” she asked as Clay gratefully sipped his water. “Given it’s a work in progress, of course.”

Clay looked around at all the chrome fixtures and sleek black leather furniture. They seemed like an odd juxtaposition with the medieval tapestries that hung on the walls, not to mention the full suit of armor standing guard by the front door, but what did he know? To him, the room didn’t look like a castle, or even a hotel, so much as an art museum. Certainly, it didn’t look very welcoming.

“Tell her it’s nice,” whispered Brett. *“But don’t sound overly impressed. Remember, you’ve been better places.”*

"Uh, it's nice. That's St. George, isn't it, fighting that dragon?" Clay indicated one of the tapestries.

"Why, yes, I believe it is!" said Ms. Mauvais, a flicker of something like surprise lighting up her motionless face.

"St. George?" said Brett. *"Where'd you pull that out of?"*

"Don't be too impressed," said Leira. *"It's the only dragon-fighting knight he knows."*

Clay squirmed. He really wished they wouldn't talk so much.

"In fact," continued Ms. Mauvais, eyeing him curiously, "that sword in there is said to be St. George's. It's called DragonSlayer." She nodded toward a glass case in the center of the room. "Of course, it's unlikely St. George ever existed, but it makes a nice story."

Feeling intensely uncomfortable under Ms. Mauvais's gaze, Clay studied the sword. The blade was long and wide and heavy-looking, and the hilt had blackened over time. In contrast to its gleaming surroundings, the sword appeared grimy and unpolished, and more than a little menacing. Had it really slayed dragons? It looked deadly enough.

"And this," said Ms. Mauvais, leading the way to an adjoining room, "is the Ryū Room."

Unlike the austere entry hall, the Ryū Room was opulently decorated with Asian art and artifacts:

intricately designed rugs, delicate vases, and silken screens. There were dragons everywhere, but unlike the flying dragons in the tapestries, these dragons were mostly wingless snakelike creatures, as the dragons in Asian art tend to be.

"The *ryū*, as you no doubt know, is the legendary Japanese dragon," she said, pointing to a dragon on one of the screens. "But we have *objets* from Korea, Malaysia, China.... Take this Ming dynasty vase." She pointed to a large blue-and-white vase that depicted all manner of animals on land, at sea, and in the air. "Now, I wonder, can you tell me which of these animals is the dragon?"

Clay hesitated; he didn't see any dragons.

"Never mind—a trick question," said Ms. Mauvais. "They're all dragons. In Chinese myths, dragons take the shapes of many animals."

In the middle of the room stood a shiny red-lacquer bar illustrated with golden dragons, as well as a grand piano that was as long as a limousine. "Now, please, I know you're exhausted, but I want you to meet your fellow guests. Don't worry—there are only a few. Our group is very intimate."

Sitting by the bar were several people wearing clothes that looked more appropriate for a night at the opera than for a day in the Kalahari. Did this mean they wouldn't be going out to see the dragons? Clay wondered worriedly. Or did these people always dress this way?

Ms. Mauvais waved to one of the guests. "Charles, darling! Where have you been hiding? You must have snuck in while I was getting my morning treatments."

A smoothly handsome man with smooth dark hair curled just so, Charles stood up from his seat at the bar and walked over to them, as comfortably as if he, not Ms. Mauvais, were the host. He wore a crisp white suit and, in place of a tie, a burgundy silk cravat around his neck. Like Ms. Mauvais, Charles was wearing white gloves, though his were not so long. Clay tried not to stare at them.

"*Chère* Antoinette," he said suavely, "do not chide me for being unable to resist your charms."

"Admit it: You wanted to see with your own eyes my *petit jardin de dragons*."

"*Oui, c'est une folie douce!*" said Charles agreeably. He reached out and took Ms. Mauvais's gloved hand in his, raising it to his lips.

"*She said he wanted to see her little dragon garden,*" Brett interpreted. *"He called it a sweet madness."*

"*Well, he's got the mad part right,*" Leira interjected.

"Shh!" said Clay under his breath.

Ms. Mauvais beckoned Clay closer.

"Charles is a dear old friend," she said.

How old? Clay couldn't help wondering. Hundreds of years?

Ms. Mauvais put a stiff hand on Clay's shoulder. Her touch was strange, at once frail and forceful. Clay tried not to recoil. "And this is Austin. His father was called away on business, so he is ours for the weekend."

"Lucky us!" Charles looked Clay over with a smile.

Ms. Mauvais next steered Clay to a table where an old man and woman were seated; that is, unlike the smooth-faced Ms. Mauvais or Charles, the wrinkles and spots on their faces showed them to be old—even older than the others, presumably. Two uniformed attendants sat across from them, cards spread out on the table between them. Judging from their unhappy expressions, the workers had been conscripted to play cards against their will.

"And here we have Mr. and Mrs. Wandsworth," said Ms. Mauvais. "They are renowned world travelers and, as you see, passionate bridge players."

Mrs. Wandsworth turned and regarded Clay over the thin gold rims of her bifocals. With her attention elsewhere, her husband frantically tried to show one of his cards to his bridge partner.

"Please don't do that, Reginald," Mrs. Wandsworth said to her husband, without turning back around. "Cheating sets a poor example for the underclasses."

Grimacing, Mr. Wandsworth re-hid his card.

Clay noticed that Mr. Wandsworth, too, was

wearing white gloves, as was his wife. They were all members of the Midnight Sun.

Clay's leg started to jiggle nervously. There was no telling what these people were capable of. If he was going to succeed in rescuing Cass and Ariella, or just get out alive himself, he had to keep up his guard at all times.

"Do you play bridge, young man?" asked Mrs. Wandsworth.

"Um, sorry, not really," said Clay.

"All the better," said Mrs. Wandsworth with a not-altogether-reassuring smile. "We'll teach you."

"She means she'll fleece you for all you're worth." Charles met Clay's eyes and winked.

Uncertain how to react, Clay looked away.

"Charles, how dare you!" Nose in the air, Mrs. Wandsworth turned back to Clay. "Despite his deep distrust of the players, Charles has consented to join us for a game after dinner, but we need a fourth. I am counting on you."

Clay opened his mouth to protest, then decided to let himself be roped in. He would just have to find a way to get out of the bridge game later. His plan was to search for Cass after dinner if he hadn't already found her.

"Yeah, okay," he said. "I'll give it a try."

Ms. Mauvais coughed to get everyone's attention. "*S'il vous plaît, mes amis,*" she said, clapping her glove-covered hands. "Now that we're all acquainted, it's time for the proverbial good news and bad news."

Clay tensed. Bad news? Had she discovered the spy in their midst?

"As you know, we hope one day very soon to fly on the backs of dragons," Ms. Mauvais continued. "Someday, we may even be able to outfit you in shining armor and let you duel with a dragon like St. George himself. No killing dragons, though—they're far too expensive!"

The Wandsworths laughed mirthlessly. Charles merely smiled. Clay had trouble simply breathing.

"Alas, our dragons aren't quite tame yet. And the largest ones are best seen from afar."

So that was the bad news. Clay swallowed, relieved that his identity had not been revealed, but worried about Ariella. What were they doing to try to tame the dragons? Nothing pleasant, he was sure.

"The good news is that we can get up close and personal with the younger dragons, and of course with our brand-new hatchlings." Ms. Mauvais looked inquiringly at her guests. "So why don't we all freshen up and meet back here in twenty minutes? The first stop on our tour will be the nursery."

She glanced at the doorway, where a young girl had appeared with a large gray bird on her wrist. "Satya, there you are!"

Hesitantly, Satya came over. She was about Clay's

age, with olive skin, freckles, and big hazel eyes; and she was wearing old jeans, a straw hat, and a long leather glove, the purpose of which was clearly to prevent the bird from digging its claws into her skin. Clay was happy to see that her other hand was bare; at least she was not a member of the Midnight Sun.

"What did I tell you about keeping that bird outside?" said Ms. Mauvais sternly.

Satya didn't say anything.

"Satya?"

"You said that if I didn't, you'd feed her to the dragons," Satya replied, expressionless.

Ms. Mauvais nodded curtly. "If you thought I wasn't being serious, then you misjudged. One more time and I will prove it."

"Yes, ma'am."

"Now, please, would you and your bird show our new guest to his quarters? He's in the Beowulf Tent."

Satya led Clay outside, stroking her bird. "It's okay. Nobody's going to hurt you," he heard her say in a low tone.

The bird squawked. Satya continued to whisper in her ear.

Clay experienced a little spark of recognition; something about the way she spoke to her bird reminded him of the way he spoke to animals.

They walked down a pathway bordered by a thicket of ferns and many brightly colored lilies.

Insects buzzed around the flowers, but Satya's bird seemed to take no notice of her surroundings; the bird's piercing gaze was fixed firmly on Clay. Meanwhile, Satya herself didn't so much as glance his way.

Clay, struggling to keep up with her, tried to think of something to say. It might be useful to make a friend, he told himself.

"What's its name?" he asked, indicating the bird.

"It's a her. And her name's Hero."

"Hi, Hero!"

Clay looked the bird in the eye, trying to communicate that he was a nice guy. The bird blinked, nonplussed.

"Ms. Mauvais wouldn't really feed Hero to the dragons, would she?"

"Oh, yes, she would, but I'm not going to let her," said Satya fiercely. "I'll kill her first."

"I guess you don't like her very much, then?"

She gave him a withering look.

"Okay. Dumb question."

"They think they own us, but they don't. Nobody owns my dad."

"Your dad?"

"Vicente. The dragon wrangler?"

Well, that figures, Clay thought.

His face must have betrayed something, because she said, "What? You think your dad's better 'cause he's a billionaire?"

"No!" Clay said, indignant. "I would never think that. I'm not really even—"

Before he could finish his sentence, Brett and Leira started shouting in his ear.

"Stop! Don't say it!"

"She's supposed *to think you're a spoiled brat, remember!"*

Satya raised her eyebrows. "Not really even what?"

Clay shook his head in frustration. "Never mind."

They came upon a row of tents, each a different color and each with a different pennant on top, as if they had been erected for knights entering a tournament.

Satya stopped in front of a bright red tent; its flag bore an illustration of a monstrous dragon and the name BEOWULF.*

"Well, here you go. . . ."

---

* *Beowulf* is the title and hero of the oldest known epic poem in the English language. He fights a dragon (or *wyrm*) after already fighting a monster (*Grendel*) and then another monster (Grendel's mother). One should never endeavor to battle a dragon, but if one must, one should do it fresh and save other monsters for later. Beowulf is bested by the dragon, who has ruled our imaginations ever since. This poem's wyrm is the origin of many modern dragon ~~myths~~ **possible truths**: such as fire-breathing and treasure hoarding. J. R. R. Tolkien used Beowulf's dragon as inspiration for Smaug, the dragon obstacle in the novel *The Hobbit* and all forty-seven *Hobbit* films.

As Satya spoke, Hero lifted off from Satya's arm. The bird landed on top of the flag, as if she were the owner of the tent.

"So this is where I sleep . . . ?" said Clay, trying to prolong the moment.

Satya looked at him.

"I know. Another dumb question."

She nodded, and a fleeting smile crossed her lips. "Got any more?"

Yeah, do you happen to know where they're keeping a woman named Cass prisoner?

"Is Hero a hawk?"

"Falcon."

"Cool. Fastest bird there is, right?" said Clay, hoping to impress the girl, if not the bird.

"Right."

Clay thought he saw a flicker of interest in her face, but she turned away too quickly for him to be sure.

Satya waved to the bird. "Come on down, Hero. We have stuff to do."

Hero squawked a warning at Clay, then flew back to Satya and resumed her perch on the girl's wrist.

"By the way, a word to the wise: You might get hot in that hat. I promise it's not going to snow."

Smirking, Satya disappeared down the path.

Annoyed, Clay watched her and Hero go. Brett and Leira were laughing in his ski hat.

"Hey, look on the bright side," Brett said. *"At least your disguise is working."*

"Thanks," muttered Clay, shoving the tent's flap open.

Why did he care so much about Satya liking him? With any luck, he would be gone before morning.

CHAPTER EIGHT

THE TRUTH ABOUT THE DRAGONS

Twenty minutes later, two Land Rovers were whisking the Keep's guests away from the castle and onto a rough jungle road—well, a rough road cutting through what was planted to look like a jungle.

Soon they had passed over a bridge, and Clay was staring wistfully out the jeep window at a thick canopy of bamboo that reminded him very much of Bamboo Bay on Price Island. Right above Bamboo Bay was the cave in which he had first discovered Ariella....

Clay shook his head, reminding himself to focus on the task at hand. Somewhere nearby Cass was imprisoned; his job was to find her. Hopefully, he would free her that evening, and then they would seek out Ariella and fly away.

As the Land Rovers bumped along, he kept an

eye out for possible holding-cell locations. Alas, they didn't immediately pass any stone towers or cinder-block storage units, or even any padlocked shipping containers or boarded-up shacks. And he couldn't imagine that Ms. Mauvais was keeping Cass outside in the jungle, tied up with vines.

Eventually, however, they stopped in front of a long warehouse-like building. A big windowless structure, it looked very much like a place in which one might lock up an unruly prisoner.

Stay alert, Clay told himself. If there was a chance to slip away from the others, he should take it. Easier said than done, of course. He looked at all the strangers around him and shivered despite the heat.

As everyone climbed out of the Land Rovers, a glass door opened and a woman wearing glasses and a lab coat stepped out of the building. She held a clipboard, and her straight black hair was drawn back in a tight ponytail. White gloves covered her hands: Was she another Midnight Sun member, or were the gloves just part of her uniform?

"Ah, there you are!" said Ms. Mauvais impatiently, as if she'd expected the woman to be outside, waiting at attention. "Everyone, this is Dr. Paru."

"Welcome," said Dr. Paru crisply, ignoring Ms. Mauvais's tone. "If everyone will please follow me..."

Clay loitered outside as Charles and Mr. and

Mrs. Wandsworth followed Dr. Paru into the building. When Ms. Mauvais stepped up, he held the door open for her, pretending he'd lagged behind out of politeness.

"After you."

She nodded, as if this behavior were perfectly normal. But why shouldn't she? How was she to know he'd never held a door open for anyone before in his life?*

After the rest of the group had disappeared, Clay walked slowly down a long, fluorescent-lit hallway, passing several open doors. These all led into storage rooms of one type or another, and not, as far as Clay could see, to any secret dungeons. There was one closed door toward the end of the hallway; steel-plated and unmarked, it looked promising. He hesitated in front of it.

Just as he was about to brave opening the door, Dr. Paru peeked her head around a corner. "I'm sorry, did we lose you?"

Clay spun around. "Sorry! For some reason I thought you guys had gone through this door," he said, his heart beating rapidly.

"Nope," Dr. Paru laughed. "That door leads to

---

* Never? I confess that is an exaggeration. But it's true that Clay was not one for the social niceties. (Here's a reason to practice your manners, if you need one: Good manners can mask all sorts of deviousness and subterfuge.)

a waste-disposal unit. You should be very glad you didn't go in."

Clay smiled weakly. So much for his first attempt at being a spy.

At the end of the hallway, Dr. Paru ushered the group into a room that looked something like a high school science classroom. As her guests took seats, a video screen came to life behind her, showing a spinning globe and a time line.

"As you know, the last dragons disappeared over four hundred years ago," she said, slipping into a rehearsed speech. "In terms of our planet's history, that is just a blip. And yet, strangely, dragons have left almost no trace in the geological record."

The image on the screen dissolved into a montage of scientists exploring mountains, deserts, caves, and even the ocean floor.

"For years, our team combed the world, searching for a stray tooth or claw, a fossilized tail, some telltale markings on a cave wall, but no—nothing. We began to fear that we would never find even a little bit of dragon DNA, let alone enough to clone. Perhaps dragons had never existed after all, we thought. . . ."

Seated in the back row, Clay wrinkled his face. *Clone?* Was that how the Midnight Sun had gotten their dragons? Had they cloned Ariella? It was an alarming thought.

"Then came the incident on Price Island—"

"About which the less said, the better," interjected Ms. Mauvais coolly.

Clay held his breath. He was sure that "the incident on Price Island" referred to the first time the Midnight Sun had captured Ariella. Hopefully, nobody was thinking about the dragon's escape and the role that certain young campers had played.

"At least we proved that dragons were real," said Amber, reddening.

"All you proved was that you don't know how to keep a lizard in a cage," said Ms. Mauvais. "And that's the last time I trust you with any responsibility. Pray continue, Dr. Paru."

Clay exhaled. They were moving on. Perhaps he would now hear how they had recaptured Ariella.

"After that we had an idea," said Dr. Paru, as if there had been no interruption. "Instead of the natural world, maybe we should be searching the human world—somewhere protected against the whims of nature and yet out of reach of most people as well."

A picture of a familiar sword flashed on the screen.

"It turned out that the thing we sought was right under our noses. DragonSlayer. In the incomparable collection of our own Mr. and Mrs. Wandsworth." Dr. Paru nodded in their direction.

Mrs. Wandsworth leaned over and whispered to

Clay: "The sword is on loan only, of course. It is of inestimable value."

"We noticed a lot of rust and grime accumulated on the blade," Dr. Paru continued. "No one had ever wiped it off. It was as if there was a taboo against cleaning it. Could that be because the rust was not rust at all? Well, I'm happy to say, this time we hit the jackpot: dragon blood, dried and preserved over the centuries."

Spinning strands of DNA filled the screen.

"We were able to reconstruct three full DNA sequences immediately. It remained only to find a means of bringing the DNA to life."

She gestured to a basket of surgical slippers waiting by the doorway. "If you don't mind putting slippers over your shoes..."

Dr. Paru led the group through a pair of sealed glass doors. "You are now entering our main laboratory, where we experiment with the most minute building blocks of life."

She stopped in front of a mysterious refrigerator-sized machine with mechanical arms and blinking lights. Another white-coated scientist was manipulating something inside the machine through rubber-lined holes in its sides. A nearby video monitor revealed what he was working on: a giant football-shaped egg in a bright shade of teal.

"Here the DNA is injected into an emu egg," said Dr. Paru. "Early enough so that a dragon develops from the emu embryo."

As Dr. Paru continued to explain what they were seeing, Clay tried to make sense of what he had just heard. If the dragons at the Keep were bred from old DNA, then they were neither Ariella's clones nor Ariella's natural offspring; they were totally unrelated to Ariella. They might differ from Ariella in any number of ways.

How well did Ariella get along with these other dragons? he wondered. How well would *he* get along with them? His mission was beginning to seem more and more complicated.

Dr. Paru looked at Clay, frowning. "Did you say something?"

Clay gulped. "I was just saying, 'Wow, cool!' That's all."

She looked pleased. "Yes, it is pretty cool. It's not every day you get to bring an extinct species back to life."

Phew, thought Clay. He'd have to hide his thoughts better.

Next, she led them into an adjoining room, where Vicente and Satya were waiting for them. The air here was warmer, and the light dimmer.

"And here are our newest additions," said Dr. Paru.

It took Clay's eyes a moment to adjust. And then he stared, awestruck.

On one side of the room sat four incubators lined with nests of hay. Inside each was a newborn dragon, no bigger than a Chihuahua. The dragons' wings and tails looked sticky, as if they'd just hatched, and their shiny, scaly skins were a range of colors: two red-brown, one blue-black, and one a pale color that almost exactly matched the hay it was sitting on. They blinked and hissed and wriggled, not fully aware of what was going on but nonetheless annoyed by the interruption.

As Clay watched, the pale dragon accidentally found its tail, then bit into it—only to shriek and turn bright red all over, just as Ariella had done when angry. Evidently, this dragon had a similar chameleon-like ability to change colors. Maybe Ariella had a relative here after all, Clay thought hopefully.

"And here we have our two toddlers...."

On the other side of the room stood a half dozen cages that looked like they might have been built to contain lions and tigers for a traveling circus. Only two of these cages were occupied, each by a young dragon about twice the size of the newborns. From the looks of the cages, though, the scientists expected them to grow. And fast.

To Clay's surprise, these two larger dragons had

cords tied to their arms, and on their heads they wore leather caps that covered their eyes but not their snouts.

"Are those falcon hoods?" inquired Charles. "And jesses, I believe the cords are called?"

Dr. Paru looked at Vicente, who nodded. "Yep. We're training these guys early. Made the mistake of starting too late with the older ones..." he said.

"But you can't train a dragon!" Clay blurted out, aghast.

The words of the *Occulta Draco* replayed in his mind: *Many are the falconers who have tried to train a dragon with hoods and ropes, as they train their birds....*

Vicente cocked an eye at Clay. "Have a lot of experience with dragons, do you?"

Clay paled, realizing his mistake. He could hear Brett's and Leira's sharp intakes of breath in his ear. "No, I just meant, uh, are you sure you can train a dragon the same way you train a falcon? Seems like they might not like it."

Vicente laughed. "Well, listen to him—the world's first dragon-rights activist!"

"Actually," said Satya quietly, trying to defuse the tension, "the hoods keep them calm. And the jesses, well, they keep the dragons from flying away."

Vicente nodded, accepting his daughter's intervention.

"It's feeding time, so the hoods come off now anyway," said Vicente. "You can relax."

Relieved, Clay watched as Vicente inserted a pair of tongs through one of the cages and pulled the hood off the dragon inside. Blinking, it hissed and batted the tongs as Vicente removed them.

"We call this guy Houdini," said Vicente.

"Because it tries to escape?" Clay guessed.

Satya nodded. "The other one's Bodhi, because it's more mellow."

She opened a plastic cooler. Inside were bright red cubes of steak, bloody and uncooked.

Dr. Paru crossed her arms and nodded at Clay. "Would you like to feed it?"

Clay blinked. "Um—sure?" He picked up a cube of meat and walked toward Houdini's cage.

The dragon inside was black, or maybe dark blue, with yellow eyes and a mane of fine black spikes like a natural Mohawk. It sniffed the air for a second and then flew to the bars, wings flapping against the cage door. Clay noticed that one of the wings had torn and was only partly healed.

Houdini's mouth opened and Clay flinched, expecting the dragon to spit fire. To his surprise, it crowed and cawed, but no flames came out. Clay took another step toward the cage and then felt a hand on his shoulder.

"I wouldn't get much closer," said Vicente. "He might be little, but he's got a mean bite." He motioned that Clay should toss the steak between the bars of the cage.

Leaning away from the flapping dragon, Clay threw the meat inside. The dragon snatched it in midair, and made a mess of chowing down. Not a very appetizing sight.

"Your dragons eat well," Mr. Wandsworth observed. "Is it always filet mignon for them?"

"No, usually their meals are..." Dr. Paru trailed off.

"Still kicking," Vicente said with a grin.

As Vicente removed the hood from the head of the dragon they called Bodhi, Satya offered Charles the open cooler of meat. "Sir?"

Charles eyed the dragon warily. "Should I be worried that it will singe my hair?"

"Actually, the fire-breathing is just a myth," Dr. Paru said. "We think the idea comes from the fact that dragons have a large amount of methane in their breath. If a dragon exhales near an open flame, then, yes, there is fire, but they don't actually breathe it."

Vicente snickered. "It's like how you don't actually fart fire when they put a match to your butt."

"Funny, I've never done that," Charles said. "Is that a habit of yours?"

Vicente looked as though he wanted to slug Charles, but he turned to the dragon instead. "I'll just feed this one myself."

Clay was confused: He had seen Ariella breathe fire several times, in the volcano and on the cruise ship. Could there have been an open flame nearby each time—close enough to ignite the dragon's breath? Unlikely, but *maybe*...

He looked at Houdini. The dragon's yellow eyes looked back at him.

"You can hold it now if you like," said Dr. Paru.

"Uh..." Clay hesitated. The coppery smell of blood was still fresh in the air.

"It's okay. They're gentler after they've been fed, aren't they, Vicente?"

He nodded curtly. "Satya, give the boy your glove."

"Sure." Satya handed Clay her big leather falconer's glove. "Don't worry, Houdini's super gentle," she said as he put it on. "Like a kitten. Except, you know, for the biting-your-hand-off part."

Smiling to herself, she stood with Clay next to the cage door and unlocked it. "Just hold out your wrist and wait."

The dragon blinked up as Clay reached into the cage and waited for it to climb on.

"Here, this ought to do the trick," said Satya, putting a cube of steak on Clay's glove-covered wrist.

Houdini immediately lunged for the steak, but Clay moved his wrist away fast enough that the dragon had to hop onto his arm in order to eat. Clay was surprised by how light the dragon felt, and at the same time how fiercely it dug in its claws. He was glad to be wearing the glove.

As the dragon attacked the meat, Clay concentrated on trying to communicate with it. "How's it going, little buddy?" he whispered. He didn't want to give himself away, but he wanted to know whether he was going to be able to talk to the new dragons at the Keep.

The little dragon tilted its head at him but didn't respond.

Clay tried again. "What happened to your wing?"

The dragon opened its mouth, and Clay flinched, but there were no flames, just as Dr. Paru had promised; the dragon was only yawning, something we're all prone to doing after a good meal.

Disheartened, Clay wondered why he couldn't reach Houdini the way he could Ariella. Then again, this dragon was so young. Human babies couldn't talk until they were—what?—two years old, he reasoned. Maybe the same thing was true for dragons.

Carefully, he set the dragon back down in its cage.

"You look pretty comfortable with that thing," said Satya, who'd been watching over Clay's shoulder.

"Huh?" Clay asked, shutting the cage door. "What do you mean?"

His mind was racing. What was wrong with him? He kept forgetting where he was.

"Did your daddy buy you a pet dragon when you were little?" Satya asked, taking her glove back from him.

"What? No!" Clay said, a bit too forcefully. "This is the first dragon I've ever seen, I swear."

Satya looked at him like he was losing his mind. "You realize I was kidding?"

"Oh, right," said Clay, his face burning.

"I mean, do you know any pet stores that sell baby dragons?"

"Actually, I had a pet Komodo dragon," Clay said as they started walking out.

"Really?"

"No." Clay smiled to himself. "But admit it—I got you, Falcon Girl."

"*Oh boy,*" Brett said in his ear. *"He likes her!"*

"*Clay!*" said Leira. *"You're not there to flirt! You've got to find Cass!"*

Satya tilted her head, just like the little dragon had done. "Why are you blushing?" she asked, which only made his cheeks flame more.

Man, thought Clay, I am going to have to think of some seriously epic pranks to pull on those guys when I get back to Earth Ranch.

If I get back to Earth Ranch...

Something disturbing had just occurred to him:

If the Midnight Sun made their dragons from old dragon DNA, then they had no need for a living dragon. No need for Ariella.

He dawdled with Satya as the others gathered around the Land Rovers. "Hey, I was just wondering," he said, as if the idea had just popped into his head. "The dragons at the Keep—are they *all* clones?"

Satya looked at him like he was nuts again. "Yeah. How else are you going to make a dragon?"

"Oh, I don't know. I just thought they might have found some old dragon somewhere...."

Clay turned away so she couldn't see his face and then headed quickly toward a waiting Land Rover.

Many thoughts and feelings swirled in Clay's head, but one thing was clear: Ariella was not at the Keep.

CHAPTER NINE

THE VIEW FROM THE HELICOPTER

As he looked out from the backseat of the Land Rover, Clay's thoughts twisted and turned along with the road.

He told himself he should be happy that Ariella was free, not a captive of the Midnight Sun. And part of him *was* happy. Really. But a bigger part of him wasn't. Because it meant facing the truth: Ariella could have come back. Ariella really *had* abandoned him.

And then, of course, with Ariella out of the picture, he had no way to get out of the Keep. His only hope was Owen. If the eruptions on Price Island had subsided, Clay's "father" would be free to come back to the Keep as expected. Then they could escape together, hopefully with Cass in tow. But if Owen was still busy evacuating campers...

Clay nervously touched his ski cap, then removed

his finger as if the hat were burning hot. Not yet! he told himself. He was desperate to contact his friends at Earth Ranch, but he couldn't risk speaking to them in front of the others. He would have to wait until he was alone.

Clay noticed that Gyorg, who was driving Ms. Mauvais and the Wandsworths in the vehicle ahead, had turned back in the direction of the castle; Vicente, who was driving Clay, Satya, and Charles, seemed to be going in another direction altogether.

"Why aren't we going back with them?" he asked Satya, who had become noticeably nicer since she saw Clay interact with the little dragon.

She looked back at him. "Don't tell me you've got a fear of heights, too?"

Clay shook his head nervously, uncertain what she meant. In fact, he did have a slight fear of heights (it was a family trait), not that he would have dreamed of admitting it.

Soon they pulled into another clearing, where he saw two cement circles dotted with lights and bright markings. On top of one sat a black helicopter. Clay stared anxiously at the massive weapons attached to the helicopter's sides. Were they there to subdue dragons or to eradicate enemy spies? Either way, he didn't like it.

A moment later, he was being strapped into a black leather seat.

Clay's stomach did somersaults as the helicopter lurched into the air, swaying with the wind as it gained altitude. But among his many skills, Vicente was a crack pilot, and they quickly cleared the jungle canopy. Soon Clay was pressing his nose against the glass to take in the view of the crater.

In one direction he could make out the castle and the tents and some sort of farm or barnyard full of livestock in the distance. In the other direction was the laboratory complex. Beyond the laboratory, standing alone, was a structure that looked something like a lifeguard station, or a guard tower in a prison yard, only much taller.

Could that tower be Cass's prison? It was definitely isolated enough. He would have to investigate later.

All other thoughts were washed away when Vicente took a sharp right turn and the glistening hourglass-shaped lake came into view directly beneath them. The lake was surrounded on all sides by a ring of boulders that looked like a necklace of giant misshapen teeth.

"Okay, keep your eyes open now," said Vicente.

He dropped the helicopter just low enough that the surface of the lake started to ripple. But it wasn't the lake that caused Clay to hold his breath; it was the two shadows passing over it.

One was unmistakably a helicopter—their helicopter. The other could have been an airplane, except that the wings were flapping and the tail was swinging. From the angle of the sun, it appeared to be right above them. Clay craned his neck but didn't see anything.

Until suddenly—

The dark, scaly underside of a dragon passed over the helicopter's cockpit. Then, with a swing of its tail, which came within inches of the windshield, the dragon dove to the lake.

As his passengers gasped, Vicente snickered. "Oh, Bluebeard's just trying to give us a scare. Doesn't like visitors. That dragon knows he can't hurt us or he gets this—"

Vicente held up what looked like a television remote control. "See that steel collar Bluebeard's wearing? If I don't like something the dragon's doing, I just press this button. Gives a ten-thousand-watt jolt to the neck."

Clay shuddered. The collar wasn't so surprising, perhaps, but it went against everything he knew and believed about the majesty of dragons.

Bluebeard skimmed the lake's surface with a claw, then landed on a broad boulder. The blue-black dragon's jagged jowls did look somewhat like a pirate's beard, Clay thought.

"Bluebeard's a wily one, though," said Vicente. "The smartest and meanest of the bunch."

Not far from Bluebeard, sunning themselves on the rocks like the pet Komodo dragon Clay had never actually had, were two other very different but equally magnificent and equally terrifying creatures. Like Bluebeard, they wore gleaming steel collars around their necks.

"Hard to believe that just a few months ago they were stuck in those little cages, being fed cubes of steak, eh?" said Vicente.

It did stretch the imagination, Clay had to admit. It was hard to tell at this distance, but Clay thought that at least one of the dragons might be bigger than Ariella.

"The biggest one, that's Rover," Vicente said.

"Rover's the dumbest—and clumsiest. That dragon'll kill you even if he's not trying to. Stay clear."

If Bluebeard was a velociraptor, Rover was a *T. rex*. Big and gray and ready to topple a mountain.

As they watched, Rover rose up on huge hind legs and then belly flopped into the lake below, making a splash the size of a tidal wave.

"And down at the south end of the lake, sleeping as usual, that one is Snowflake."

Clay was about to ask about the name, when the smaller, bright green dragon turned its head. Right above its snout was a white snowflake-like spot.

"Don't be fooled by how relaxed they look," Vicente said. "I chose this time on purpose because the sun is high and it makes them lazy."

As he spoke, Snowflake batted something away from its eyes, rolled onto its back, stretched, then went back to sleep.

"These dragons may be born in a lab, but they're wild animals all the same," said Vicente. "They're mean and unpredictable, and they'll pounce on you in a second if you're not careful."

"Perhaps they are so wild because they have no adult dragons around to model proper dragon behavior," Charles suggested mildly.

Vicente looked over his shoulder. "Don't worry. They know who's boss." He pointed to himself.

"You believe yourself to be the alpha, do you?" Charles said.

"I *know* I'm the alpha," Vicente corrected. "That's part of it. You have to be one hundred percent confident."

"But how can you be so sure dragons have alphas?" Charles persisted. "In legend, dragons are a rather independent species."

"They are independent," Clay said. "Very."

Charles, Satya, and Vicente all turned to look at him. Clay felt the blood rushing to his head; he'd done it again.

Vicente raised an eyebrow. "And how would you know that, kid? From *The Hobbit*?"

"Don't tease him, Dad," said Satya. "You've never even read *The Hobbit*."

"Touché," said Charles, amused.

"The point is, there are alphas in every species," Vicente said, glaring at his daughter. "Ours included."

Clay decided it was best to change the subject. "What are those poles?" he asked, pointing to a line of white poles stuck into the ground. There was a blinking light at the top of each one.

"They mark the perimeter of the dome," said Vicente.

He explained that around and above the dragons' habitat, there was an invisible perimeter—a "dome"—made of electric currents. The dome signaled the collars to shock the dragons whenever they got too close.

"So this dome, if it were to be turned off... the dragons could fly anywhere they liked?" Charles peered at the sky around them as if he thought the dome itself might be visible.

"And attack anyone they like, that's right," said Vicente. "Especially since the dome is connected to this." He held up his remote again. "If the dome turns off, the collars turn off."

"Sounds like we might want to keep the dome on, then," said Charles with obvious understatement.

Unless you wanted to fly away on the back of a dragon, thought Clay. In that case, you'd have to turn off the dome beforehand. Of course, you'd have to convince the dragon to let you climb onto its back first. And that would likely be much harder.

The helicopter did a slow figure eight, looping back around the dragons, then gradually descended, getting even closer to the sunbathing beasts. By now two of the dragons—Bluebeard and Rover—had raised their heads to look at the helicopter through squinty eyes. Snowflake was still lying on the rock, like an overgrown cat lazing in the sun.

Clay watched with anxious awe. Was this his new plan B, to fly out of the Keep on the back of one of these dragons? Or rather his plan C. Owen coming back was his plan B. (Ariella had been plan A.) Still, it couldn't hurt to think of options. He might very well need to leave before Owen could come get him.

Would he be able to befriend one of the Keep's dragons—*ally* with one of them, as the *Occulta Draco* put it? He hadn't been able to communicate with the baby dragons in the nursery, but these dragons were fully grown, or close to it; hopefully, their language skills were more advanced.

He stared out the window, trying to discern whether the dragons were communicating with one another.

As the helicopter drew closer, he started sensing something coming from them. Not words or thoughts. It was more of a feeling than anything else.

A *strong feeling.*

It was rage.

Suddenly, Bluebeard reared back and spread a pair of enormous blue-black wings. Clay flinched.

Roarrrrrrrrr!

Vicente pulled up sharply but then hovered not too far away.

The dragon stared at them, looking as though it wanted to rip the helicopter to shreds.

"Isn't it time to push that button of yours?" asked Charles.

"Or maybe just fly away," said Clay.

Vicente laughed. "Don't worry. He can't reach us before getting zapped."

"Maybe not," Clay argued. "But his breath can!

Look at him—in a second he's gonna turn this chopper to toast!"

Shaking his head, Vicente turned around to look at Clay. "Like Dr. Paru said, dragons don't really breathe fire...."

Suddenly, Bluebeard jumped into the air. Then the dragon reared its head back in a way that was all too familiar to Clay. Clay braced himself, waiting to get lit up like a torch.

But when the dragon opened its mouth, exposing rows of sharp, gleaming teeth, no fire came out—not even a spark. Only a very loud and very frightening

ROARRRRRRRRR!

At the same time, Vicente pressed down on his remote. Bluebeard made a sound of strangled fury, then dropped back to the rock below.

"What did I tell you?" Vicente grinned as if to say, *See, I'm the alpha*.

Clay nodded, his heart racing. This was the second dragon that hadn't breathed fire when he thought it was going to. Maybe Ariella was an exception? Or maybe there really had been an open flame nearby every time he saw fire come out of Ariella's mouth.

Maybe he just didn't know as much about dragons as he thought he did.

CHAPTER TEN

THE TERRORS OF DINNER

When he reached his tent, Clay made three complete turns, checking that nobody was nearby. (And perhaps it's just as well nobody was; he looked pretty silly spinning around like that.) Satisfied, he pushed open the flap door and ducked inside.

"Guys, are you there?" Clay tapped the side of his ski hat. "I've kind of got a situation here."

"*Yeah, we're here,*" said Leira. It was unnerving to hear her voice in his ear even when he expected it. *"You've got a situation? You shoulda heard Mr. B chew me out when I told him you were staying. It was like we were leaving you alone with dragons or something."*

"Very funny."

"Seriously. He was raging. In his mind, it's all my fault. You know, the whole shoot-the-messenger thing? Of course, I blamed it on you and Owen. . . ."

"Can we worry about Mr. B later?"

All in a rush, he told her that Ariella wasn't at the Keep and that he was hoping Owen would be able to come back soon.

"*Yeesh*..." said Leira, aghast. "*Owen isn't even back here yet; it's a long flight, remember? Plus, the lava is still headed right for us. Everyone's counting on Owen to get us out. Or else we're all going to be inflating life rafts.*"

"So basically I'm on my own...."

"*What about the other dragons? Can't you fly out on one of them?*"

"Yeah, maybe," said Clay. Or maybe not. "Did you get the *Occulta Draco* back from Flint?"

"*No. Sorry. He swears he doesn't have it.*"

"You searched all his stuff?"

"*Of course I did!*" said Leira, offended. "*Am I not the best cabin raider at Earth Ranch?*"

"Okay, well, thanks for trying," said Clay, forcing himself to keep going and not collapse in despair. "Ms. Mauvais told me not to be late for dinner. She says they're very Old World here. Whatever that means."

"*Dinner? What about looking for Cass?*"

"I know. But if I don't show up, they'll start looking for *me*...."

It was the sort of room that would have been intimidating even if it weren't inhabited by ancient bloodthirsty alchemists.

As Clay entered, he faced a glass wall with a view of the jungle outside and the lake in the distance. The other walls, as well as the floor and ceiling, were covered in mirrored tile, so they reflected each other in an infinite regression, giving Clay the vertiginous sense that he was falling through space.

But it was the long, elaborately carved dining table that was most striking. It looked much like a table you might see in an old movie, with a king and queen sitting at opposite ends—with one exception. Instead of wood, the table was made entirely of glass, legs and all. Likewise, the tall dining chairs had an ornate baronial aspect, but they too were all glass. Glittering crystal candelabras and giant glass goblets completed the effect. It was as though some fairy-tale snow queen had waved her wand and turned the dining room to ice. Even the expressions on the faces of the guests appeared frozen.

Clay had a feeling the whole room might shatter at any moment, diners included.

"Austin, darling, how... *you* you are," said Ms. Mauvais, glancing at the ski hat still on his head. She was wearing a shimmering silver evening gown, in which Clay could see tiny pieces of himself reflected. "Come, sit right next to me."

A waiter pulled out his chair for him, but Clay didn't notice and he almost fell as he sat down. "Oh, sorry!" he said.

Mortified, he tried to take stock of the situation. He had planned to eat quickly, then excuse himself and go hunt for Cass, but in this intimate environment, peeling himself away was going to be tough. Maybe impossible.

Ms. Mauvais *ping*ed her goblet with a spoon to get everyone's attention.

"You are about to have a medieval feast," she informed her guests. "Every dish served is exactly like a dish you might have found on a castle table in the Middle Ages. But we have modified the presentation, and the size of the portions, to suit modern tastes."

"Of course, we must make everything modern these days," complained Mrs. Wandsworth.

Charles smiled thinly. "Even dragons."

"We call our cuisine nouveau moyen-âge," said Ms. Mauvais, studiously ignoring them.

Brett, who evidently had been listening, translated in Clay's ear. *"That means new Middle Ages, which is a paradox, or maybe an oxymoron."*

Clay stared at his place setting. Lined up on either side of his plate were approximately fifty forks. Well, at least ten.

Pretending he was scratching his temple, he discreetly pressed the side of his ski hat.

"*What?*" Brett asked. *"You want to know the difference between a paradox and an oxymoron?"*

Not for the first time, Brett reminded Clay

strongly of Max-Ernest. He pressed the side of his hat again.

"Wait, you're at dinner, right? Is it... is it the forks?"

Clay coughed meaningfully.

"*Well, this will teach you to pay attention next time, won't it?*" Brett chastised, before reminding Clay to start from the outside in.

"A toast," said Charles, standing. "To the dragons and their queen." He raised his glass toward Ms. Mauvais. She acknowledged him with a slight nod.

Mr. Wandsworth shouted, "Hear! Hear!" and they all clinked goblets.

“What is this, anyway?” asked Clay, looking at the amber liquid in his goblet. He liked it.

“Mead,” said Mr. Wandsworth. “Beer made from honey.”

“I wouldn’t drink too much of it,” said his wife. “We’ve got that bridge game.”

“Don’t be silly. Clay’s is nonalcoholic,” said Amber. “Drink as much as you want, sweetie.”

Clay took a big gulp, then laughed, mead dribbling down his chin to his lap. “Oops.”

Ms. Mauvais gave him a chilly look, and Clay immediately sobered up. This was not the time to relax.

The meal was possibly the best, definitely the fanciest, and by far the most frustrating Clay had ever eaten. It was true about the portion sizes; the bits and pieces on his plate were nothing like the giant mutton legs and huge apple-biting roast pigs one imagined at a medieval feast. It was as if they were being served sniffs and glimpses rather than actual food. Not that anybody else seemed to mind. Maybe after a certain age—a hundred years, say—one no longer needed to eat.

Clay did his best to fill up on honey cakes, the one thing in generous supply.

“You seem to have built up quite an appetite,” said Charles, catching Clay’s eye. “Must be all the excitement from seeing a dragon...for the first time.”

Clay nodded slowly. Something about the way Charles said *for the first time* seemed a little odd. Had he overheard Clay's conversation with Satya?

"Uh, well, yeah... this food is basically the best I've ever had," he stammered.

"*Stop that!*" Brett hissed in his ear. "*Blasé, remember?*"

"Well, maybe not the best," Clay corrected hastily. "The food was better in Gistopp."

"*No...!*" Brett groaned.

"Gistopp?" Charles repeated, confused. "Oh! You mean *Gstaad*." He smiled. "So then, you're fond of fondue, I take it?"

Clay paused, listening to Brett in his ear. "Actually, uh, I prefer raclette."

Charles nodded judiciously. "*Bien sûr. Moi aussi.*"

Avoiding the eyes of his fellow guests, Clay looked through the big window across from him. Above the lake, two of the dragons—Bluebeard and Rover, Clay thought, though he couldn't be sure—could now be seen silhouetted in the twilit sky. From here they looked no bigger than dragonflies, and yet there was something about the way they circled that made their fury and frustration obvious. How would he ever be able to approach them?

Clay turned to see Gyorg entering the room. Unceremoniously, Ms. Mauvais's muscle-bound henchman marched up to his mistress and whispered in her ear. Clay strained to listen as he sipped his mead.

Gyorg had a thick Slavic accent, and Clay could make out only two words, *escape* and *tower*, but they were enough to make him sit up straight. Gyorg must be talking about Cass! And maybe about the tower he'd seen from the helicopter! Had she escaped from the tower, or merely tried to?

Clay watched Ms. Mauvais's face for clues, but she was as unreadable as ever.

"Very well, Gyorg," replied Ms. Mauvais icily. "But next time, a little more discretion, please. We are in the middle of dinner."

Gyorg nodded curtly and marched out.

Ms. Mauvais stood, leaving her napkin carefully folded next to her untouched food. "I am terribly sorry, but I must cut our meal short."

Immediately, the attendants began removing plates and clearing the table. While Mr. Wandsworth helped his wife out of her seat, Clay grabbed a honey cake off the table and then started inching out of the room, hoping to get away without drawing attention to himself.

Before he was fully out the door, Mr. Wandsworth called to him: "We'll see you in the Ryū Room in five minutes for our game."

Clay clutched his stomach dramatically. "Actually, I'm...all that food...I think I'm going to be sick...."

Without waiting for a response, he hurried down the stairs and out of the castle.

Clay didn't stop until he was most of the way down the open-air hallway, near the path to his tent. He took a bite of his honey cake, thinking about the guard tower. Where was it in relation to the castle? Could he get there on foot? What would he say if he were caught on the way?

He needed to talk it over with his friends. "Leira?" he whispered, crumbs falling from his mouth. "Brett? Whose shift is it?"

"Who are you talking to?"

Clay whirled around and clamped his mouth shut. Satya was leaning against a column, Hero sitting patiently on her shoulder.

"Oh..." Clay fought the blush creeping up his neck. "Uh, just myself. It's this weird habit I have."

"Like wearing ski hats in the desert?"

Clay silently cursed Brett again

"Sorry, that was mean," said Satya.

She pushed herself off the column and walked toward him. Hero's head was cocked like she was listening closely to their conversation.

"You're not like the rest of them, are you?" Satya asked. "You're not wearing gloves, and you eat."

"How do you know I eat?"

She pointed to the half-eaten cake in his hand.

"Oh, right. Duh." Clay laughed, embarrassed.

"And..." She pointed to the stains on his shirt.

This was getting worse and worse. If only he could tell her the truth, at least he would be able to explain the ski hat. Could he trust her?

"Oh, um, well..."

Clay was saved from having to form a full sentence by a figure emerging from the darkness. The moonlight revealed Vicente, still wearing safari fatigues. He looked from his daughter to Clay, and his scowl—already quite impressive—grew somehow even more menacing.

"Satya," Vicente said, his eyes not leaving Clay's face, "don't you have chores to do?"

Satya scowled right back at her father, and suddenly Clay could very clearly see the resemblance.

"If you say so," she muttered after a moment. She looked like she had a hundred more questions she wanted to ask Clay, but she turned and walked away nonetheless.

That left just Clay and Vicente.

"Well," Clay said. "I guess I'll be off...."

He backed up and headed away in the direction of his tent. He would have to get out of Vicente's line of vision before he went anywhere else.

"Austin," Vicente called after him.

Clay paused and turned around. Was Vicente going to warn him off his daughter? All he'd done was have a conversation with her. Talk about overprotective.

"Be careful out there," Vicente said.

"I thought you said we were safe from the dragons?"

Vicente shook his head. "I'm not talking about the dragons."

With that, the man melted back into the shadows just as quickly as he'd appeared.

CHAPTER ELEVEN

THE ENCOUNTER BELOW THE TOWER

Now that Clay was no longer playing tourist and was officially sneaking around, Leira and Brett were eager to help with "tactical ops," as they called it.

First goal: the guard tower. If Cass was still imprisoned there, he would free her. If she'd already escaped, Leira and Brett said they would help him "pick up the scent of her trail." Clay was skeptical—if Cass was hiding from the Midnight Sun, how was he supposed to find her?—but he didn't say so aloud.

Clay told his friends that the tower was out past the lab building, at least a half mile deeper into the crater.

"*Why don't you just steal one of the Land Rovers,*" Leira suggested. "*I can talk you through hot-wiring it....*"

"Terrible idea!" said Brett. *"There's a big difference between him being caught snooping around on foot and him being caught stealing a car."*

"I thought he was supposed to be a rebel," Leira protested.

"A rebel, yeah. Not a thief!"

"Anyway, there's no point," said Clay. "I don't know how to drive."

"*You don't?*" Leira sounded shocked.

"I'm not even fourteen for another week!"

"So? I learned when I was nine."

Brett snorted. *"Yeah, and look where that got you."*

As Brett and Leira squabbled in his ear, Clay began jogging down the road to the laboratory—or at least what he *thought* was the road to the laboratory. Luckily, the moon was bright, and he had little trouble seeing, even if he wasn't exactly certain where he was going.

After about five minutes, he reached the bridge that he remembered crossing; now he was definitely going the right way. As he mentally congratulated himself, he heard a strange whirring noise.

"*What was that?*" asked Leira.

"I don't know—shh!" Clay whispered.

Then he spotted a figure buzzing toward him from around the bend. It was one of the park security guards on some sort of motorized three-wheeled standing scooter.

With no time to second-guess himself, Clay

dove into a nearby shrub, scratching himself badly. He hoped the scratch wouldn't raise questions later.

The guard wheeled down the road slowly, giving everything around Clay a long, hard look. He must have heard something when Clay launched himself into the landscaping. Admittedly, it hadn't been the smoothest hideaway strategy.

But after looking closely at the shrubs, the guard sniffed and leaned forward, spinning on.

Clay waited until all he could hear was the buzzing of insects before stepping back onto the road.

"*Well? What was it?*" asked Leira.

Whispering, Clay told his friends what had happened.

"*Nice work,*" said Leira approvingly. "*It isn't a proper operation until you've hidden in the bushes and gotten scratched 'til you bleed.*"

"*Sure, but you'd better hope the Midnight Sun didn't plant any poison ivy,*" said Brett.

Not bothering to respond, Clay headed across the bridge.

Eventually, he reached the guard tower. At the top, sitting on its tall, rickety scaffolding, was a square structure that looked like a little house, with windows on all sides. Light flickered in the windows, as if there were a television playing behind them. Below, attached to the scaffolding, was the kind of huge round spotlight you might expect to see in a prison yard; it was dark now, but when it was lit, it must have been bright enough to be seen for miles.

A narrow and very perilous-looking ladder led from the ground to the top of the tower. Clay looked around, wondering how likely it was that he would be seen climbing up. On the one hand, the tower was visible from all directions; on the other hand, it was fairly dark out, and the ladder was partly obscured by the scaffolding. Most of the time, he would be in shadow. He decided to chance it.

The ladder clanged and vibrated as he climbed, causing him to keep looking over his shoulder to make sure that no alarms had been sounded. He didn't see anyone, but the surrounding jungle seemed to move and shift in the darkness.

At the top of the ladder was a hatch door. There was no lock that he could see, but he hesitated before opening it.

He pressed the side of his ski hat. "What if there's someone inside—I mean, besides Cass?" he whispered. "What's my alibi? Why am I here?"

"*Curiosity,*" said Brett. "*Simple as that. Remember, you're used to owning the world. Why shouldn't you check out the tower? You're a paying guest.*"

Cautiously, Clay pushed open the door—

Then pulled himself up into the tower room. Nobody was there. Cass must have escaped.

No, actually, she'd never been there. And I'm an idiot, he thought, shoulders slumped.

It had been silly to think Cass might be inside;

he had obviously misunderstood the message that Gyorg whispered to Ms. Mauvais. Far from having the walls of a prison cell, the room had a 360-degree view of the crater around it. The interior was filled with computer screens and surveillance monitors and various other blinking and beeping machines.

"*Well . . . ?*" asked Leira, startling him.

"It's some sort of control tower." Clay sighed. "Definitely not a place where you'd keep a hostage."

The largest screen showed what appeared to be a digital relief map of the crater. A thin red circle in the center pulsed with light. Within the circle, three flashing orange lights were moving erratically.

Clay squinted to look more closely. "I think this is where they monitor the dragons and the dome—that's the electric force field that keeps them from flying away and terrorizing the world."

As he examined the confusing array of technology around him, Clay was suddenly aware of a terrible sound:

ROOOOOOOOOOOOOOOOOOOOAWRRRRRRRRRR!

His heart racing, Clay dropped to his knees so he wouldn't be seen. Then he peeked out a window.

About twenty yards away from the tower, Snowflake was crouched on the ground. The dragon's big yellow eyes were staring straight ahead, its bristly tail swinging back and forth, like a cat stalking a bird.

Still trying to stay out of sight, Clay cracked open a window so he could better hear what was happening.

"Mr. Schrödinger, no!"

A safe distance away, right behind the perimeter marked by the blinking dome posts, Ms. Mauvais was beckoning to a scraggly old man who was standing directly in front of the dragon. He wore a straw cowboy hat and had a big, drooping handlebar mustache.

"Be reasonable and back away from the dragon right now," said Ms. Mauvais, her voice calm but strained.

Gyorg stood beside her, shaking his head solemnly. "Mr. Schrödinger, you listen to the lady!"

Ignoring them, the man they called Schrödinger stepped closer to Snowflake. In one hand he was holding an apple; in the other, a riding crop. He looked ready to break a pony.

"Here you go, Snowflake. There's a good girl," said Schrödinger. His voice was warbly and uneven, and he had a raspy Old West sort of twang. "Old Schrödy's got an apple for you! We're going to go on a little trippy-wippy."

He tossed the apple at the dragon, which was something like tossing a raisin at a horse. Uninterested, Snowflake let the apple fall on the ground. The dragon's tail continued to twitch back and forth.

Clay watched in horror. Any moment now, Snowflake was surely going to pounce, and the old man was going to be chewed up or ripped to shreds.

"I know you can't wait to get on that dragon again, Mr. Schrödinger," said Ms. Mauvais. "You want to go back—we understand that—but the conditions aren't right at the moment. We are conducting controlled experiments."

Clay scrunched his face in confusion. It sounded as if this guy had ridden the dragon before. Where did he want to go back to?

"But don't you see? I never left," Schrödinger shouted back nonsensically. "I'm still there—I'm not here at all!"

"Have patience, dear. Soon you'll be yourself again, I promise. And when we get you back there, you'll be better than that. You'll be a young man."

Young man? What did that mean? He looked plenty old to Clay.

"You don't know what you're talking about," yelled Schrödinger. "And you can't stop me!"

Gyorg leaned into Ms. Mauvais. "Madame, let me go inside and grab him—"

"No, let him be," she said wearily. "No sense in your dying, too. If he wants to feed himself to a dragon, that's his affair. We can always find another test subject."

She took a last look at Schrödinger and turned as if about to leave.

Then a Land Rover screeched to a stop in front of Ms. Mauvais, and Vicente sprang out.

Spurred to action, Schrödinger yelled, "Yeeeee-hawwww!" and started running toward the dragon, clearly intending to leap right onto its back, although there was little chance he could actually jump that high. Clay held his breath, ready for the worst.

But just before Schrödinger could reach Snowflake, Vicente sprinted toward him and grabbed him around the waist.

"All right, ya rodeo clown," Vicente said, dragging the old man outside the dome perimeter. "That's enough action for you for tonight." He gave Ms. Mauvais a sharp look. "I told you it was too soon to put anybody on a dragon's back. Those were just supposed to be speed trials. Not a round-trip ticket to . . . wherever the heck it is you're trying to get to."

"Thank you for your help, Vicente, but please keep your opinions to yourself," said Ms. Mauvais. "You may drive me back to the castle now. Gyorg will make sure that Mr. Schrödinger is settled in his quarters—and that he stays there."

Vicente nodded and released Schrödinger.

The old man lunged toward the dragon, but Gyorg grasped him firmly by the shoulders and lifted him off the ground as if he weighed no more than a child.

"How dare you!" shouted Schrödinger. "Unhand me, sir!"

Clay descended ten minutes later, the scene he had witnessed still replaying in his mind.

"This old dude, Show-ringer—you think he really flew on that dragon's back?" Clay whispered.

"How should we know?" said Leira. *"But come to think of it, wouldn't this be a good time to try to make friends with the dragon—what's his name, Snowball?"*

"Snowflake. And you don't make friends; you make an alliance. But, yeah, I guess I could try."

As terrifying as the idea was.

By the time he got to the bottom of the tower, however, Snowflake was no longer in the clearing. Clay stepped up to the dome line and peered into the darkness, wondering whether he should look behind the trees for the dragon, but he decided against it. Running into Snowflake was one thing; running into Bluebeard was another.

Feeling as though he was disappointing Brett and Leira, he headed back down the road. *I'd like to see you guys walk into that jungle,* he thought. Funny how even when his friends weren't providing running commentary, he still felt like they were inside his head.

What next? Cass could be anywhere, he thought glumly. He'd been so excited when he thought he overheard Gyorg saying she was in the tower. Now he had no idea what to do or where to go.

When he got near the tents, he heard more outraged shouting.

"Inside-outside-you-side-me-side! Don't tell me to stay inside! There are no sides here!"

Schrödinger. The man's raving made even less sense now. He sounded insane.

As Clay listened, somebody coughed. He wheeled around and saw Gyorg walking up the path from the castle.

"Why you are still outside?" said Gyorg sharply.

"Sorry, just, uh, getting some air." Then, remembering he was supposed to be cocky, not defensive, he added, "Is that a crime?"

Gyorg said nothing.

"Hey, what's with that guy shouting back there? Who is he?" Clay figured it was a normal question to ask under the circumstances.

Gyorg looked at him as if debating whether to answer. "He is first guest at Keep," Gyorg said finally.

He stared, unmoving, until Clay said an awkward "good night" and headed for his tent. Further investigation would have to wait.

CHAPTER TWELVE

THE DISCOVERY IN THE BARNYARD

Clay's eyes blinked open.

Heart racing, he lay stiff in bed, not daring to move.

It had been a roar that awakened him. A loud, angry roar. A much-too-close-sounding roar.

He waited for a monstrous silhouette to appear on the walls of his tent. Or for a long sharp talon to tear into the canvas. Or for a burst of fire to burn the whole thing down. (Sure, Dr. Paru had said the fire-breathing was a myth, but he still wasn't entirely convinced. . . .)

The minutes ticked by. And . . . nothing.

Perhaps the dragon had been farther away than Clay thought. Or perhaps he had dreamed the roar.

Some Dragon Tamer he was, shaking in his bed, afraid of shadows.

Clay shook his head in dismay. He had been crazy to come here alone. Crazy to think he would be able to save Cass. Crazy to think he would be able to fly away on a dragon. He was no better than that kooky old cowboy, Schrödinger. He was stark raving mad.

With a shiver, he remembered how Ms. Mauvais had been ready to leave Schrödinger to die. And Schrödinger wasn't even a spy. He, Clay, would be lucky to get out alive.

Clay had intended to get up at dawn to search for Cass, but the sun was high in the sky by the time he exited his tent and headed to the castle.

He would have to find an excuse to slip away later. Then again, he thought bleakly, what was the point of finding her when he had no idea how they were going to get out?

Breakfast, he was relieved to discover, was a more casual affair than dinner. There was a buffet on the patio behind the castle, and he gladly filled his plate with waffles and eggs and bacon and sausages and then more waffles and a pancake for good measure.

"Feeling better this morning, I see," said Mr. Wandsworth, looking at the pile on Clay's plate. "Too bad you didn't recover in time to play bridge last night. Maybe this afternoon?"

"Don't badger the boy, Reginald. He obviously doesn't want to play with us," sniffed Mrs. Wandsworth. "No doubt he prefers video games or some such."

"Yeah, that's right," said Clay, forcing a smile. "Er, sorry."

He grabbed a table by himself, then tapped the side of his hat. "Leira? Brett?" he whispered, covering his mouth. "You there?"

"Yeah, and guess what—camp is safe! Everybody got together and built this crazy-big dam. And with a little bending of the no-magic rule, we diverted all the lava to the ocean."

"Hey, that's great!" Clay felt himself relax a bit. "So Owen can come back here, then?"

"Well, that's the thing." Leira's tone changed. *"We kinda sorta forgot to tell Owen about the lava situation, so he just, um, landed in the water where he always does.... And he's totally fine... but the lava sort of hardened around the plane? They're trying to salvage it, but it might be a while...."*

"Oof." Clay's relief evaporated.

"I know, it's a serious bummer," said Leira. *"How'd it go with Snowball? Any chance that dragon could be your ticket out of there?"*

Before Clay could respond, there was a loud squawk.

Satya had stepped up behind him. Hero, sitting

on Satya's shoulder, studiously ignored Clay, as if she had not just squawked in his ear.

"Talking to yourself again?" said Satya. "It really is a thing for you, huh?"

Quickly, Clay pulled off his ski hat. No doubt he had terrible hat head, but he couldn't worry about that now. "Why not. I don't know if you've noticed, but I'm really great company."

"Can't say that I've noticed that, no," Satya said.

Clay didn't want to stare, but he was pretty sure she was trying not to smile.

"You should see me around llamas—they love talking to me," said Clay, as if he were joking (although, as you know, it was the truth).

"Riiight." Satya laughed. "Actually, we do have some llamas here."

"You do?"

"Yeah. A lot."

"Why?"

Satya made a face. It was too gross to say aloud.

"You mean, they're . . . dragon food?" said Clay, his mouth suddenly dry.

"Kind of horrible, huh? But it's the circle of life, I guess. The lions eat the antelopes, and the antelopes eat the grass or whatever."

Clay thought guiltily of Como. If he ever saw that llama again, Clay owed him an apology.

"Seriously, the llamas don't have such a bad

life—I mean, until... Anyway, I can take you to see them if you want." Satya smiled mischievously. "So you can talk to them."

Clay paled, then realized she was referencing his joke. "Ha-ha."

"No, really, you want to go?"

Clay hesitated. It would be awful to see the llamas, knowing what their fate was going to be. On the other hand, he wasn't helping them by pretending they didn't exist. If he went, at least he might learn a little more about the dragons. And he was going to have to know a whole lot more about the dragons if one of them was going to be his ride out of there.

"I'm not gonna force you—"

"No, no, I want to," said Clay hastily.

"Okay, but we'd better ask her first," said Satya, indicating Ms. Mauvais, who was standing some distance away, in conversation with Charles. "I don't want to make her mad. Well, I do, but I don't. If you know what I mean."

Happily, Ms. Mauvais thought a tour of the barn was a great idea.

Unhappily, she thought the idea was so great that she insisted everyone go. Everyone but her. She didn't want to get her clothes dirty. Amber would lead the group in her place. "Gyorg will give you his keys," Ms. Mauvais told her.

And just like that, Clay's hopes of a solo trip with Satya were dashed.

With Ms. Mauvais absent, Satya felt comfortable bringing Hero along. When Clay got into the Land Rover, his ski hat now firmly back on his head, he found Satya sitting next to her dad, with the bird on her shoulder. Hero leaned around the seat and stared right at Clay. *I will peck your eyes out*, she seemed to be saying, *if you come a single inch closer.*

They drove off in the opposite direction from the laboratory, and Clay tried to keep track of their twists and turns on the map he was building in his mind. And tried not to think of how itchy his scalp felt under the hat.

Vicente pulled over in front of a tall wire-mesh fence that ran the length of a large barnyard—the very one Clay had seen from the chopper the day before. No doubt the fence was sturdy enough to keep animals inside, but Clay couldn't help thinking it would be of little use keeping out certain predatory beasts. If for some reason a dragon couldn't fly over the fence, the dragon could slash right through it.

As Clay walked through the gate, he thought again of Como. There were at least two dozen llamas, a few that Clay would have trouble telling apart from his llama friend back at Earth Ranch. They lazily chewed grass and rolled in the dirt, seemingly unaware of the dragons that lurked not so far away.

The llamas shared space with a handful of other animals, including one pig, two goats, and nine or ten chickens that scuttled between the llamas' legs, pecking at the ground.

"They tried other animals—goats and sheep and whatnot—but the dragons liked the llamas best," Satya explained matter-of-factly.

She pointed to an adjacent, smaller barnyard in which several flightless birds could be seen standing around. "Emus. For the eggs."

Past the barnyard and the enormous barn were three tall gray cylindrical structures—storage silos. The silos formed a semicircle and looked a little foreboding and fortress-like. At the bottom of each was a pair of double doors, closed with heavy chains. Clay stared at the silos. The more he looked at them, the more they resembled prison towers.

"What's inside those things?" he asked Satya as casually as he could.

"Those silos? Feed for the animals, mostly. You know, grain and hay and stuff... Oh, no you don't—" Satya put a hand on Hero, who was looking very purposefully at a nearby chicken. "Not now..."

As Satya tried to keep Hero from making a meal out of the chicken, Clay slipped away from her and sidled up next to a pair of llamas that were grazing on their own, near the barnyard's back gate.

"*Hola. ¿Cómo estás?*" said Clay in Spanish because that was what he was used to speaking with Como.

The llamas looked blankly at him. But one cocked its head, as though trying to figure out what sort of animal he was.

"*Yo me llamo* Clay. *¿Habla español?*"

The llamas said nothing.

"Is English better?"

He wasn't certain the language selection mattered—he was pretty sure that his communication with animals operated on a different, more telepathic level—but it didn't hurt to ask.

One of the llamas nodded. Or maybe it was just chewing.

Clay plunged ahead. "So how's it going? How's that grass?"

The other llama snorted and spit.

"The grass gets a little warm this late in the morning, doesn't it?" Clay guessed. "But what can you do, right?"

This time, the llamas definitely seemed to be nodding.

Encouraged, Clay leaned in and lowered his voice. "So, hey, you know those buildings over there, where they keep your food?" He discreetly tilted his head in the direction of the silos.

The llama on the left made an inquiring noise.

“No, no, I can’t open them for you—wish I could!” Clay smiled apologetically. “I was just wondering if they might be keeping anything else in there, like a two-legged animal, maybe? You know, like me. A human. But a girl human . . . or a woman human, I mean,” he corrected himself. Cass was twice his age, after all.

The llamas exchanged a glance before the one on the right spit casually and whinnied.

“So you think somebody does live in there?” said Clay, trying not to sound too excited.

The llama on the right conferred with the other, then whinnied again.

"You don't know what they look like, but they smell like a two-legged animal? And they get special food delivered in the mornings?"

Yes! He made a fist. At last he knew where Cass was!

The llamas whinnied again, but now their whinnying was beginning to sound like whining.

"What? Why don't you get special food like she does?" Clay shook his head sympathetically. "I don't know. That's a bummer. At least you're not stuck inside a silo though, right? You have your freedom... sorta...for a while...."

The llamas looked at him expectantly, waiting for him to finish his thought.

"Anyway, thanks for your help!" said Clay cheerily. "You guys are really cool."

He was about to turn to go, when they started nudging him with their noses. "What? Oh, man, I'm sorry, I would totally give you guys a carrot if I had one, but..." He shrugged helplessly.

Just then Satya walked over, shaking her head. "You really commit to a joke, I'll tell you that much."

"What do you mean?"

"You've been talking to those llamas for almost five minutes."

"I was waiting for you to notice," Clay improvised.

Shoot. He thought he was being more discreet. Had anyone else seen?

"Oh, I noticed, all right. Not too many people have full-on conversations with farm animals. Plants maybe."

Satya leaned against the fence near him. Hero was perched on her shoulder again.

Tentatively, Clay reached out, intending to pet the bird's cheek. Hero squawked angrily, and Clay jerked his hand away.

Satya laughed.

"Does she eat chocolate?" Clay pulled a leftover piece of chocolate out of his pocket. It was melted.

"No, she eats meat. And, by the way, that's gross." She reached into her own pocket and pulled out a cube of meat—just like the cubes they fed to the baby dragons. "Here, give her this."

Clay made a face as he took it. "That was in your pocket? And you thought the chocolate was gross?"

Clay was about to say something else (devastatingly charming, no doubt), when a jangling sound announced that Amber was strolling toward them, wearing a ridiculous army-green safari bodysuit.

"Heyyyy, guys! How's everything going over here?"

As Amber came closer, Clay saw what had made the jangling sound: Gyorg's brass key ring, hanging from a belt loop on Amber's bodysuit. There were so many keys on the ring that Clay was sure one of them *must* be for the silo. . . . But how to get it?

"Such a beautiful eagle you have," she said.

"Falcon," Satya corrected.

Amber leaned in and tried to pet Hero. Hero snapped at her, even more fiercely than she had snapped at Clay, he was happy to see.

Insulted, Amber pulled away from the bird. "Sheesh, you're not the friendliest thing in the world, are you?"

"She's a bird of prey, not a pet," said Satya stiffly.

Clay thought back to what Leira had taught him on his last day at Earth Ranch: What were the three Ds of pickpocketing? Oh, yeah. Divert. Detach. Disappear.

"Hey, Amber," said Clay, acting fast, "if you want to make friends with Hero, hold still."

Before Satya or Amber could see what he was doing, he showed the cube of meat to the hungry bird, then placed it on Amber's arm, just the way Satya had placed meat on his arm a day earlier.

Immediately, Hero spread her wings and lunged for the meat.

Amber screamed and swung wildly. The bird clung to her in a panic, wings flapping.

"Oh, sorry, sorry!" said Clay.

"Hero, stop that!" shouted Satya.

Clay's heart thumped. It's now or never, he told himself.

Under the guise of helping, he leaned into

Amber, unhooked the key ring from her belt loop, and slipped it into *his* jeans. Success! He felt light-headed.

"Ugh, Satya," Amber scolded when Hero was safely resting on Satya's wrist. "That bird is a menace. I'm going to have to talk to Antoinette about it." She rubbed her arm where she had been scratched by the bird's claws.

"Sorry," Satya said, calming Hero down. "I don't know what happened. Just...just don't get so close next time."

Satya darted a look at Clay. If she didn't know what he had done, she definitely suspected it.

"Come on. The Wandsworths have a question about the llamas that I need you to answer," Amber said, dropping the sweet girlie tone of voice. "I guess it's obvious I don't know anything about animals."

Satya shot a last accusatory look at Clay, then followed Amber out the gate to where the Land Rover was parked and the others were already waiting.

Clay felt bad; he had acted impulsively, without thinking about how it would affect Hero or Satya. However, he had the keys now; there was no backing out.

Glancing around to make sure there were no human eyes on him, he stepped over to the gate and lifted the latch. Quickly, he shoved the gate open a few inches and beckoned to the llamas nearby.

"Hey, guys, wanna get out and see the world?" he said, nudging the gate with his foot. "Here's your chance—run!"

The llamas blinked at him for a minute, but then the pig came squealing past them and shoved its way through, forcing the gate open even wider. Blazing out of the barnyard, the pig ran right through Amber's legs, making her scream and grabbing the attention of everyone else on the tour.

Soon the goats, the chickens, and even the llamas were making for the fence and scattering in a million directions. While Amber continued screaming and Charles retreated to the safety of the Land Rover, Satya and her father sprinted after the rampaging animals, trying desperately to steer them back toward the barn.

The Wandsworths, meanwhile, stood in the middle of the melee, scowling at everyone, apparently counting on their aura of disapproval to keep the animals from trampling them to the ground.

Under the cover of all that chaos, Clay ran to the third silo. Luckily, the door was on the far side of the silo, out of view of the group. Breathing heavily, Clay chose a key from Amber's ring at random and fumblingly inserted it into the padlock. The first one didn't fit, and neither did the second, third, fourth, or fifth. Just as he was getting really worried, Clay tried the sixth key....

Click!

The door swung open and Clay peered in, trying to make out any shapes in the silo's dark interior.

A second later, there was an arm around his neck, and he was being dragged, choking, into the silo.

CHAPTER THIRTEEN

THE PRISONER IN THE SILO

Moments earlier

The beetle must have thought it was safe.

It was the middle of the day, the middle of summer, the middle of the desert. (Well, the desert-turned-jungle, but how was the beetle to know that?) Most of the beetle's natural predators—the owls, the anteaters, even the snakes—would be fast asleep. And if they weren't asleep, they wouldn't have been able to get in here anyway, this cool, dark space that could only be entered through cracks and crevices in that round metal wall.

With single-minded determination, the beetle tiptoed across the dirt on its six bent legs. The goal: a lone crumb lying on the ground, in a narrow shaft of light.

Alas, before the beetle could reach its target, a hand darted out from the darkness—and snatched up the beetle.

The hand belonged to a woman whose nose was smeared with dirt, who hadn't washed her hair in weeks, and whose black clothes had long ago turned a dusty gray. And yet her pointy ears were as alert as ever.

She held the beetle between her thumb and forefinger, admiring its shell in the sliver of sunlight. A Namib Desert beetle! Adapted for the arid conditions in just the way the San people had described. At any other time, the Namib would have made an excellent specimen for study.

"I'm so sorry about this," she whispered.

CRRRUNCH—

Cass sighed discontentedly.

She was still hungry, though she hated to admit it. Gram for gram, insects are a great source of protein. Unfortunately, you have to eat a lot of them (hundreds, probably) to equal what you would get in a peanut butter and jelly sandwich, let alone in a hamburger. Not that she would ever eat a hamburger. She'd been a vegetarian—okay, vegetarian-ish—for as long she could remember. She ate meat, even bug meat, only when it was a matter of survival.

Naturally, she had been doing her best to maximize the meager rations that were delivered to her every morning. On the ground in front of her were tiny seedlings sprouting up in the spots most often hit by the sun: There was a tomato plant grown from a seed extracted from a quarter of a cherry tomato that had miraculously appeared in a so-called salad, a potato plant grown from a barely cooked potato that was supposed to have been her dinner one night, and an entire row of oats grown from a sack that had spilled before being removed from the silo. Soon she would have a veritable indoor farm.

Based on the tally marks she'd carved into the metal wall, it had been three weeks to the day since Ms. Mauvais had found her attempting to save a baby dragon on the lip of the crater. Three weeks that she'd been living in *silo-tary confinement*, as she'd taken to calling it. A pun she thought worthy of her friend Max-Ernest. (I'm not so sure about that, but who am I to judge?) Her goal was total self-sufficiency. Every day she followed an intense workout regimen to keep her body in tip-top shape: push-ups, sit-ups, lunges, and squats, followed by an hour of running in place. To keep her brain sharp, she challenged herself to recite facts about Richter scale earthquake measurements and the epidemiology of infectious diseases. And, of course, she kept a journal, writing on the paper she made from pulped hay, with a quill made from a stray pigeon feather and ink made from crushed leaves and an old goji berry she'd found stuck in a fold in her pocket.

Ms. Mauvais had been visiting almost daily, sure that she could make Cass crack and reveal the secrets of the Terces Society, but Cass had only grown more resolute over time, and Ms. Mauvais more frustrated. "For your sake, I hope you have some information of value in that dull, plodding brain of yours," Ms. Mauvais had said the previous evening. "The Secret Keeper, they used to call you. But do you really know how to get to the Other Side? Alas, I think not, and I'm beginning to tire of our little chats."

The fact that the Midnight Sun knew of the existence of the Other Side was a huge blow. Exactly how much the members knew about it—and what their activities at the Keep had to do with the Other Side, if anything—Cass had yet to ascertain. Her hope was to keep the conversations with Ms. Mauvais going for as long as possible; every question Ms. Mauvais asked told Cass more about what the Midnight Sun knew or suspected. By the time Ms. Mauvais gave up on her, Cass intended to have a comprehensive outline of the Midnight Sun's plans and, of course, to have her own exit strategy worked out in detail.

That was the idea, anyway, until Max-Ernest's little brother showed up.

The rattling of keys and fumbling attempts to open the door came as a surprise; Ms. Mauvais customarily visited Cass at night. As the struggles with the padlock became more and more frantic, Cass became increasingly suspicious. Whoever was at the door, it wasn't Ms. Mauvais. And moreover they were very clumsy.

Clumsy enough to let Cass overpower them and escape from the silo? The timing wasn't perfect, but experience had taught her to take advantage of opportunity when it knocked—or in this case, when it broke in.

When the door finally burst open and a boy stepped in, squinting, Cass was waiting, ready to put him in a headlock.

"Hey! Ow!" the intruder said in a muffled wheeze. His voice was oddly familiar, like the voice of a sitcom star or some Internet comedian. Then again, Cass never watched sitcoms or funny online videos.

Cass loosened her headlock and leaned around to see the intruder's face. "Paul-Clay?"

"It's just Clay now," he said, coughing.

Cass released Clay and pulled him inside the silo, shutting the door behind him. "When did you get so tall? And more to the point, what the heck are you doing here?"

"Max-Ernest sent me to rescue you," said Clay, dusting off his shirt and pants.

"You're kidding."

"Nope." Clay looked over his shoulder. "I got her!" he said excitedly.

Cheers erupted in his ears. *"Awesome!" "Congrats!"*

Cass whipped around. But there was nothing behind her except her empty silo cell. "Um—who are you talking to? Is your brother here somewhere?"

"Oh, no—" Clay pointed to his ski hat. "My hat is like a walkie-talkie. My friends at Earth Ranch say hi."

"A walkie-talkie? This isn't cops and robbers! The Midnight Sun don't play games—do you know how dangerous this place is?"

"She says hi back," said Clay.

"You know we can hear her. . . ."

"Why don't you guys just take a break for a while, huh?"

Cass shook her head. "What was Max-Ernest thinking, sending a child!?"

"Didn't you and my brother go on Terces Society missions when you were my age?" said Clay, more than a little miffed. "And you're welcome, by the way."

"Okay. You're right." Cass held up her hand—a truce. "So tell me, Special Agent Paul-Clay—sorry, Special Agent *Just Clay*—what's your big escape plan?"

"Uh." Clay shoved his hands in his pockets. "To fly out of here on a dragon."

"I'm serious. You must have some idea."

"That is the idea."

Cass stared at him, incredulous. "You've been reading too many fantasy books."

"I've done it before," said Clay defensively. "I've flown on a dragon."

"Your brother might have said something about that," Cass admitted.

"Well, it's true. We thought Ariella would be here, but, anyway, there's no reason I can't fly on another dragon," he said, trying to sound confident. "I know the *Occulta Draco*."

"The what? Never mind. Say you can fly a dragon, even though . . . well, say you can—isn't there something stopping them from flying away?"

"You're talking about the dome," Clay said. "I found the tower where they control it. We just have to go there, turn it off, and then . . ."

"Find a dragon and ask it politely not to eat us?"

Clay took a breath. "If you really want to know, Owen was supposed to be here, too, but he got called back to the island. And his plane got stuck in some lava. So..."

"Dragons are all we've got," Cass finished for him.

"Yeah. Pretty much."

Cass nodded. "All right, then."

She made a quick circle around the interior of the silo, saying a silent good-bye to her seedlings, then looked at Clay.

"Well?"

"Well what?" Clay asked.

"Lead us to that tower. I assume you've got the password or key or whatever we need for the job?"

"Um..." Clay paused.

Cass pursed her lips. "Right. Well, we'll figure it out."

"Yeah," said Clay, relieved. "Hey, it's really good to see you."

Cass patted him on the head. "That's nice, but let's have the tearful reunion later, okay?"

"Okay." Clay gave her a little salute and turned around to lead them out of the silo.

Outside, the rest of Clay's tour group was still battling renegade llamas.

It meant he and Cass had to take the long route,

but Clay figured it was best to run in the opposite direction. They crept from the silo door toward the tree line, glancing backward the entire way to make sure they weren't being seen.

Once under cover of the jungle, they doubled back and started pushing their way through bushes and vines. They tried to stay parallel to the road as they went, but even so they almost lost their way a few times.

It took more than thirty minutes to come in sight of the clearing where the control tower was located. Cass was too busy looking at the tower to notice that Clay had stopped in his tracks. She was about to step into the clearing, when Clay grabbed her arm and put his hand over her mouth. "Shh! Don't move!"

Lying on the ground in front of them, no more than ten feet away, was the spiky end of a huge green tail. It twitched, then swung out of the way, but when they leaned forward to see where the tail had gone, it swung back toward them, coming within inches of where they stood.

The tail was attached to a gigantic green body topped with delicately folded wings. On the dragon's snout was a distinctive white mark.

"That's Snowflake," Clay whispered.

"Cute," Cass whispered back.

He pointed to the line of white posts on either side of the dragon. Snowflake's tail was sticking out from between them.

"See those posts with the blinking red lights—they send out the electric currents or whatever that make the dome. The good news is that the dragon can't go all the way outside that line. Only up to its collar."

"And the bad news is . . . ?"

"The rest of the dragon is outside the line."

"And to get to the control tower . . ."

"We have to pass the dragon, yeah."

Cass nodded, calm and businesslike. "Is it sleeping?"

"Yeah . . . Well, maybe . . . not . . ."

Frozen in place, they watched as the dragon heaved itself up and stretched. Then it turned its massive head their way, nostrils flaring.

"Ow!" Clay squeaked. As calm as Cass seemed, she was digging her nails into his shoulder.

"Sorry." She released Clay and took a step back. "Does it see us?"

"No . . . Well, maybe . . . yeah . . ."

The dragon was staring at them but not making a move.

"If it wanted to kill us, it already would have, right?" Cass asked after a moment. "I mean, you think we can just walk by it?"

"Yeah . . . Well, maybe . . . ?"

"I thought you were the dragon guy," said Cass.

"You're going to have to be a lot more decisive if we're going to get out of here."

"Okay, let's walk, but... be prepared to run."

Palms sweating, they started to walk as quickly and quietly as they could across the clearing.

The dragon watched, its strange lizard eyes giving them no clue whether it was happy, mad, or indifferent. Then, all of a sudden, one of its wings unfolded and stretched to full length, blocking them from seeing its face. With a quick move, the dragon shifted its weight and craned its neck around. It looked at them and roared briefly, just enough to make Clay feel like his heart was about to stop.

Cass looked from the dragon to Clay. "You're sure you know how to handle these creatures? Better to tell me now..."

"I'm sure." Clay avoided her gaze.

The dragon had bent its head and started licking its wings. Grooming itself.

"If you say so," said Cass. "Looks like what we really need is some dragon catnip."

As soon as they were safely past the white posts, Clay tugged on Cass's arm and they hurried toward the tower. When they got to the ladder, they glanced around—they seemed to be alone—and started climbing.

Clay pushed opened the hatch door, and they pulled themselves into the room at the top of the tower. Cass took in the banks of computers and the beeping, blinking radar. Then she stepped to the window to observe the green dragon, now stretching out in a patch of sunlight.

"Okay," said Cass. "As soon as you turn the dome off, we're going to have to move fast. We slide down the side of the ladder like it's a fire pole, then jump right onto that dragon."

Clay nodded uncomfortably. There was no sense saying that they wouldn't be able to jump onto a dragon like that. They would just have to try.

His hand hovered over a big red button beneath the digital map tracking the dragons' movements. "I think it's this one."

"Well, press it."

Taking a breath, Clay put his forefinger on the button and pushed.

"It doesn't go down."

"Maybe you have to unlock that first," said Cass, pointing to a small keyhole.

Clay pulled Gyorg's key ring from his pocket. He tried a few keys until he found one that fit.

Just as Clay's hand hovered over the red button again, Cass tensed. "What was that sound? The dragon?"

"Actually, it was a car," said a voice. "Parking."

Clay quickly tucked the key ring under his waistband. Then turned around to see Gyorg pointing some kind of rifle at them.

"This is tranquilizer gun," said Gyorg. "It will not kill you. But it will put you to sleep. And then when I push you out, there is very good chance you will die from fall." He motioned to the open hatch door at his feet. "Or you climb down. You choose."

Ms. Mauvais was waiting for them at the bottom with an expression of mild interest. Behind her, looking exceptionally smug, was Charles.

"Well, well," Charles said. "What have we here, *Austin?*"

"Austin?" Cass repeated.

Clay nodded, trying to convey with his eyes that she should play along.

"I told you he was with the opposing team," Charles said to Ms. Mauvais. "Or should I say the *other side.*"

Clay's stomach lurched. He'd had a feeling Charles was onto him.

"No, he's not," said Cass quickly. "He's not on any side. I just met him."

"Somebody left the padlock open and dangling," Clay jumped in, "and I . . . decided to look inside."

Ms. Mauvais regarded him with undisguised skepticism. "Left it open, you say? How careless."

"Happens to the best of us," said Cass. "So anyway, he found me inside and took pity on me. Some people are like that. It's called compassion. Let him go."

"Oh, you know me better than that, Cassandra,"

said Ms. Mauvais scornfully. “I don’t *let people go*.” She made it sound like a silly new dance she would never try.

She turned to Clay. “It seems I was wrong to hope your father would continue investing in our little project here. But perhaps you will be valuable in any case—as a hostage. Now turn out your pockets so we know you’re not hiding any keys in there.”

His heart beating uncontrollably, Clay did as he was told. Luckily, he hadn’t had time to move the keys from his underwear to his pockets.

Ms. Mauvais nodded curtly, then snapped her fingers. “Gyorg—”

Gyorg reached for Clay. Clay jerked away, and Gyorg wound up pulling the hat off Clay’s head.

“No!” Clay shouted before he shut his mouth. They were taking away his link to Leira and Brett and all of Earth Ranch, but he couldn’t risk letting them know that. “Hat head,” he said in response to Ms. Mauvais’s raised brow.

“You’ve got a lot more to worry about than hat head, young man,” Ms. Mauvais said.

She turned toward a waiting Land Rover. “Put that riffraff somewhere, Gyorg. I’ll deal with them later.”

CHAPTER FOURTEEN

THE VISION IN THE TOILET

Meanwhile, back on the ranch...

Jonah, dude, you okay?" asked Pablo.

"I'm fine."

"You've been in there for two hours. People are getting worried, man."

"I said I'm fine. Go away."

"Plus, you know, they need to go. You're not the only guy in camp who has bodily functions to take care of."

"Tell them to find a tree."

"Let me talk to him," said Kwan.

They were standing in line in front of every camper's favorite outhouse. Favorite because it was isolated on a hill and therefore more private than the others (usually). Also because it had no roof and therefore was not smelly and even had a bit of a view.

"Jonah, if you can't pinch a loaf in two hours, it ain't happening," said Kwan. "So pull up your pants, open the door, and get your plugged-up butt over to Puke Yurt. Nurse Cora will give you something that will straighten you out in no time."

"And if she can't, I've got more of that exploding gum I made," said Pablo. "That might help."

"You guys are disgusting," said Jonah from the other side of the door. "And, FYI, I'm not trying to poop, okay?"

His friends looked at each other. "You're not?"

Leira and Brett walked up.

"I think he's worried about Clay," whispered Leira. She held up the conch shell walkie-talkie. "We told him the phone line went dead."

"He's probably crying in there," Brett mouthed. "But don't say anything, okay?"

"Jonah, are you crying in there?" asked Pablo loudly, grinning at the others. "Brett thinks you are."

Brett rolled his eyes.

"We don't care—you can cry in front of us," said Kwan. "There's no shame in that."

"Yeah, just man up and own those tears, bro!" said Pablo.

"Anyway, it's just us. It's not like there's"—Kwan

looked down the line and counted—"ten kids waiting to use the toilet or anything."

"Okay," said Jonah. "You really want so badly to know what I'm doing, come in and see for yourself."

"No, that's okay, some other time," said Kwan quickly.

"Yeah, man, your business... is your business," said Pablo.

The door opened, and Jonah beckoned them inside. He was standing up and fully dressed.

"No, please, come on in," said Jonah. "I insist."

Reluctantly, his friends all squeezed inside.

"Well, this is cozy," said Brett cheerily. "Thanks for inviting us in."

"Look—" Jonah pointed to the toilet.

"Do we have to?" said Leira.

"Yep."

Jonah's four guests looked into the toilet and were relieved to see nothing except water.

"So what are we looking for?" asked Brett. "Just out of curiosity."

"You don't see any swirling shapes?"

"Not really."

"Or, like, sparkles or shimmers?"

"Nope."

"I guess that's 'cause you guys don't have second sight." Jonah pushed his friends out of the way and looked down at the toilet himself. "I didn't want to say, because it's kinda embarrassing, but this is where I have my best visions."

Leira laughed. "Oh, so you weren't crying in the toilet. You were—"

"*Scrying*, yeah. And it's not a joke," said Jonah. "I've been trying to see what's happening with Clay, but he's half a world away, and I've never been there, and that makes it harder...."*

Then Jonah leaned farther in. "Wait, I think I'm seeing something!" he said excitedly.

"Is it yellow or brown?" Pablo snickered.

"Shut up, I'm serious."

The water in the toilet bowl, which had been reflecting the clear blue sky, now seemed to darken.

Jonah peered in, trying to discern what the darkening gray blob in the water could be. "I think that might be the body of an animal, and those—could those be wings?"

The others gasped as the vision in the toilet bowl suddenly became clear.

"It's a dragon!" Jonah shouted. "But what's happening? Is it attacking Clay?"

---

* When *scrying*, a fortune-teller looks into a reflective surface to see a future, past, or simply distant event. Typically, this is done with a mirror or crystal ball, but one can scry with any old reflective object lying around the house—a licked-clean chocolate wrapper, say. Jonah uses a toilet bowl. However, I don't suggest you follow his lead unless the past you want to see happens to be your last meal.

Heart in his throat, Jonah concentrated still harder on what the toilet bowl was showing him. The dragon's features became clearer and clearer, and closer and closer, as if it were coming right at Jonah. "It's getting bigger, and it looks vicious!" he shouted.

Leira tapped him on his shoulder, but he ignored her.

"Where is it?" he asked frantically, still staring at the water. "Where's it going? Has it already attacked him? Clay, can you hear me, buddy?"

The shoulder tapping turned to shaking.

Finally, Jonah leaned back. "What do you want?! There's a dragon out there somewhere, and I think it might be eating Clay!"

"There's a dragon, all right, but it's nowhere near Clay," said Leira.

"Huh?"

"That wasn't a vision you saw. It was a reflection."

Jonah glanced around; his friends' faces were all turned upward, their necks craned.

"Oh, wow," he said when he finally saw what they were seeing. "Sure looked smaller in the toilet."

Swooping low over the island, like a great eagle returning to its nest, was a dragon—the dragon known as Ariella.

CHAPTER FIFTEEN

THE PRISONER IN THE SILO II

It's the principle of the thing," Cass said, shaking her head at the patch of freshly trampled dirt. "Do you know how hard I worked getting those seeds to sprout?"

Cass walked over to the door, where a security guard was now posted twenty-four hours a day. She and Clay wouldn't be able to sneeze without Ms. Mauvais knowing about it.

"Did you even wait to apprehend us before destroying my garden?" Cass shouted at the door. "Strange set of priorities, if you ask me!"

I could say the same to you, Clay thought, but he didn't say so aloud.

He sat against the wall, slumped down with his chin on his knees. He wished Cass would stop yelling so he could be miserable in silence. He had failed—totally, utterly, no-bones-about-it failed. No, it was worse than that. What was it called when you double down on failure? Instead of rescuing Cass, he'd been thrown into jail with her; there were now two prisoners rather than one.

All they could do was sit and wait...for what? Who would come save them? Owen and the Earth Ranch crew were grounded, thanks to the volcano's appetite for seaplanes, and who else was there? Max-Ernest? Yeah, right, Clay thought. Fat chance.

Cass stopped pacing and looked at Clay, as if noticing him for the first time. "Clay? I hope you're not just sitting there moping," she said sternly.

"That's exactly what I'm doing."

"That's ridiculous. Things could be much worse."

"Worse?" Clay said, exasperated. "How?"

Cass shrugged. "We could be trapped in here with one of those dragons. Or they could be torturing us for information. Or we could be shipped off to some supersecret Midnight Sun prison in Antarctica...."

"Okay! I didn't actually want examples," Clay said. "I just can't believe I messed this up so badly."

"Don't blame yourself. It's very self-indulgent."

"Thanks," said Clay sarcastically. "That makes me feel a lot better."

Cass seemed like she was about to lecture him some more, then stopped herself and sat down next to Clay. "Look. Back in the day, your brother and I got in much worse scrapes, and we always got through it."

That was the last thing Clay wanted to hear about. "Yeah, yeah," he muttered. "My brother never would have screwed things up so bad. And I'm sure if he was here, he would tell me all about it." He paused. "If he talked to me at all."

"Uh, excuse me?" Cass said, leaning back to look at Clay. "Max-Ernest screwed things up plenty of times, believe me. And let's face it: He has a lot of faults, but *not* talking has never been one of them."

"Oh yeah?" Clay scoffed. "The last time I saw him, the *only* time he visited in two years, he talked a lot, sure—to you, on the phone. But he only talked to me for a minute, and that was about what kind of helmet I should wear when I skateboard. I don't think safety lectures really count as quality time."

Cass looked at him with what for her passed as sympathy. "You know what he was talking to me about that day?" she asked.

Clay shook his head.

"He was trying to convince me not to come here alone." She glanced around their silo prison. "And, in hindsight, he had some good points."

"Okay, so he doesn't even convince you not to go on a suicide mission—sorry, it's true—and then the minute he gets off the phone he runs off to Mexico with that Anthony dude. He barely said good-bye."

"Well, he and Anthony had to go talk to this man named Perry about the Keep."

"Perry? You mean Brett's father. The guy who kidnapped Ariella for the Midnight Sun."

"Well, whatever he did in the past, he's a broken man now. The Midnight Sun beat him up and left him on the side of the road in Baja. More or less."

"He deserves it," said Clay, remembering the moment when Brett's father left him and Brett under the volcano to die.

"Maybe so... Your brother and Anthony didn't get anything useful out of him, but they had to try." She sighed. "Anyway, I'm sure they enjoyed themselves. It was their first trip together and all."

Clay looked at her askance. "Wait—you don't mean *together* together?"

"Oh, you didn't know?" Cass asked, flustered.

Clay shook his head.

Cass could see the wheels turning inside him. "Are you surprised that he's with a guy?"

Shrugging, Clay considered this. "I guess I'm surprised he's with anyone at all...."

Cass smiled. "I know what you mean. Max-Ernest isn't exactly the dating type." She nudged Clay with her shoulder. "That's why we should be happy for him, right?"

"I guess so," said Clay, not entirely convinced.

"But maybe a little sorry for Anthony," Cass joked.

"Yeah, heh..." Clay chuckled. "I hope he likes puns. Like, a lot."

(I'm afraid I don't see the humor here.)

"At least he'll get chocolate," Cass reflected.

"What about you?" Clay asked. "Weren't you with Yo-Yoji?"

Cass threw her head back and laughed so loud it echoed in the silo. "Oh that was a *long* time ago! Yo-Yoji has had a lot of girlfriends since then. Comes with the territory, traveling the world as a DJ. You know he's designing his own product line now? It started with headphones. Now there are phone cases, sneakers, sunglasses..." Cass shook her head, lost in some memory. "I'm counting on him to start funding the Terces Society.

"And you?" she asked. "You seem a little more... advanced than Max-Ernest and I were when we were your age.... Do you have a girlfriend?"

"Er, no, but..." Clay could feel his face turning red. He was grateful for the darkness.

"There's a girl you like?"

"Sorta." Clay avoided meeting Cass's eyes.

"She has a boyfriend?"

"I don't think so...."

Just then there was a loud tinny banging sound from above, and then an echoing caw.

Clay looked up in surprise. Satya's falcon, Hero, was swooping down from an air vent with something hanging from her beak.

"She has a bird, though," he said, staring.

"That one?"

"Yep—ow!"

Hero landed on Clay's shoulder, digging her claws in, and dropped Clay's ski hat into his lap.

"Thanks," said Clay to Hero as calmly as he could.

The falcon bowed her head in acknowledgment. Then, job done, she lifted off and flew back up and out of the vent, leaving Clay rubbing his shoulder.

Inside the hat, there was a folded-up piece of paper.

Cass raised an eyebrow. "Well, that's one way to send a love note."

Blushing even harder, Clay opened it. Satya had scrawled a few words in pencil:

Be ready in five—

Reading over Clay's shoulder, Cass smiled. "Hmm, I think I like this girl."

They were waiting right beside the door, when Satya stepped into the silo, leaving the door cracked open behind her. Hero was sitting on her arm.

"You guys ready?"

Clay nodded, his ski hat now back on his head. "What happened to the guard?"

Satya grinned and held up a walkie-talkie. "I used my dad's walkie to call him off. But he won't be gone long. We have about three minutes to get out of here, tops." She looked at Cass. "I'm Satya, by the way."

"Cass. And thanks," said Cass.

"Yeah, thanks. This is so . . . awesome of you. . . ." After his confessional conversation with Cass, Clay was having a hard time looking Satya in the eye.

He made for the door, but Satya pressed a hand to his chest.

"Wait—first I want to know who you are. Really."

"I wanted to tell you," said Clay eagerly, "but—"

Cass clasped them both by the shoulder. "I don't want to ruin the moment, but can we do this later?"

"Sure." Satya nodded and pushed open the door.

"Clay! My name is Clay!" Clay said as the three dashed outside.

CHAPTER SIXTEEN

THE RUN THROUGH THE JUNGLE

As they ran through the jungle, with Cass shushing them and hurrying them along at every step, Clay did his best to explain to Satya who he was, why he was at the Keep, and how he planned to escape. And even though it wasn't strictly necessary, he told her why he wore a wool hat in hot weather. Just so she wouldn't think he *really* thought it was cool.

In most circumstances, his tale about a magical camp for juvenile delinquents and an evil society of centuries-old alchemists, not to mention his desire to become a Dragon Tamer and follower of the Occulta Draco, would have seemed far-fetched, to say the least. However, Satya had been living for weeks among the Midnight Sun and had seen dragons up close, so she was inclined to believe him.

"The way you handled Houdini—I *knew* you looked a little too comfortable for it to be your first time with a dragon."

Predictably, the part of Clay's story Satya had trouble with was the part that had him and Cass flying away.

"Be serious—you can't just fly those dragons out of here. First of all, there's the electric dome, remember?" Satya pointed at the sky. "Plus, I don't know what Ariella was like, but those dragons aren't really hop-on-board types."

"What about that crazy guy with the mustache and the cowboy hat?" said Clay, trying not to let her see how winded he was. "Show-ringer or something. He was trying to jump on Snowflake like it was a horse. He even had a bullwhip in his hand. . . ."

Clay held up an invisible whip, imitating. Satya looked at him like he was nuts, until it dawned on her.

"Wait, are you talking about Mr. Schrödinger? They told me he was gone. . . ."

"Well, maybe gone in the head, but he's still around." Clay almost tripped over a root, then righted himself. "I overheard him talking, and it sounded like he'd actually ridden the dragon before. He wouldn't stop babbling, saying he had to go back somewhere, that he'd never really left."

Cass stopped and looked back at Clay. "What else did he say?"

"Uh, not much. Nothing that made any sense, anyway. Ms. Mauvais promised he would be able to go back eventually, and that when he did, he would be a young man again."

"*A young man again*—she said those exact words?" asked Cass sharply.

"Uh-huh," said Clay, surprised by her tone. "I mean, I think so."

She silently considered what Clay had said.

Clay turned back to Satya. "Well, anyway, I still have Gyorg's keys, so I can turn off the dome if—"

Satya shook her head. "You can't go back to the control tower; they'll be watching it now." She hesitated. "But I guess if somebody else went—like me, for instance..."

"No way," Clay said quickly. "You've done enough."

"Very gentlemanly," said Cass. "But isn't this her choice to make?"

"Here's the thing," said Satya. "If we turn the dome off, the other dragons will get out, too, and they'll attack everyone here. I don't like those white-gloved weirdos very much, but I don't want to kill them. Plus, my dad would totally get fired."

"Trust me, you don't want your dad working for them," Cass said.

"And anyway, even if they get out, the dragons will still have their collars on," said Clay. "So your dad can still control them, right?"

"Maybe. Once the dome is turned back on," said Satya. "But let's try not to let them get out in the first place."

She looked from Clay to Cass and back again. "Okay, if you give me the key, I'll create a distraction, then shut off the dome. But only for, like, a minute. Seriously"—she held up her index finger—"*one* minute. And it has to be at night so nobody sees me. Let's say right after sunset."

"That should be about eight twenty-one tonight," Cass said. At Satya's look, Cass shrugged. "Always good to know what time the sun sets, just in case."

"Fine. Say, four minutes after that, to give you guys time. At eight twenty-five, I'll shut down the dome. You'd both better be on a dragon and flying the heck out of here by then, because a minute later—" She made a buzzing sound to indicate the dome turning back on.

"You realize the Midnight Sun will be very unhappy with you if you're caught," said Cass.

"They won't catch me," Satya said confidently.

"You're sure?" prodded Clay. "Because we can do this ourselves, really—"

"No, you can't, and it's gonna be fine."

"Okay, thanks," Clay said awkwardly. "This is really cool of you."

"Yeah, it is," said Satya, businesslike. "Now, where are you going to hide in the meantime?"

Clay stared into the jungle. "I think it's time for me to ally with a dragon."

"Ally?"

"Like, make an alliance? That's what it's called in the *Occulta Draco* when you make friends with a dragon. Except you can't ever make friends with a dragon. So...yeah."

Both Cass and Satya blinked at him.

"You're not exactly inspiring confidence," said Cass.

"Oh, no worries," Clay said with an effort at heartiness. "I've read all about it, and I've got a couple of hours, right?"

"If you say so..." Cass was looking upward and frowning.

While they were talking, the clouds had parted and the mysterious line had appeared in the sky again. It flashed in the sunlight.

"That line in the sky—I saw it three weeks ago. Has it been there this whole time?"

Satya shrugged. "I think so? I mean, I only notice it sometimes. Why?"

"I'm just thinking about my original mission, that's all," said Cass, still focused on the sky. "What are they *really* doing with the dragons here? This guy Schrödinger—I have a hunch that he might be the answer." Cass looked at her young companions. "Where do I find him?"

"Um, he's in one of the tents, unless he got out again," said Clay. "But you're not thinking of going now, are you?"

"I'll meet you at nightfall."

"Where?" asked Clay as she ran off.

"At the edge of the clearing, near the tower," Cass called over her shoulder.

And with that, she disappeared into the shadows of the pathless jungle, leaving Satya and Clay alone.

"I have to get back," Satya said. "They're going to freak when they realize you two have broken out again."

She backed up and paused.

"What?" said Clay.

"Nothing. Just... your watch is working, right?"

Clay nodded, suddenly very grateful that Owen had given him the watch.

"Good. Remember: 8:25."

"I will. Don't forget this—" Clay handed her Gyorg's key ring, with the dome key sticking up. "Hey, Satya?"

"Yeah?"

"Well, now that you know who I am..."

"What?"

"Nothing," said Clay helplessly. He wouldn't

have known how to tell her he liked her, even if they'd been in the normal world and not in an unbelievable, life-threatening situation.

Satya looked at him, a little confused. "Okay, well, I'll be at the guard tower tonight," she said, then turned to run off. Hero squawked something that Clay hoped meant *she likes you, too*—although it sounded more like *I'm hungry*—and flew after her.

Suddenly, Clay felt very alone. He tapped the side of his ski hat, hoping to hear his Earth Ranch buddies on the other end. There was no response.

He tapped again. Still nothing. Could something have happened to the hat while it was out of his hands?

Clay sighed. Oh well. It wasn't as though Leira or Brett could really advise him on how to ally with a dragon. He considered taking the hat off—it was as hot and itchy as ever—but he was loath to. Even if it wasn't working, it made him feel a little more connected to his friends.

CHAPTER SEVENTEEN

THE FIRE IN THEIR BELLIES

Clay loved the *Occulta Draco* and the whole idea of becoming a Dragon Tamer too much to think ill of that ancient memoir-slash-instruction manual, but I have no such scruples: It was, and is, a singularly unhelpful document.

Clay well remembered the page in *Secrets of the Occulta Draco* where allying was discussed. According to the author, most Dragon Tamers formed an alliance by bestowing a gift, performing a favor, or singing a song. Well, he had no gift to give and no idea what favor to bestow; and as for a song, he could hardly carry a tune.

He would just have to improvise.

During the helicopter tour, he'd seen all three of the grown dragons hanging out at the big lake near the center of the crater. If he didn't run into any of them sooner, he decided, he would make his way there. He only hoped he'd find a dragon before a dragon found him.

Taking a deep breath, he walked between two poles and crossed the border of the dome.

Clay might not have had a good singing voice, but unlike his older brother, he had a decent sense of direction (perhaps because he had been left to navigate for himself so often as a young kid). Watching for telltale footprints, listening for telltale footsteps, and even smelling for telltale, well, dragon patties, Clay pushed his way deeper and deeper into the jungle, terrified all the while that he would be caught unawares.

Soon enough, he could see cracks of light between the trees, and he could hear what sounded like a distant waterfall. A moment later the jungle suddenly ended, and Clay was squinting against the bright late-afternoon sun. He'd found the lake, but as far as he could see, he hadn't yet found a dragon.

He started walking around the water's edge, looking for any talon or tail that might happen to be peeking out from behind a boulder, listening for a roaring yawn or a stomach rumble that might be coming from a hidden cave. The lake was perfectly clear, and Clay could see the sandy bottom—probably the only part of the crater that looked the way it had before the Midnight Sun arrived.

Then Clay heard a loud metallic scratching that made the hair on his neck stand up. It was coming from a little ways down the lake, just inside the tree line.

Clay proceeded with caution, peering around the trunk of a giant banana tree. There was Snowflake standing up on two powerful hind legs. The smallest of the three grown dragons, Snowflake nonetheless looked huge in this posture. The dragon was backed up against a tall boulder, scraping its back and neck against the rock's surface. From the expression on Snowflake's face, the dragon was having a difficult time scratching whatever spot was itchy.

As Clay watched, unsure what to do, the frustrated dragon let out a roar of aggravation and slumped onto its big scaly rear end.

Was there a way Clay could help?

He stepped out from behind the tree and approached slowly.

"Hey there, buddy," Clay said, putting on a big smile. "Whatcha doin'? Can't get to that itch, huh?" He took one step forward, then two. "I hate that feeling."

Snowflake turned toward Clay and gave him a sullen, withering look.

Silently, Clay cursed himself, remembering how Ariella had reacted every time Clay suggested there was any similarity between a human and a dragon. On the upside, at least Snowflake appeared to understand him.

"Oh, sorry!" Clay said. "You're totally right. I have no idea what you feel. I'm just a lowly creature who can't fly or do anything cool."

He paused for a moment, then took another step. "I wouldn't bring it up except—if you wanted—I could help you out and give you a scratch. I mean, *if* you had an itch. Sometimes you need a second pair of hands . . . or, er, claws or whatever."

Snowflake continued to stare dubiously at him but seemed to be considering Clay's offer. With a resigned snort, the dragon slumped down on its belly, wings folded at its sides and front legs folded underneath like a cat's.

Clay glanced around quickly and spied a palm frond lying on the ground. The leaves had fallen off, leaving a long serrated edge.

"Hey, now, this looks like a good back scratcher, doesn't it?"

Holding up the palm frond so Snowflake could see it, Clay approached slowly. The dragon followed his movements with a dark, unblinking eye. Cautiously, Clay leaned against the dragon's side, feeling its great belly rise and fall as it breathed. He reached up as far as he could with the palm frond and started scratching the sharp ridges of Snowflake's back.

"Here? No—a little farther up... Here? Okay, to the left..."

Clay scratched and scratched, following Snowflake's directions, until he was scratching along the dragon's neck. Clay was momentarily confused by a strange buzzing sound, then realized it was coming from the gleaming steel ring around Snowflake's neck.

"Er—uh—" Clay stalled, nervous about getting too close to the mysterious piece of technology. But the dragon twisted its neck, urging Clay forward, until Clay got the message and slid the end of the palm frond under the collar and started scratching as best he could.

The dragon shut its eyes and made a rumbling sound almost like a purr. "Aha, found it, huh?" Clay said, scratching harder. He wasn't sure how vigorously dragons liked to be scratched, but there wasn't much chance of damaging the steel-hard scales.

Could he really be making an alliance this easily? Clay wondered. What would happen if he were to try to climb onto the dragon's back right now?

He was on the verge of asking for a ride when the dragon abruptly shook itself and knocked Clay onto his butt.

"Hey!" Clay said, getting up. "What did I do?"

With a casual swing of a wing, the dragon swiped at Clay, brushing him away. Clearly, petting time was over.

Blinking lazily, Snowflake stretched, then readjusted, seemingly ready for a nap. Seeing that Clay was still standing there, the dragon swiped once more. Clay leaped backward, barely avoiding the knife-sharp talon at the end of Snowflake's wing.

"Jeez!" Just when he thought he was making progress...

The dragon twisted its neck around and roared into the air. Clay scrambled back to the edge of the lake, unsure whether Snowflake would pursue him.

When Clay looked back, there was no sign of the dragon. Snowflake didn't want to play cat and mouse after all.

He leaned over, resting his hands on his knees while he caught his breath. Should he go back and continue trying to ally with Snowflake? He didn't relish the idea, especially if the dragon was taking a nap. But he had so little time; he couldn't afford to wait a few hours before trying again.

Before he could decide on his next move, a wild rustling in the trees caught his attention. Something very big was tromping through the jungle, and it was causing quite a ruckus.

Could Snowflake have gotten over there so fast?

Clay didn't exactly like the idea of walking *toward* whatever monster was tromping through the jungle, but there was no time for hesitation. He stood up straight, set his jaw, and marched in the direction of the rustling trees.

It wasn't Snowflake; it was Rover. The gigantic gray dragon was hopping and skipping around, thrashing its head and whimpering. The sight of the great beast in such distress was a little bit comical, but a lot scary. Clay was almost clawed, walloped, and trod upon—all before the dragon had even glimpsed him.

Rover hopped around a few more times before Clay could see what was upsetting the dragon so much: a honey-dripping beehive nestled in the crook of a tree—a crook too narrow for the dragon's massive claws to squeeze into. Clay watched as the dragon tried once, twice, and a third time to stick its long twisty tongue inside to get to the honey.

The bees were onto Rover, though, and they flew into the dragon's mouth and buzzed around the dragon's eyes, sending Rover into fits of fury. There was probably no way the bees could sting through the dragon's armor of scales, but by all appearances they were driving the dragon crazy nonetheless.

Clay stepped closer, smiling wide to show he was friendly (though come to think of it, baring his teeth at a dragon wasn't necessarily the greatest idea). "Hey—hey there, Rover," said Clay, his hands sweating. "Are you trying to get some honey?"

The dragon spotted him—and let out a roar that shook the trees.

Clay swallowed but didn't move. "I'll take that as a yes," he said. "Why don't you give me a shot?

The dragon roared again, a little more angrily this time.

"Sorry!" Clay said quickly. "I didn't mean so I could have it. I meant, why don't you let me get the honey for you?"

Rover's eyes looked confused and suspicious. Generosity seemed to be a new concept for the dragon.

"Really, I just want to help."

Rover seemed to get the gist and reluctantly backed away from the beehive, but only a few feet. The dragon wasn't about to leave this strange human alone with such a treasure.

Last summer at Earth Ranch, Buzz had taught

Clay the most common beekeeper trick for extracting honeycomb from a beehive: smoke.* Alas, Clay had no matches or lighter, and he couldn't just snap his fingers to create a flame, like Flint could. But Buzz, quite unintentionally, had also taught Clay a little about talking to the bees.

Clay approached the beehive slowly, with steady footsteps. He carefully stuck an arm out, not flinching when first one and then a dozen angrily buzzing bees landed on his hands and arms. They tickled a bit as they walked on his skin, and Clay was certain he would be stung at any second, but he reminded himself that getting killed by a dragon, or by the Midnight Sun, would be much worse.

"I need to take a little bit of your honeycomb," he told them, in the peculiar humming voice Clay had heard Buzz speak in. "It is for your own good. It is the only way the dragon will leave you alone."

It took a few tries and some more coaxing, but apparently he was doing a passable imitation of bee-speak, because eventually the bees allowed Clay to get a handle on the hive and to snap off a Frisbee-sized piece of honeycomb.

---

* Smoking a beehive calms the bees so that they are less likely to sting you. Blow smoke in the face of almost any other creature, however, and you will get a very different reaction.

Clay backed up a few steps until only the very curious—or very lazy—bees were left on his hands.

"Thank you, thank you, thank you," he said, relief washing over him. "I will never get mad at Buzz's bees for bugging me again."

Then he tossed the honeycomb in a big arc toward Rover. The dragon lifted its head and snatched the honeycomb out of the air with about the closest thing a dragon can get to a grin.

The dragon dropped the honeycomb on the grass and, awkwardly holding the honeycomb with its talons, started licking pockets of honey with its tongue.

"How is it?" Clay asked.

Rover looked at Clay, tongue lolling like a big, dopey golden retriever's.

Clay laughed. "Awesome."

He was about to sit down and try to work his way into a conversation with Rover, when a telltale rumbling came from deep within the forest. The steady plodding of heavy footsteps grew closer and closer, until Clay was nearly bonked on the head by a coconut that had been knocked loose from a palm tree.

Clay backed up until he was half inside a shrub, trembling a bit as the other dragon drew nearer.

Bluebeard entered the clearing on slow and steady feet, the dragon's long sharp claws digging into the ground, ripping the earth apart with every step. The blue markings on Bluebeard's face made the dragon look especially fierce as it searched the clearing, sniffing around for the human intruder.

Then Bluebeard noticed the honeycomb dripping from Rover's talons. With a contemptuous growl, Bluebeard looked from the hard-to-reach beehive to the big oaf of a dragon. It was pretty clear that Bluebeard didn't think Rover capable of stealing that sweet golden treasure without assistance.

It was also pretty clear that Bluebeard didn't like the idea of Rover's cozying up to a human.

Clay considered his options: Give up on the dragons and run away—and most likely be found and eaten anyway. Or face Bluebeard and try to ally with the toughest, meanest dragon of the bunch.

Clay took a deep breath and stepped forward.

Bluebeard regarded the puny human through slit eyes; the ends of the dragon's blue mustache-like lips curled upward as if to say, *Aha! I knew it was you!*

"Hey," Clay said, trying to sound relaxed, though his heart was beating wildly. "Do you want some honeycomb, too?"

Bluebeard snorted, then turned to Rover and, with a lightning-fast swipe of a talon, knocked the honeycomb out of the clearing. Rover whimpered. The message: Bluebeard didn't want any honeycomb that Clay had touched, and Rover wasn't to have it, either.

"Right," Clay said. "I know humans haven't really been the coolest to you guys."

Bluebeard stared at him. Rover lowered its eyes.

"Those collars—they really suck."

At the mention of the collars, Rover sat up straight, and Bluebeard emitted a low rumbling growl.

"Oh, heh," Clay said, raising his hands and backing up a little. "I'm just trying to say I'm not like those other humans."

For some reason, this seemed to puzzle Bluebeard.

What is a human?

It took Clay a moment to realize that Bluebeard had asked him a question—telepathically—and that the dragon expected an answer.

"Me, I'm a human."

Ah, a two-leg-no-wing. You put the collars on our necks.

"Yes. I mean, no, I'm not the one who—"

You try to control us, but soon we will kill you.

There was a chilling confidence to Bluebeard's assertion.

"No, don't kill me! I'm going to...turn off the collars and get you out of here. I'm not like the other...two-leg-no-wings. I'm friends with a dragon!"

Bluebeard looked at him contemptuously. *What is a dragon?*

"A dragon? You're kidding."

No, Clay thought, Bluebeard's not kidding. How would these dragons know what a dragon was? They're the only ones they've ever known.

"You. You are a dragon. You and Rover and..."

Bluebeard roared in fury. *Liar!!! We are not dragons!*

"Um, okay," said Clay backing away farther. "But why do you say that?"

You said you were friends with a dragon. One of our kind would never be friends with a two-leg-no-wing monster.

Well, if anything proves you're a dragon, it's your attitude, thought Clay.

Aloud, he said, "Well, you don't have to call yourself a dragon if you don't want to, but I would be stoked to be one if I were you."

Bluebeard nudged Rover, and they both roared at Clay.

We. Are. Not. Dragons.

The two dragons were standing on all fours now and looked like they were waiting for one more reason, any reason, to toss Clay in the air like a human volleyball. Panic like he'd never known engulfed Clay.

At least they couldn't breathe fire. That was something.

Sing. He should sing. Like the *Occulta Draco* suggested. It was the only thing left. But he couldn't think of a single song that seemed remotely applicable to the circumstances.

So just make one up, he told himself.

"*Dragons are awesome. They're old and wise,*" he sang-shouted, aware that he sounded terrible, but pushing ahead as if his life depended on it (which it did). "*They're pretty much the all-around coolest guys. . . .*" Bluebeard looked at him with a fury like Clay had never seen; it was as if he had just insulted Bluebeard, the dragon's family, and everything the dragon held dear.

We. Are. Not. Dragons.

Singing wasn't the answer.

The incensed dragon rose up on hind legs and opened its mouth, taking a big, deep breath. . . .

Clay inched backward, feeling the blood drain from his head.

Bluebeard let out a deafening

and then suddenly, as if it had been waiting there all along, fire blasted out of the dragon's mouth like out of the back of a rocket ship.

A few stray hairs sticking out of Clay's ski hat were singed; he'd narrowly avoided being burned alive.

So they *could* breathe fire after all. He had never been less happy to have been proven right.

Bluebeard looked briefly stunned. Then, with the thrill of a toddler taking her first steps—or, more to the point, the thrill of a caveman who has just discovered fire—the dragon reared back and released another fiery plume, even bigger and more powerful than the first.

Their conversation was over. Summoning his nerve, Clay forced himself to move.

With the sulfurous odor of dragonfire in his nose, he ran blindly into the jungle. Heedless of the branches scratching his arms and legs, he scrambled over rocks and tripped on tree roots. Anything to get away from Bluebeard.

Around him, one tree after another burst into flame. The dragon was in pursuit.

As he ran, panicked, panting, Clay gradually realized he wasn't heading to the dome's perimeter, as he'd intended; he was circling back in the direction he'd come from. When he broke through the tree line, he found himself once again facing the lake, but now he was at the upper end, which was bordered by a sheer rock cliff. A natural wall that Clay would have had trouble climbing even if he'd had all the right equipment and all the time in the world. He had reached a dead end.

Behind him, still partly hidden among the trees, but getting closer with every earthshaking step, was Bluebeard. And not far behind Bluebeard followed Rover, and now Snowflake as well, galloping after their leader.

One after another, the dragons spit triumphant fireballs into the air, leaving tree after tree in flames.

A trio of dragons that had *just* learned they could breathe fire.

In seconds, Clay would be at their mercy.

But out of the corner of his eye, Clay detected something: a dark sliver in the cliff, almost like an opening. . . .

The entrance to a cave?

Yes.

Clay sprinted toward it, relieved to see that the opening was big enough for him to get through comfortably, but much too small for a dragon. Consciously deciding not to consider what creatures *besides* dragons he might encounter inside, Clay slid into the cave just as Bluebeard burst from the trees.

The dragon roared upon seeing his human quarry disappear, then repeatedly rammed the side of the cliff in frustration. Clay backed up against the inside wall of the cave as pebbles and loose dirt showered down on him.

Bluebeard, agitated, backed away from the cliff, huffing and puffing angrily. Then the dragon let out a roar and charged at the cliff again, sending a wall of fire inside the cave. Holding his breath, Clay jumped out of the way just in time to avoid being engulfed in flames. He could smell his arm hairs as they curled in the heat. If Bluebeard kept this up, he would be no better off than a chicken in an oven. Perhaps sitting in a cave and waiting to be roasted alive wasn't exactly the best plan.

"Hey, Bluebeard," Clay called out. "I just thought of something."

Bluebeard huffed angrily, a puff of smoke rising out of the dragon's mouth. Clay winced, worried that anything he might say could push the dragon over the edge.

"I know you're all into your new firepower, but think about it: If you keep breathing fire into this cave, I'll die in here, and you'll never be able to get me out and eat me."

Bluebeard made an incredulous sound.

What makes you think I want to eat you? Maybe I just want to kill you.

"Oh, well, then..." Clay stumbled, trying desperately to think of another argument. "Then maybe you should go find something else to eat now? I mean, you must be hungry. And you need energy to kill me, right?"

The cave shook again, but when Clay peered out the entrance, he saw that it was because Bluebeard had taken an emphatic seat right in front of it. Clay was now stuck inside a dark cave, smelling the lasting effects of dragon breath and staring out at a dragon's immense butt.

No longer much concerned with their human prisoner, the other dragons lounged by the lake's shore, intermittently practicing their fire-breathing technique. Rover took to this new talent with fervor, blasting a spray of white-hot flame through the air along the brush at the edge of the lake. Snowflake, meanwhile, breathed fire as lazily as if blowing smoke rings.

Clay watched them disconsolately. To think that only moments earlier he'd been trying to befriend the dragons—he'd even imagined that he would fly away on a dragon's back! Now he couldn't imagine any scenario in which they would let him out of the cave alive. Soon the world would have no more to remember him by than a pile of scorched bones.

All this time, the sun continued creeping westward across the sky. The dragons' shadows grew long and thin, and Clay's worries multiplied. He thought guiltily of Cass and Satya. Where was Cass now? Was she waiting for him by the clearing? What would Satya do when she turned off the dome and didn't detect any of the dragons leaving?

He tried creating a distraction by tossing out a large stick he found inside the cave. But Bluebeard torched the stick before it hit the ground—target practice.

Clay felt around in his pocket for the exploding gum Pablo had given him, but decided that an explosion would only serve to further infuriate the dragons.

As for trying to reason with the beasts, so far he'd gotten exactly nowhere, and every wasted second brought him closer to the meeting time.

When the sun dipped below the edge of the crater's rim, Clay was in a full-blown panic. He stared at the hands on his watch as they got closer and closer to 8:25. *Tick tick tick.* Soon his flight window would be closed. The best thing he could hope for at this point was to be caught by the Midnight Sun. At least they might save him from the dragons.

Eight twenty-five. He peered out into the night as if he might see Satya or Cass coming to save him, but how would they even know where he was?

And then something happened—a strange reaction from the dragons outside the cave entrance. Snowflake's head was shaking back and forth. The dragon was fussing with its collar again, but tentatively, as if confused. Carefully, the dragon contorted its body enough to touch the collar with a talon.

Rover's head was shaking as well. The big dopey dragon looked questioningly at Bluebeard, but Bluebeard was scratching, too, and looked lost in thought.

Finally, Bluebeard eyed Snowflake and barked at the smaller dragon, unmistakably giving an order.

Snowflake remained sitting. *No way*, Snowflake seemed to say. *Not doing that again*.

Bluebeard nodded insistently, looking upward. It was clear to Clay that Bluebeard was telling Snowflake to fly.

They must realize the dome was shut off, he thought excitedly. Would they leave?

Snowflake didn't make a move.

Bluebeard grew impatient and let out a fiery roar. *FLY!* Snowflake growled a bit but finally stood up and, with a single flap of wings, launched into the air.

Snowflake flew up, and up, and up—to a point about as high as the helicopter had been on Clay's tour of the crater—and then tentatively poked at the sky with the tip of a wing. Apparently hitting no barrier, the dragon joyfully spread its wings, dove briefly, then rose again in triumph.

Watching in disbelief, Rover jumped clumsily into the air and, flapping wildly, started flying loops around Snowflake.

Snowflake swooped down over Bluebeard's head, seemingly expecting Bluebeard to join them. *We can fly anywhere we want! This is our chance!* Clay could feel Snowflake saying. The dragon waited, but Bluebeard didn't make a move. *Come on*, Snowflake seemed to urge. *Let's move!*

We will, Bluebeard said ominously. *But first we eat.*

The dragon spread its enormous wings and took off, rising up into the dark sky and turning to head toward the castle. Snowflake and Rover followed, thinking hungry thoughts.

CHAPTER EIGHTEEN

THE GUM IN CLAY'S MOUTH

When the sun dipped low in the sky and the first few twinkling stars were visible, Satya stood in the control tower, watching the seconds tick away on her wristwatch. She'd managed to finagle quite a distraction: After making sure that all the doors and windows in the nursery were closed so that the little dragons couldn't escape, she'd released them from their cages. At this very moment, Hero was flying through the nursery, wreaking havoc and taunting the dragons, who would be trying to get to the open coolers full of prime red meat. Every security guard at the Keep would be called in, as would her father.

Satya scanned the clearing again and again, but to no avail. She'd been standing in the tower for almost thirty minutes without seeing any sign of Clay or Cass—or of a dragon. But a plan was a plan, and at

8:25 on the nose, Satya took a deep breath and turned the key in the dome's master lock. She pointed her finger at the big red button, then pressed down without allowing herself another second of hesitation.

The dome died with a strange electric hiss, as if it were deflating. Satya hadn't noticed how pervasive the sound of the dome had been until it was gone. Suddenly, the sounds of dusk—the buzzing of insects, the cooing of hunting birds, and the whispering flaps of bats' wings—seemed as loud as fireworks.

Come on, Clay, she thought. *Come on.* The seconds on her watch ticked on and on, but still there was no sign of a large winged creature escaping with two puny humans on its back—not in the dark jungle depths, not in the starry night sky.

Thirty seconds...

Forty-five seconds...

A minute.

The time Satya had promised had come and gone. Her heart sank. Clay must have failed to mount a dragon; she only hoped he had survived the attempt.

Just as Satya's finger hovered over the button, preparing to turn the dome back on, a large figure flew into the night sky, its blue-black body a shifting shadow in the dark. Bluebeard. Satya's heart lifted—Clay! He made it!—until the dragon opened its mouth and...

Unlike the other times Satya had seen a dragon roar, this roar was accompanied by a blinding streak of fire. Her jaw dropped almost as fast as her stomach. Clay had been right; dragons could breathe fire after all. As if that wasn't terrifying enough, the white-hot exhalation lit up the night long enough for Satya to be sure of two things: Bluebeard was loose, and there was nobody on the dragon's back.

"Oh no."

As she watched, aghast, Bluebeard slowed and started circling above like some monstrous bird of prey.

Shaking with fear and adrenaline, Satya tapped the dome button, about to turn the power back on, but then she realized Bluebeard was already well outside the boundary. If she turned the dome on now, it would actually repel the dragon, rather than keeping Bluebeard enclosed.

"Oh no. Oh no. Oh no."

Bluebeard was soon joined by the two other dragons. They circled one another, looking as though they were discussing their plan of attack. Or at least two of them looked that way. Rover was doing cartwheels in midair, like a frolicking puppy who happened to have wings and to be the size of a whale.

Suddenly, Bluebeard's head spun in Satya's direction. The dragon was too far away for her to really see its face; nonetheless, Bluebeard seemed to her to be looking through the dusky night, right into her eyes.

Then, with a single stroke of wings, Bluebeard was off like a shot—diving straight toward the tower.

At the same second, the hatch door flung open with a *bang*, and Satya screamed. She spun around and saw Clay, his feet still on the ladder, sticking his head through the hatch.

"C'mon!" he shouted, breathing heavily. "We've gotta run!"

Clay grabbed Satya's hand and dragged her toward the hatch. "There's no time to climb down. Slide, like this—"

He grasped the side of the ladder and started sliding down as if it were a fireman's pole. She followed close behind.

"Faster!"

They were descending quickly, but not quickly enough. Bluebeard was closing in. In a second they would be within range of the dragon's breath. Another second and they would be within range of the dragon's teeth.

They were still a dozen feet off the ground, but Satya and Clay looked at each other, both thinking the same thing:

"JUMP!!!" "JUMP!!!"

With not a moment to spare, they dropped to the ground and rolled in the dirt. Scrambling to get away, they looked back just before Bluebeard unleashed a fireball at the tower. The dragon hung in the air, blasting the tower again and again, until the scaffolding buckled and the structure burned to the ground. Then, just as quickly as the dragon had turned on Satya, it was off—in the direction of the castle.

"Well," Clay wheezed, "I guess the dome is down for good. And now the collars on the dragons are useless."

"Actually, there's a backup," Satya said, panting. "But it'll take them a while to boot it up."

"Where's Cass?" asked Clay.

"I was going to ask you the same thing."

"You think she's still with Schrödinger?"

"Unless the dragons got her."

"Or the Midnight Sun . . ."

Clay and Satya sprinted along the dark path to the castle and tents. In the distance, they could hear the sounds of crackling flames and people shouting, and above it all, the roars of dragons. Clay hoped that Cass and Schrödinger were somewhere safe. In hindsight, splitting up had been a very bad idea.

All of it had been a very bad idea.

The path wound around the laboratory building,

which miraculously was still standing. They rounded the corner, approaching the bridge that separated the lab from the castle. Both Clay and Satya stopped in their tracks at a loud *crash*.

The AUTHORIZED VISITORS ONLY sign that marked the entrance to the Keep hadn't escaped the dragon's wrath. It had collapsed onto the bridge in a heap of burning rubble, blocking the path entirely. Clay was about to suggest that they walk under the bridge and take their chances wading through the shallow river, when he caught sight of a long green twitching tail. Snowflake was crouched beneath the bridge and, judging by the tail, was a little agitated.

"Great," said Clay under his breath.

Then came an ominous vibration in the ground beneath them.

"Don't look now, but there's somebody behind us," Satya whispered.

Clay gulped and glanced over his shoulder. Rover was approaching on foot, the dragon's plodding steps rumbling the ground.

"Which way?" Satya asked.

Clay tried to think quickly. They couldn't cross over the bridge because of the burning sign, nor could they run under it because of the dragon lurking there like an oversized troll. But they had to cross somehow, and soon, or else be trampled by the even bigger dragon that was approaching from behind.

What to do? The simplest thing would be to push the burning sign aside, but it was too big and the flames too hot.

Wait—the exploding gum! All he had to do was chew, throw the wad at the wreckage on the bridge, and two seconds later—*kablam!*—the way would be cleared for them. Unless the whole bridge collapsed. In which case, Snowflake would be forced to flee.

Anyway, it was worth a try.

Clay unwrapped the gum and stuck it in his mouth.

"Is now really the time to worry about fresh breath?" Satya asked, looking at him askance. Then her eyes widened like she'd just had an epiphany.

Clay pointed at his mouth and started to pantomime an explanation. If he stopped chewing, the gum would blow up right between his incisors.

Satya stopped him, grabbing his hands. "Wait—I think I know what you're going to say," she said. Her dark eyes were big and round. There was no hint of her usual sarcasm.

Clay struggled to remember to keep chewing.

"We're toast, right?" She squeezed his hand "And this is really cheesy, but... well, I don't want to die before I ever get to kiss anyone." Lifting herself up on tiptoe, Satya leaned in to give Clay a kiss.

Clay nearly choked on the gum. Of course, he was no expert in kissing, but he knew enough to know that chewing while a person is trying to kiss you is rude at best, and mortifying at worst. Especially when it's that person's very first kiss ever. And, to be honest, your very first kiss, as well. But he couldn't stop chewing or they'd both be blown to smithereens!

"Clay!" Satya pulled her head back and wiped her hand across her mouth. "What are you doing? Stop chewing already!"

Shaking his head vehemently, Clay put his hands on her shoulders and pushed her back.

"Jeez!" exclaimed Satya, insulted. "Sorry, forget I ever—"

Clay took the wad of gum out of his mouth and threw it on the flaming wreckage of the sign.

"Get down!" He pulled Satya to the ground by the arm, and they crouched with their backs to the bridge.

"Three... two... one..." he whispered.

The explosion scattered the flaming pieces of the wooden sign, clearing a narrow path across the bridge.

Behind them, Rover roared and took off into the air.

Beneath the bridge, falling debris conked Snowflake between the eyes. The dragon swung woozily back and forth in the riverbed.

Satya looked at Clay in amazement. "Who are you—James Bond?"

Clay smiled. "Funny, that's just what I said to Pablo when he gave me that gum."

"Who?"

"Never mind—time to run!"

Clay jumped to his feet, dragging Satya after him. They bolted across the bridge, not daring to look back. Or below.

As Clay and Satya ran down the path toward the tents and the castle, they could see security guards sprinting back and forth in the distance. Air horns blasted around them.

Suddenly, Satya grabbed Clay's wrist and pulled him behind a shrub.

"What is it?" Clay whispered, hoping he was going to have another chance to kiss her, though questioning the timing.

Satya pointed. Approaching one of the tents, without much stealth, was Rover. The dragon had taken off when they blew up the bridge, but hadn't gone far. And now it had set its sights on something—or someone—in one of the tents.

Satya and Clay watched in horror as Rover lifted a claw and sliced through the tent like it was a soft cheese, revealing the sight of a scraggly gray-haired man standing at the ready, a ten-gallon hat firmly affixed to his head.

With a cry of "Yeehawww!," Schrödinger launched himself at Rover, grabbing the dragon's tail with all his strength.

And yet, as remarkable as it was to see an old cowboy attempt to ride a giant dragon, something inside the tent drew Clay's attention away from the spectacle. There, behind Schrödinger's desk, Cass was crouching low, trying her best to avoid becoming the dragon's next meal.

CHAPTER NINETEEN

THE MAN WITH THE TEN-GALLON HATS

*One hour earlier**

With so many security guards running all over the Keep looking for her, it had taken Cass a frustratingly long time to reach the tents, but as soon as she did, she could tell which one was Schrödinger's: The array of ten-gallon hats hanging from the post in front was a dead giveaway.

She found the craggy old man at his desk, scribbling furiously on a stack of papers. Instead of the Midnight Sun's traditional white gloves, he wore calfskin riding gloves, which were stained with dirt and ink. Yet another cowboy hat sat beside him.

---

* More or less. Time is not my strong suit.

"Excuse me," Cass said, shutting the tent flap behind her. "Mr. Schrödinger?"

She had to repeat his name several times before he looked up, his eyes wild and unfocused.

"Schrödinger...Schrödinger...I know that name!" he said excitedly.

"It's not yours, then?"

"What's not mine?" He smiled broadly, lifting his huge mustache up at the ends. "Never mind, young lady. Whatever it is, take it. I have no use for material things anymore."

"I was talking about the name. Schrödinger."

"Schrödinger? Yes, I remember. He was a sheriff. Or was he that snake-oil doctor who sold me that worthless hemorrhoid cream?"

Cass tried a different tack. "What are you writing...sir?"

"Oh, this—?" He looked at the pages in front of him as though surprised to find them there. "Am I writing?"

He held up a page. Instead of writing, there was a line drawing of a great dragon with a large snowflake on its snout, its wings spread wide in flight. And in the corner of the page, Schrödinger had drawn a dark gash in the sky.

"That line again..." Cass muttered, her brow furrowed. "Mr. Schrödinger, did you go somewhere on one of the dragons? Is that why the Midnight Sun is breeding them—to get to this place?"

Schrödinger nodded. A light seemed to switch on behind his eyes. "So fast the dragons fly. Faster and faster. You ain't seen nothing like it. And then...it stops...and there you are....She thinks I want to go back, but I don't."

"You mean Ms. Mauvais thinks you want to go back?"

He stared at her, twisting his mustache. "Antoinette, yes."

"Where? Where does she think you want to go back to?"

"The place where I am! That's what the lady doesn't understand. I'm still there." Schrödinger shook his head, as though Ms. Mauvais were being exceptionally thick. "I told her, I don't want to go anywhere. I want to come back."

"Come back where?"

"Here!" he said, exasperated.

Cass stepped closer, pressing her finger against the gash in the drawing. "This line in the sky—does it lead to the place where you were—I mean, where you are, Mr. Schrödinger?"

Schrödinger's mustache twitched. "Schrödinger... Schrödinger...I know that name....Cattle rustler, wasn't he? Terrible man, but what a charmer..."

He scratched his head until his gaze landed on Cass. "Hello, young lady. Who are you?" he asked as though she had just arrived. "Can I get you some coffee? I make a mighty fine brew." He looked around, confused. "Darn it! My campfire must have gone out."

"That's okay, I don't need coffee, Mr. Schrödinger. Thanks."

"Schrödinger! Now, there's a name with a story. . . ."

"Please concentrate," said Cass, putting her hand on his shoulder. "This place you're talking about, this place where you are—does it have anything to do with this line?" Once again, Cass pointed to the line in the sky. "Does the line lead the way?"

But Schrödinger wouldn't or couldn't focus on anything in front of him. Then, just as Cass was thinking she should run and meet Clay, the old cowboy at last seemed to understand what she was asking him.

"Oh, that line in the sky?" he said, as if she had only just mentioned it for the first time. "That's what is left after a dragon flies there, of course. So fast the dragons fly. . . ."

Cass glanced at Schrödinger's pocket watch, lying on his desk. The dome was going to be turned off in exactly one minute, but she was finally getting somewhere with Schrödinger—she couldn't leave yet. She was on the verge of solving the mystery that had brought her to the Keep.

“You mean the line is like a trace of the dragon’s flight?” she asked.

Schrödinger nodded vigorously. “A rip in the fabric.”

“The fabric?”

“The fabric between the sides.”

“What sides? Do you mean this side and . . .” She didn’t like to say it aloud, but he probably wouldn’t remember a word she said anyway. “Do you mean this side and the Other Side? Have you been to the Other Side?"

He didn't answer. His eyes were starting to glaze again.

"That's what this is all about, isn't it?" Cass persisted. "The Midnight Sun wants the dragons to fly the members to the Other Side? They think going there will make them young again, don't they?"

"They think it is the Fountain of Youth," Schrödinger whispered. "It is not."

"What is it, then?" Cass asked urgently. "What's on the Other Side, Mr. Schrödinger?"

Schrödinger sat up straight. "Schrödinger? Now, that rings a bell!"

"Yes, it's a very familiar name, isn't it?" said Cass, gritting her teeth. When was she going to learn not to say that name?

She pressed him several more times before admitting defeat.

Finally, she looked at Schrödinger's pocket watch again. Fourteen minutes late. For his sake, she hoped Clay had left without her.

"Thank you, Mr. Schrödinger—you've been a lot of help."

Before she left, she saw something behind Schrödinger's scraggly-haired head: A shadow was growing against the canvas side of the tent.

"If I'm not mistaken," he was saying, "that poor

old sot Schrödinger landed in Truckee during the gold rush...."

"Shh," Cass hissed. "Mr. Schrödinger, look behind you!"

The shadow loomed ever larger and began to take shape. Long neck...jagged back...big talon-pronged wings...

"Never found much gold, did he?"

"Shush, please," Cass pleaded, whispering.

Confused, Schrödinger turned around. A grin spread beneath his mustache. "Well, I'll be—my pony is here!"

As the dragon's shadow grew so large it darkened the interior of the tent, Schrödinger reached for his hat. "You'll have to excuse me, ma'am—it's time for me to go home," he shouted gleefully, clicking his spurred heels together.

With a heart-stopping *rrrrrrrip*, the side of the tent sagged. A razor-sharp talon was cutting through the canvas, exposing Schrödinger and Cass to the outside, and to a row of shining dragon teeth.

It was the big gray dragon with the lolling tongue—Rover. The dragon's eyes rolled around the shredded tent and then fixed on the two humans.

With most wild animals, as Cass knew better than anyone, the trick is to wave your arms and make yourself look as big as possible so that the animal leaves you alone. But with something as big as this dragon, Cass thought, arm waving might seem more like a dinner invitation. Another approach was needed.

Cass was about to urge Schrödinger to stay absolutely still, when Schrödinger raised a hand, shouted, "Yeehaww!," and leaped right for the dumbfounded dragon—

Only to trip and land on the dragon's tail.

CHAPTER TWENTY

THE DESTRUCTION OF THE CASTLE

About twelve yards away, Clay and Satya watched, aghast.

Clay wanted to run to Cass, but there was a gigantic dragon named Rover in the way, and a crazy man was holding on to the dragon's tail like he was riding a bucking bronco.

"Giddyap!" Schrödinger shouted, now trying to pull himself onto the dragon's back.

Roaring angrily, the dragon thrashed this way and that. Schrödinger's legs flew into the air.

"Easy, boy!" he cried, sounding like he was having the time of his life. "Easy!"

The dragon thrashed around for a moment longer and then finally spread its wings and jumped into the air, throwing Schrödinger to the ground. The old cowboy bounced on his butt, clutching his back in pain.

"Ouch," said Satya, wincing on Schrödinger's behalf.

"C'mon, let's go," Clay said.

They ran to the torn-to-shreds tent, where Cass was standing in a posture that indicated she was very ready to run but very uncertain about which direction to take.

"You okay?" Clay asked her.

"Never better," said Cass drily. "But I have to admit I'm having second thoughts about flying home on one of those things."

"Don't worry about it," said Clay glumly. "They're not too hot on us riding them, either."

Cass looked at him. "So no luck, huh?"

He shook his head.

"Let's go find my dad," Satya said. "He'll know what to do."

"I thought he worked for the Midnight Sun," said Cass, furrowing her brow.

Satya furrowed her brow in response. "My dad works for the dragons."

Sure he does, thought Clay. By putting blinders, and ropes, and electric choke collars on them. But he figured it wasn't the time to argue.

"My dad and I have an emergency plan," Satya explained as they started running toward the castle. "If something like this goes down, we're supposed to meet by the fountain. He'll be waiting there—I know it."

"And I'm sure he'll be just thrilled to see you harboring a pair of escaped convicts," said Cass, with a wry smile.

The castle courtyard was flooded with people running helter-skelter: security guards, butlers, gardeners, cooking staff. Satya led Clay and Cass through the crowd, then stopped short and motioned urgently for them to back away.

Standing next to the fountain was not Vicente but Ms. Mauvais, looking as imperious and unruffled as ever. If there was a storm raging at the Keep, then Ms. Mauvais was the eye of the storm—the calm but deadly powerful center.

"Vicente! Somebody get me Vicente!" she commanded. "Satya! Where is your father?"

"Uh, I'll go get him!" Satya shouted nervously.

Without waiting to hear more, Satya motioned to the others. They snuck around the periphery of the courtyard, out of sight of Ms. Mauvais, then ran up the steps and into the castle. "He's probably in the emergency control booth." She pointed to the Ryū Room. "Through there—c'mon!"

They sprinted across the marble foyer, toward the Ryū Room. But as they passed the glass case containing DragonSlayer, Clay stopped and turned, skidding briefly on the marble. Unbidden, the ridiculous image of Kwan with a butter knife between his teeth had come into Clay's mind. *Always handy to have a weapon on you, right?*

"Wait for me!" he shouted at Cass and Satya, and he raced back across the room to the suit of armor that stood by the entrance.

"Sorry, gotta borrow this," he muttered. He grasped the double-sided ax held in the hollow knight's metal hand and pulled.* The armor collapsed to the floor, loud clangs lost in the general din. Clay swung the ax, almost dropping it (it was quite heavy). Then he ran lopsidedly back to the display case.

The sword inside looked like it hadn't been touched since King Arthur's time. But of course it had been touched, and very recently, too—not to slay dragons but to create them with the ancient blood caked on the blade. Reason enough to take the sword, Clay thought.

Without worrying about who was watching, he raised the ax high in the air, then let it fall. The glass

---

* A METAL GLOVE LIKE THIS IS CALLED A *GAUNTLET*, A WORD YOU MAY RECOGNIZE FROM THE PHRASE *THROW DOWN THE GAUNTLET*. AND YET IT WAS THE DOUBLE-SIDED AX, KNOWN AS A *FRANCISCA*, THAT A MEDIEVAL KNIGHT WAS MORE LIKELY TO THROW BEFORE HAND-TO-HAND COMBAT COMMENCED. THE GAUNTLET HE KEPT ON, TO PROTECT HIS FINGERNAILS FROM CHIPPING. KNIGHTS, I'M TOLD, WERE VERY PARTICULAR ABOUT THEIR MANICURES.

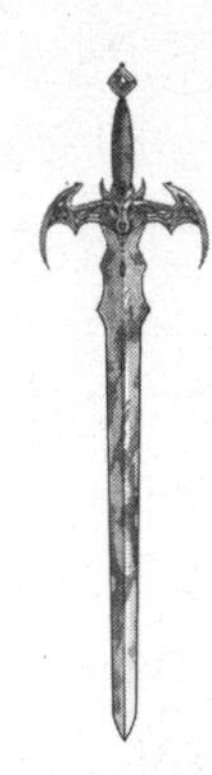

shattered and an alarm went off—yet more noise added to the cacophony.

The sword felt better in his hand than the ax did, which is mostly to say it wasn't quite as heavy. Clay slashed experimentally through the air once in each direction. He hated the thought that the sword had killed dragons; nonetheless, wielding it was almost, well, fun—or would have been in other circumstances.

"Hey, easy with that, Sir Lancelot!" said Cass. "At least give me the ax if you're gonna be swinging that sword around."

As she took the ax from him, there was a huge thundering **BOOM!** that made them all cry out. The building shook as if there'd been an earthquake.

"In there!" Cass shouted. All three of them lunged for the Ryū Room as another **BOOM!** rocked the castle.

The Wandsworths were at their table near the

bar, playing cards as if there were nothing untoward going on. Two terrified-looking staff members sat opposite them. As one made to get up, Mrs. Wandsworth put her hand on his.

"Tut, tut. You know nobody moves until the game is done."

Mr. Wandsworth nodded in agreement, then helped himself to a generous pour of mead from the big keg sitting on the bar.

A gigantic **ROAR** nearly split everyone's ears.

Clay, Satya, and Cass dove under the closest cocktail table.

Around them, priceless ceramic vases started shattering one by one, as if they were being shot by a sniper. Artwork fell from the walls. Bottles toppled from the bar to the floor, until the bar itself crumpled.

Finally, the shaking stopped. Clay opened one eye, then the other. Cass and Satya were looking around, too.

Just in time to see a column buckle and an entire wall crumble. The room was literally collapsing around them.

"What happened?" Satya whispered.

"It's like a bomb went off," said Clay.

Cass crawled out from under the table. "Sturdy little thing, this table."

Clay and Satya crawled out after Cass and stood

up in the rubble. Half of the castle was gone. Where the roof had fallen in, they could see a starry sky.

Not far away, the Wandsworths and their bridge partners were still seated at their table, but they were now covered with dust and plaster.

"That was the best hand I've had in ninety years!" Mrs. Wandsworth complained. "What do you mean, the game is forfeit?!"

"Maybe you'd prefer to have a dragon as a partner," said her husband, pointing.

Everyone turned and stared. Where the marble foyer used to be, Rover was now sitting on a pair of massive hind legs, tongue lolling out, as usual. The dragon looked at them hungrily. If only I had some of that honeycomb now, Clay thought.

"The mead!" he shouted to the Wandsworths. "Give the dragon some mead."

"What? We will do no such thing," said Mrs. Wandsworth, offended. "Do you know what happened to my shih tzus when they got into the champagne?"

But Clay wasn't paying attention; he had grabbed the keg of mead himself and was now dropping it in front of Rover—not too close, of course, but close enough.

"Here, Rover. You'll like this; it's made with honey."

While Rover sniffed curiously, Clay unscrewed

the lid of the keg, leaving what for the dragon would be a smallish bowl of mead. Then he hopped away.

Seconds later, the dragon was happily lapping up the mead, as predicted. But all too soon the keg was empty. Rover picked it up and started drunkenly shaking it, hoping for more.

As Clay tried to think of other ways to divert the dragon's attention, a shadow crossed over the moon and Rover pulled up short.

Roooooooooooaaaaaaawrrrr!!!

It was Rover's black-and-blue boss, Bluebeard. Responding to some secret signal, Rover started backing away out of the ruins of the castle and into the courtyard. With apparent difficulty, the dragon then spread its wings and jumped into the air, bumping into the dragon fountain on the way, but eventually catching flight.

For a moment all was quiet. Leaving the Wandsworths and their hapless bridge partners behind, Clay, Cass, and Satya gingerly picked their way through the rubble.

The moonlit courtyard appeared to be empty save for the bronze dragons in the fountain, silhouetted against the purple evening sky. Had Bluebeard gone somewhere else? Is that why Rover had been called away?

They stepped cautiously into the courtyard and looked around. Then all three screamed at once.

"Run!"

Bluebeard had not gone away but was merely circling above, waiting to strike. And now the dragon was diving straight for them.

They headed to the jungle for cover, but they weren't fast enough.

"Aaaayyh!" Cass screamed. A wing talon ripped her sleeve off as Bluebeard flew past her.

"Are you okay?" Clay shouted.

"Yes!" Cass said, but Clay could see blood on her arm. "Where's Satya?" she asked.

They looked around. The dragon had landed in front of the fountain—separating them from Satya. She was backed up against one of the castle's few remaining walls.

Bluebeard blew a puff of smoke in Satya's face, toying with her.

Not fully aware of what he was doing, Clay raised DragonSlayer over his head and barreled toward Bluebeard.

"Get away from her, or deal with this!" he yelled, with what you might fairly call foolish courage.

Bluebeard's neck craned around, and the dragon looked at Clay. For a moment it seemed like Clay's words were sinking in. Was it possible that the huge beast was afraid of the little sword? But then Bluebeard let out a scornful roar and swung at Clay. Just in time, Clay squatted down, out of the way, while holding DragonSlayer aloft with both hands.

Bluebeard's shriek was bloodcurdling.

The dragon thrashed around in pain, then gave another cry and fell on its side, shuddering.

Clay watched in surprise. Had he sliced into Bluebeard's belly without realizing it? He examined the blade in his hands; there was no blood.

Then Satya pointed—

"I told you he would come."

Behind Bluebeard stood Vicente, holding a familiar weapon. Clay glanced back at the dragon. A red feather—the end of a tranquilizer dart—poked out of the side of Bluebeard's belly where the scales were smooth and thin.

"Satya!" Vicente yelled. Satya took off for her father, hugging him tightly.

"That horrid scientist told me they couldn't breathe fire!" Ms. Mauvais appeared out of nowhere, lit by the glow of the fountain, shouting at no one in particular. "I specifically requested nonflammable dragons!" For the first time, a smudge appeared on her perfect face, and there was even a little rip in her otherwise immaculate dress.

Suddenly, her focus shifted from the unconscious

dragon lying on the ground to the other humans in the courtyard.

"Well, don't just stand there," she said to Vicente. "Shoot them, too!"

Vicente glared at her. "Satya is my daughter!"

"Cassandra and the boy, then," responded Ms. Mauvais impatiently. "It's just a tranquilizer gun—there's no need for melodrama!"

"I'm out of darts." Vicente held up the gun as if demonstrating that it was empty.

"Do I have to do everything myself? Don't let them go." Scowling, Ms. Mauvais quickly disappeared into the ruins.

"You're not really out of darts, are you, Dad?" asked Satya.

Clay looked from Bluebeard to Vicente. "Well, I guess you showed Bluebeard who was boss after all."

"No, it was just a lucky shot," said Vicente. "We all could have been killed easily. Looks like you were right about the fire-breathing. And maybe about the way I've been training them, as well."

Clay didn't say anything. He figured it must be hard for a guy like Vicente to admit he was wrong, and Clay didn't want to push it.

"I'm going to see about getting the dome operational again—you may not like those collars, but right now they're our only hope," said Vicente. "You guys stay out of sight."

As her father ran off, Satya noticed Cass's arm. It was covered in blood. "What happened? Do we need to do something with that?"

"Probably—I'm losing a lot of blood," said Cass, her face very pale. Her voice was calm and matter-of-fact, but it was obvious that she was in a great deal of pain.

"Okay," said Clay, trying hard to remain as calm as Cass was. "What do we do?"

"Can one of you rip off my other sleeve for me?"

Methodically, Cass talked her companions through the making of a tourniquet.

They were just about finished when they heard Ms. Mauvais's voice: "Don't move."

She had returned, this time with Gyorg. He was pointing a gun at them. Not a tranquilizer gun. A machine gun.

Looking like a warrior with her sleeveless shirt and bloody armband, Cass stepped in front of Clay and Satya and addressed her age-old adversary, Antoinette Mauvais.

"Go ahead, kill us. You've killed so many—what are a few more?" Cass said, her voice surprisingly strong. "But you'll never win. You know that, right? Even if you get to the Other Side. Because the one place you can really live forever is the one place where you'll never find a home."

"Oh, where is that?" said Ms. Mauvais carelessly.

"In someone else's heart."

For a moment Ms. Mauvais just stared at her, and it almost seemed as though Cass's words had struck a nerve, but the woman quickly recovered. "How long have you been waiting to give that little greeting card of a speech? Gyorg, get rid of them. For good this time."

Her cold tinkling laugh was soon lost in a deafening **ROARRRRR!**

Another dragon was entering the fray, but this roar was new and unfamiliar. Unfamiliar to everyone except Clay, that is.

He would have known that roar anywhere.

Bearing down on them, making right for the courtyard in front of the crumbling castle, was Ariella.

From *Secrets of the Occulta Draco; or, The Memoirs of a Dragon Tamer*

We humans are pathetic creatures. Sniveling crybabies, every one of us. Other species are weaned in months, at most a few years; we cling to our parents all the way into our teens, and sometimes even longer.

Dragons, though they live to a much older age than we do, grow up much faster. They are extremely independent creatures. Even in birth. Neither male nor female, they reproduce alone. A dragon simply lays an egg, and once laid, the egg does not need to be sat upon or cared for in any way.

Dragons do not have the same ideas about parenthood and family that we do. When a dragon hatches, it may wander around on its own for days, perfectly content. And yet an adult dragon would never leave a baby dragon entirely to its own devices. The young are considered a group responsibility, and baby dragons are schooled in the Dragon Way by older, mentor dragons.

The Dragon Way is something like a language and something like a moral code, but mainly it is something we cannot understand because we are not dragons. In dragon communities, all dragons are equal; there are no rulers. The Dragon Way makes this kind of egalitarian society possible. A dragon who does not follow the Dragon Way is referred to as a Lost One and is an object of scorn and pity for other dragons.

Of course, since humans do not follow the Dragon Way, we also are objects of scorn and pity.

CHAPTER TWENTY-ONE

THE ARRIVAL OF ARIELLA

Clay never saw Ms. Mauvais slip away with Gyorg, and he didn't care where they'd gone. For the moment, even Cass and Satya were invisible to him. He only had eyes for the gentle—or gentle-ish—giant that was now landing in front of them. Never in his life had he been so grateful to see another living creature, human, dragon, or otherwise.

He ran up to Ariella, ready to throw his arms around the dragon's neck. Yet something in Ariella's demeanor stopped him from taking the liberty.

He settled for a smile and an enthusiastic hand wave; you couldn't shake hands with a dragon, after all.

"Hey, Ariella," he said awkwardly. "Thanks, uh, for coming."

There was no return greeting, only silence. Ariella's coloring, which was naturally a pale gray, tended to change along with the dragon's mood and environment. At the moment, it looked like a dark storm cloud was passing over the dragon, even though the sky above was clear.

This was not the reunion Clay had imagined.

His leg started to jiggle with anxiety. Did Ariella not remember him? Had Ariella not come to save him?

Ariella looked from Clay to the inert dragon lying on the ground. Bluebeard's eyes were closed, but an expression of outrage was frozen on the dragon's face.

Who did this?

Clay felt Ariella's fury. It was a deep dragon anger.

Did a human do this?

Desperately, Clay tried to think of a way to respond. *Yes, but the dragon deserved it? Yes, but the dragon is only unconscious, not dead?*

Before Clay could say anything aloud, there was a low rumbling growl that seemed to shake the ground. Bluebeard was waking up.

Clay exchanged glances with Cass and Satya. Uh-oh. They each took a step back.

Groggily, Bluebeard opened an eye and started to stretch. Then all the dark steely scales on the dragon's back seemed to rise at once, like hackles on a rooster:

Bluebeard had noticed Ariella.* With a quick shake, the no-longer-sleepy dragon pushed itself to its feet.

Seeing Bluebeard waken, Ariella made a low sonorous sound, almost like a whale call, that Clay sensed meant something like *Hail, fellow dragon*. And then the old dragon bent its neck, lowering its head almost all the way to the ground, in what was unmistakably a gesture of courtesy and respect, though not at all of submission.

Growling, Bluebeard regarded the newcomer suspiciously. *Why does this big interloper look so much like me?* Bluebeard's eyes seemed to say. *And what are they getting at with this bowing business? It must be a trap.*

Then, with no warning but a snarl, Bluebeard pounced—taking advantage of Ariella's posture to go straight for Ariella's neck.

"No!" Clay cried.

If you've ever watched another dog attack yours, then you know a little bit how Clay felt. (Not that a dragon is anything like a dog! And not that Ariella belonged to Clay! But...oh, just forget I made the comparison.)

---

* *Hackles* are errant feathers along a rooster's back. They can also refer to cowlick hairs on a dog's neck, which stand up with annoyance or fear. Agitating things are said to raise one's hackles. Never raise a dragon's hackles. A hackle feather is also used when fishing. But information on that is just as boring as actual fishing.

Ariella was taken by surprise but was strong and fast enough to throw off Bluebeard before the attacker's teeth penetrated the scales on Ariella's neck.

Once free, Ariella barked at Bluebeard—a fast and furious reprimand—then blew a warning plume of fire into the sky. To Clay, the meaning was clear: Ariella was giving the ornery young dragon a chance to apologize to an elder, and quickly. If not, it would be war.

Bluebeard hissed in response. No apologies for this dragon.

Never taking its eyes off Ariella, the mean, unrepentant dragon whipped its tail in the air, making a loud *crack*. Then, dark wings flapping, Bluebeard lifted off the ground and hovered low over the courtyard, baiting Ariella to follow.

Ariella just watched. The seconds ticked by.

Growing impatient, Bluebeard screeched threats to Ariella, then finally unleashed a long rope of fire. Ariella jumped out of the way, blocking the fire with the wave of a wing.

Clay, Satya, and Cass huddled under the one small overhang that remained amid the castle ruins.

"What do I do?" asked Clay, stricken. "I can't just let—"

Suddenly, Bluebeard dropped from the air; at the very same time, Ariella reared up, talons flashing. For a moment, they both stood on their hind legs, eyes

wild. They looked much like the two bronze dragons standing in the fountain behind them.

Ariella roared, a loud, bellowing roar, and then attacked, swiping Bluebeard's neck with a long, sharp talon and then sweeping Bluebeard's legs with the full weight of a twelve-foot-long tail. Bluebeard stumbled but quickly stood up again, spitting with fury. The two dragons bared their teeth at each other, then joined in movements so quick the dragons became a blur. One second they were in the air, flying at each other. The next second they were on the ground, wrestling.

For a while they appeared evenly matched: Ariella's size and experience versus Bluebeard's energy and youth. But there was something that Bluebeard had that Ariella lacked: the instinct to kill. When it seemed they might fight forever, Bluebeard let out a roar and sent a fireball bigger than any Clay had ever seen, directly at Ariella's chest. The older dragon dodged as best it could, but a shoulder and part of a wing caught the full force of the flame.

Ariella staggered backward in pain.

"Ariella!" Clay shouted, panic-stricken. "Are you okay?"

Clay raised DragonSlayer in the air, but before he could even consider using it, Ariella rebuked him.

Stay away! You are never to strike a dragon, even one who would hurt us.

Clay looked back at Satya, but she was looking up, preoccupied with something in the sky. She put two fingers in her mouth and let out a shrill whistle.

Suddenly, something was spiraling toward them. Another dragon?

No, too small.

Before anybody could tell what was happening, a certain gray falcon had dive-bombed into the dragon fight and was flying straight for Bluebeard's eye.

Clay cheered. "Go, Hero!"

Confused and infuriated, Bluebeard thrashed this way and that, trying to bat the falcon away. Undaunted, Hero pecked and pecked at the screaming dragon.

Ariella watched from a safe distance. (A human was not allowed to attack a dragon, but a bird—this, it seemed, Ariella would allow.)

Finally, Hero let out a victorious squawk and flew high into the air, leaving Bluebeard with a bloody mess where a big yellow eye had been. The half-blind dragon continued to spin around in pain, seemingly afraid that the falcon would return at any second.

For one harrowing moment, Bluebeard's good eye found Clay, and it looked as though the dragon might take out its rage on this easy human target, but Ariella immediately stepped in front of Bluebeard and growled a warning.

Screeching furiously, Bluebeard flew off into the night—like a bitter one-eyed pirate setting out to sea.

We must go.

Ariella lay low on the ground, so the dragon's human passengers could climb on more easily. Still, Cass winced with pain as Clay and Satya helped her onto Ariella's back. How was it that something could be so slippery and so spiky at once?

"You need to get her home right away," said Satya, after Cass was securely in place and they'd jumped down to the ground.

Clay looked back up at Cass, struggling valiantly to sit upright. Beneath the smears of blood, her arm was turning a strange yellowish color. Satya was right. Cass needed medical attention as soon as possible.

"What about you? What about the baby dragons? What about—" Clay gestured helplessly. "I can't just leave."

"You have to."

Before she could respond, Clay was startled by a crackling in his ear: *"Clay, are you there?"*

"Uh—" It was Leira. The hat was working again.

"Where've you been?! Never mind. Guess what—Ariella came back! And we all played charades and drew a map to show where you were, and now—"

"I know. Ariella's here. Cass, too. But she's hurt. Make sure Nurse Cora is ready. Sorry, gotta go—"

"Wait–"

Clay pulled off his hat and looked at Satya. "Come with us," he said urgently.

"I can't."

"Look around. You can't stay here."

As he spoke, Hero returned and landed on Satya's shoulder.

"See, I'll be fine. I've got Hero. And my dad. Now go. Before Ms. Mauvais sees you."

"I'm coming back," said Clay, reluctant to leave her side.

"No, you aren't."

"Will you kiss me when I do?" he blurted, then reddened.

Satya laughed, reddening as well. "Sure."

Clay grinned. "Then I definitely am coming back."

Feeling much better than he had in a long time, Clay picked up his sword and jumped easily onto the dragon's back. Well, almost. He wound up with his feet dangling down the dragon's side. Trying to keep a straight face, Satya gave him a push, and he swung his leg up and over, taking a seat in front of Cass.

He didn't need to tell Cass to hold on tight. The minute Ariella unfurled those massive wings, flapping up into the sky, Cass's good hand was digging into Clay's shoulder.

They lifted up, and instantly the night became quieter and cooler, the stars brighter. Tentatively, Clay stroked Ariella's back. He was unsure whether the dragon would appreciate, or even notice, his small human hand, but he felt the need to make contact.

When Clay had last seen Ariella, the dragon had recently molted, and its skin was smooth and sleek. In the year since, the scales had become rougher, careworn. Clay could see various lines and scars crisscrossing the dragon's back. Where did the lines come from? What had Ariella been doing? He wanted to know, but it was not the right time to ask. He was certain that Ms. Mauvais would not let them go so easily. At any second he expected to see Gyorg piloting a helicopter behind them, the chopper's missiles firing—straight at Ariella's rear end.

He was right: They were being pursued. But not by a helicopter.

Cass lifted her head. "Oh no—behind us!" she rasped.

Screeeeeeeeeeeeeeeeeeeeeeeeeech!

A bright green dragon was streaking through the sky, directly toward them. It was Snowflake, apparently recovered from being hit on the head, and now chasing after them—under Bluebeard's orders, no doubt.

That dragon—another Lost One? Ariella asked.

"Lost?" repeated Clay nervously.

A dragon who does not follow the ways of a dragon.

"Yes, another Lost One. Sorry." He hoped Ariella wouldn't choose this moment to try to school Snowflake in the finer points of proper dragon etiquette.

Very well.

The determined dragon leaned forward, flapping its wings with tremendous force, then holding them tight against its sides, picking up speed. Still, Ariella had been wounded in the fight with Bluebeard, and Snowflake covered the distance between them with shocking velocity.

"Hurry!" Clay urged.

Ariella responded with something that Clay couldn't totally understand, but he guessed it was probably some dragon form of swearing.*

Breathing heavily, Ariella flew a little faster, but Snowflake kept gaining. By then Snowflake was almost upon them. Smelling victory, the green dragon stretched out its neck and opened its jaws, revealing several rows of sharp teeth. Clay was afraid Snowflake was about to bite down on Ariella's tail, when he was startled by a sudden crackle, followed by a loud buzzing.

---

* It was indeed a dragon swear, which I wouldn't dare repeat in print. Nor could I. The real language of dragons is not something that can be reproduced in Roman letters.

"What's happening?" asked Cass, roused by the noise.

Just as they came level with the crater's rim, Snowflake gave a strangled roar and stopped abruptly, swatting at the air. Confused, the dragon fell backward for a second before regaining equilibrium and flying back toward them at double speed—only to stop again, screaming with fury.

"It's Snowflake's collar!" Clay yelled. "I think the backup power finally kicked in! Vicente's calling the dragons back."

Sure enough, as Ariella soared farther and farther from the Keep, Snowflake spiraled downward until once again trapped inside the dome, like a flying goldfish in a giant bowl.

It looked, at last, like they were safe.

Clay turned around to share the moment with Cass, but her eyes were closed and her head drooping. Alarmed, he put his hand on her good wrist. She still had a pulse; she'd only fallen asleep.

CHAPTER TWENTY-TWO

THE RETURN TO EARTH RANCH

The flight from the Keep to Earth Ranch was much shorter on Ariella's back than in Owen's seaplane—much, much shorter. The dragon didn't necessarily fly faster than the plane—not in terms of actual, measurable speed, anyway. Instead, there seemed to be a kind of supernatural teleportation at work, so subtle that Clay didn't even notice when it was happening. He would blink, and suddenly he'd have traveled a hundred miles farther than he'd thought.

So it was unexpected, but *expectedly* unexpected, when Price Island suddenly appeared, a puffy gray mass on the horizon.

Seconds later they burst through the clouds of vog, and Clay could see the distinctive profile of Nose Peak. Two figures were straddling the topmost rock, staring at the sky, just as Clay had done on so many

mornings. They waved wildly. Clay didn't have to see their faces to recognize Leira and Brett. Leira raised her conch-shell communication device to her lips and blew it three times like a trumpet. It blared painfully in Clay's ear but also echoed around the island, announcing their arrival.

"Looks like they're expecting us!" he said, his ears ringing.

He looked back at Cass, whose eyes were partway open. She smiled briefly before passing out again.

As soon as they landed, Cass was rushed to the infirmary, where her arm was re-bandaged and she was given one of Nurse Cora's mysterious transfusions.

Cass would live, the nurse said. Her arm—that was an open question. It had become infected, and there was a chance they would have to amputate. Cass took the news stoically, as if she'd always expected to lose a limb one day or another.

Nurse Cora insisted she rest; Cass insisted she go to the all-camp meeting.

It was just after dawn. Awakened by the blowing of the conch shell, if not by the thunderous arrival of a thirty-foot-long dragon, campers had stumbled out of their cabins and over to the geodesic dome, rubbing sleep from their eyes. And now Clay was being overwhelmed with people patting him on the back, including a very relieved Owen, and gawking at

Ariella, who was sitting claws forward, like a sphinx, next to the dome.

Jonah shook his head. "I'll never go to the toilet again without thinking of that dragon."

Clay looked at him strangely. "What?"

Before Jonah could explain, Kwan grabbed Clay's arm. "Wait, are you carrying a sword?"

Pablo shook his head in exaggerated amazement. "You give a guy an exploding gumball, and the next thing you know he's a full-on soldier."

"That's full-on knight to you," said Clay, equal parts proud and abashed. "This isn't just any sword; it's DragonSlayer."

Kwan laughed. "Okay, so you're doing some kind of fantasy cosplay now?"

The camp's geodesic dome was about thirty-five feet in diameter—an open grid of steel like you might see being used as a climbing structure at a grade school, only bigger. A few holdouts perched themselves on top of the dome, but most of the campers and staff gathered underneath, around a pile of logs—an unlit campfire. Just outside the circle of campers, Cass sat on a rock, conferring with Owen and Buzz and Mr. B.

"Hey—where's Flint?" said Pablo, looking around. "This is when he usually lights the fire with a snap, the show-off."

Clay tensed, hearing Flint's name. "We don't

need that guy." Except to give me back the *Occulta Draco*, he thought. He turned to Ariella. "Hey, could you . . . ?"

The dragon looked wearily at Clay as if to say, *Are you really making me do this?* Then the dragon leaned over the dome and sent a burst of fire right onto the waiting logs. The campfire crackled, and the other campers broke into applause.

"Thanks," said Clay, suddenly wishing Flint had been there after all, to witness the moment.

Mr. B clapped to get everyone's attention, then rested a hand on Cass's shoulder. "Some of you know Cassandra here, a longtime warrior for our side, who now returns to us wounded but unbroken."

There were a few cheers, but Cass waved them away with her good arm.

"She has been filling me in on the latest doings of the Midnight Sun," continued Mr. B. "It is worse than we imagined. Under the guise of running a dragon preserve, they've been training dragons to fly Midnight Sun members to the Other Side. . . ."

Cass nodded and then spoke with effort. "Or trying to. They seem to have had some problems making the trip, and Clay's and my exit probably set them back a little, but I know the Midnight Sun: They don't give up. They're going to keep at it until they get what they want."

Clay raised his hand.

"We're not in class anymore, Clay," said Mr. B. "Speak."

Clay blushed. Usually it was Mr. B who wouldn't let Clay forget that he'd once been Clay's language arts teacher. "Okay, well, I just thought you should know that the dragons at the Keep are Lost Ones—or at least that's what Ariella calls them. They don't know what it means to be dragons. It makes them more dangerous."

"How so?"

"For one thing, they don't know how to fly to the Other Side. Ariella says it takes years for a young dragon to learn how to do it right, but all these dragons are doing is flying superfast. That's why there's a rip in the sky above the crater. Ariella says if they keep at it, the rip is going to keep getting bigger and bigger until, well, I didn't really understand the rest...."

Buzz, sitting on the other side of Mr. B, looked grave. "I think what the dragon's saying is that the separation between our world and the Other Side will be destroyed. I can't imagine what that would mean. The laws of physics, everything we think know about the natural world, would be in question."

"That's why we have to stop them," agreed Mr. B.

"How?" Leira asked. "The Midnight Sun already has three big dragons, and a half dozen others that are catching up."

Clay nodded. "It would take an army of dragons

to stop them. Hey—cut that out!" Something big and sharp was poking him in the back.

He looked over his shoulder and saw Ariella's tail nudging him. The dragon let out a low rumble.

"There're more dragons?" Clay said, incredulous. "Why didn't you say so?! Oh...so that's what you were doing all year—looking for them?"

Then you weren't intentionally avoiding me, he almost added.

As Clay listened to the dragon's response, the others glanced between Clay and Ariella, confused.

"Does Ariella think these other dragons can help us?" asked Mr. B.

"Maybe," said Clay. "There's only one problem. The dragons are all on the Other Side. And they intend to stay there—away from us. From humans."

After what everyone had seen and heard about the Midnight Sun, hearing that dragons held grudges against humans wasn't exactly a surprise.

"Can they be convinced to come back?" Cass asked.

"What about it, Ariella?" Clay asked. "Even if they don't care about people, what about the baby dragons? Maybe they could be saved."

The dragon shook its massive head.

"What do you mean, *I* need to explain it to them?!" Clay demanded.

Gulping, Clay turned to the others. "Ariella says

the only way that the other dragons might come back is if I go to the Other Side to ask."

"What!" Leira squeaked. "Why?"

"To make the case for why they should even care about our world. Ariella can't do it, because they would automatically consider any dragon who spoke for a human to be a traitor."

Mr. B frowned. "Are you saying Ariella wants to take *you* to the Other Side?"

"I'm not sure that's such a good idea," Cass said. "You saw what happened to Schrödinger." She turned to Mr. B. "The Midnight Sun sent this guy to the Other Side as a test, like they were sending a monkey into space to see whether he'd make it back alive. And believe me, he wasn't all there when he got back."

Clay swallowed, remembering Schrödinger jumping up and down like a crazed clown.

Flint had arrived in the middle of the conversation and was leaning casually against the dome. "Are you seriously going to let this kid go to the Other Side?" He nodded scornfully toward Clay. "Look at him. He barely got out of the Keep alive. And then only because his precious dragon saved his butt at the last minute. And now you're gonna send him on probably the most dangerous journey any of us have ever been on? Isn't this a job for a counselor?" Flint grinned. Evidently, he meant himself.

Clay found himself standing up, his fists balled at his sides.

Mr. B shook his head. "Clay, whatever you're about to do, don't. Flint, that wasn't very constructive."

"I'll be back," said Clay through clenched teeth. He grabbed DragonSlayer, which was leaning against a rock, and walked out from under the geodesic dome. Only to be confronted by Ariella's golden eyes staring at him.

"What?" he muttered angrily. "Am I not following the rules of the Dragon Way?"

Back in his cabin, Clay sat on his bed and fumed. Next to him was the cheesy neon faux-graffiti skateboard helmet that Max-Ernest had sent only two days earlier. It seemed like a long time had passed since then.

Clay picked up the helmet and was about to throw it against the wall, when the cabin door creaked open. Leira and Brett came over and sat on the bunk opposite him.

"Don't listen to Flint," said Leira.

Brett nodded. "He's not the biggest jerk there is, but he's up there—and I'm an expert."

"Yeah, he's a jerk," said Clay. "But he's right. I was crazy to stay there without Owen."

He hit his skateboard helmet in frustration.

"What are you talking about?" said Leira. "You got Cass out. Mission accomplished."

"Only because Ariella miraculously appeared. Or not miraculously. More like 'cause of you guys."

"Well, don't sound so mad about it," said Leira.

"Sorry." Clay smiled—briefly. "I guess I should say thanks."

Brett shook his head. "So you're just going to sit here banging on your helmet while you let Flint go to the Other Side?"

"Why not? I know he denies it, but he's got the *Occulta Draco*—I'm sure of it," said Clay, repeatedly hitting the helmet. "He knows as much as I do. And he practically breathes fire himself."

"Dude, will you stop it with the helmet already?" said Leira.

Clay stopped, an idea hitting him. "Wait a second.... Wasn't there something in the *Occulta Draco* about a helmet?"

He shut his eyes and thought back to what he'd read in those pages just days earlier.

Ten minutes later, Clay was standing with Ariella outside the dome, trying to persuade his fellow campers not to get too close to the dragon, while simultaneously assuring them that they needn't be afraid.

"Pardon me... excuse me..."

The crowd parted and Leira emerged, carrying Clay's garbage-lid sled over her head and looking very irritable.

"Okay. Now do you want to explain why the heck you needed your old volcano sled to go to the Other Side?"

"Not sled—shield!" said Clay, with considerably more liveliness than he'd shown only moments before.

"Right. Of course. Silly me."

Ignoring her, Clay took the board and grabbed its strap, looping it over his head so it rested against his back. He put on the skateboard helmet and raised DragonSlayer into the air, a little bit embarrassed, but determined nonetheless.

"I'm ready!"

Kwan shook his head. "Dude. You are *so* happy I don't have a camera right now."

"No, seriously," said Clay. "Listen to this. . . ." He recited the words from memory:

"Let not a dragon leap when you're astride,
Lest you lose your mind on the Other Side.
Yet if you must this dizzy journey make,
Three things will keep you woozy but awake:
First, your enemy's sword will point the way.
Next, the shield you made will keep ghosts at bay.
Last, if you'd not return your brain half-dead,
Please, a helmet from home put on your head."

"A nursery rhyme?" guessed Kwan.

"No! It's from the *Occulta Draco,*" Clay said. "Don't you see? The sled is the 'shield I made.' "

He tapped his helmet. "The helmet my brother gave me is a 'helmet from home'!"

He waved DragonSlayer. "And this right here is my 'enemy's sword.' "

Brett looked impressed. "It's not exactly how *I* would dress you. But, you know, I think you're onto something."

Pablo reached over and grabbed the hilt of the sword, adjusting Clay's grip. "You hold it like this."

"How do you know?" Clay asked skeptically. "You took fencing?"

Pablo shrugged. "Table tennis."

Leira looked Clay up and down. "You're really doing this?"

Clay nodded.

"Do you need a snack to take?" Brett asked. He flashed a candy bar from his secret stash.

Clay laughed, accepting the candy bar. "Thanks, I guess I could get hungry," he said as a sobering thought hit him. "I don't know how long I'll be gone."

Mr. B walked up, taking in Clay's outfit. "That's very true. I don't mean to scare you, but you could take off and be gone for five minutes or five years. Time is different on the Other Side, if it exists at all."

Jonah glanced around. "So for all we know, he

came back yesterday and he's hiding behind a rock, watching us right now?"

Mr. B nodded.

"Whoa," Pablo said, shaking his head. "Trippy."

"Trippy," Mr. B agreed.

"Well then, I'd better get going, I guess," said Clay, whose nerves were beginning to fray. "There's that whole time-travel thing where you're not supposed to run into yourself, right?" he joked half-heartedly.

Clay climbed onto Ariella's back—no easy task with his sword and shield—and awkwardly saluted his friends. "Wish me luck."

His friends saluted back. "Good luck!"

"Wait," said Kwan. "What if everything is all reversed on the Other Side? You know, parallel universe-style. Shouldn't we wish him bad luck, too—just in case?"

But it was too late. Ariella lifted off the ground, sending the group scattering with a great flapping of wings. The campers held their hands to their eyes, squinting as Clay and Ariella flew higher and higher, until they were nothing more than a dark speck in the clear blue sky.

After a moment, breakfast was announced, and all the campers started walking toward Big Yurt. A mood of quiet anxiety pervaded the group; so much seemed to rest on Clay's trip to the Other Side, and yet the nature of his destination was totally mysterious.

Suddenly, Jonah stopped and pointed. "Hey. What's that?"

As one, his friends turned their heads to look in the direction opposite from the way Ariella had flown. There was another spot in the sky, but this one was getting bigger and bigger.

"What the . . . ?" Leira said as the spot got closer. It was starting to look like . . . Could it be . . . ?

"Ariella?" Brett said, incredulous. "Already?" It had been less than three minutes since they'd left.

The dark spot was indeed Ariella, returning to the island at breakneck speed. The dragon coasted over the volcano and came to a rest on the shore of the lake. Leira and everyone else sprinted past the yurts to where Ariella had landed.

As they got closer they could see Clay, but something wasn't right. He was lying facedown across Ariella's back, completely still. He was still wearing the helmet, but the sled-turned-shield was cracked in half, and the sword was gone.

Leira and Brett ran across the beach as the dragon hunched its back and Clay slid to the ground.

"Clay?" Leira asked, lifting her friend's head from the sand. "Clay?"

Clay's face was pale and sweaty. He opened his

eyes, but his pupils were dilated and he was breathing unevenly.

"I've got to go back..." Clay muttered deliriously. "Back there... not here..."

Jogging up to them, Cass slapped a hand over her mouth. He sounded just like a certain deranged cowboy back at the Keep.

"Back... back..." Clay repeated, and then his eyes shut.

CHAPTER TWENTY-THREE

THE TRIP TO THE OTHER SIDE

Three minutes earlier

Ariella rocketed through the layer of vog that surrounded the island. In seconds, they were sailing through a cloudless sky, above a sparkling ocean. The wind tugged on Clay's garbage-pail shield as if it were a kite, and Clay felt like he might fly off the dragon's back at any second. And yet he couldn't resist letting go for a moment and raising his hands in the air, sword flashing in the sunlight. For one exhilarating moment, he forgot about everything—the people who were pinning their hopes on him, the dragons he was supposed to bring back with him, all the dangers he would soon confront—and he was lost again in the thrill of flight.

This was the feeling he remembered.

"So how long does it take to get there?" he asked, finally lowering his arms.

To what you humans call the Other Side?

"Yeah. . . . Wait. If you don't call it the Other Side, what do you call it?" Clay asked.

Home.

"Oh, wow, like that's where you grew up?"

Not that kind of home.

"What kind, then?"

Another kind.

"Well, how do we get there?"

We're there now.

"We are?"

Look around.

Clay looked around. They were still flying over the ocean. The sun was high in the sky.

"It looks the same."

That's because your mind hasn't opened yet. You are seeing only what you expect to see. Try again.

Clay closed his eyes, then opened them.

"Still the same."

Not your eyes, your mind.

"How do I open my mind?"

Ariella was silent a moment, perhaps thinking about how to translate dragon knowledge into human terms.

Jump.

"What?"

*Jump. Don't worry. I'll catch you. You won't need me to, but I will.**

Clay jumped.

Well, first, he stood on Ariella's back—helmet still on his head, sword still in his hand, shield still over his shoulder—with his arms outstretched.

And then he jumped.

Or dove, really. Somewhere in his mind was an image of a skydiver diving headfirst through the air with his arms spread-eagled, and Clay unconsciously copied it.

Of course, a skydiver has a parachute. All he had was the word of a dragon. He was terrified.

He was in free fall. Or he should have been. He'd never been in free fall before, but he assumed it would feel faster, colder, windier.

Instead, he seemed to be falling in slow motion. And then he didn't seem to be falling at all but rather floating through space. No, not space. Light. It seemed like he was traveling through light—pure and bright, but also somehow soft and gentle.

---

* YOU'VE PROBABLY HEARD THAT YOU SHOULDN'T JUMP JUST BECAUSE A FRIEND TELLS YOU TO JUMP. BUT WHEN THE FRIEND IS A DRAGON, IT'S A LITTLE DIFFERENT... EVEN IF TECHNICALLY YOU CAN'T BE FRIENDS WITH A DRAGON.

He never saw Ariella fly past, but there Ariella was, waiting to catch him, as promised. Clay drifted down, as if he were no heavier than a leaf, and settled gently onto the dragon's back.

And then he became very, very tired.

He blinked a few times. His eyelids felt heavy.

Don't go to sleep, Ariella warned him. *Or you will not go back.*

"What? Oh, right!"

Clay shook his head and sat up straight, remembering what the *Occulta Draco* had said: his sword, shield, and helmet were supposed to keep him "woozy but awake." Forcing himself to keep his eyes open, he adjusted his grip on DragonSlayer, rattled his garbage-pail shield, and tightened the strap of his skateboard helmet.

"So is this it?" he asked, looking around. There still wasn't much to see, but the light had become sparkly and iridescent, as if at any moment something spectacular might pop out of it. "Or is there, like, a particular place we're going to?"

You tell me. This is your trip.

"What do you mean? Where are the dragons?"

Wherever you find them.

"You don't know where they are?"

Where they are for me is not where they are for you. On the Other Side, you make your own path.

While Clay tried to digest this, a shape appeared

in the air in front of them. Clay peered at it as it came closer. "Is that a . . . house?"

Do you see a house?

"You don't?"

Everyone sees different things on the Other Side. Even dragons do not see everything here.

It was a little white cottage floating toward them. Clay was reminded of *The Wizard of Oz*, except that there was no tornado whipping them around; there wasn't even a breeze.

As they approached, Clay saw that the door of the cottage was ajar. (He remembered learning the word *ajar* when he was little: "When is a door not a door?" his brother would ask—one of his many corny jokes and riddles.)

"Do you think I should look inside?" Clay asked. He felt somehow that the door had been left open—ajar—for him.

Perhaps.

"Can you stop—"

I can . . .

"Will you?" said Clay impatiently.

Ariella had pushed him to go on this journey to the Other Side; couldn't the dragon be a little more helpful?

Ariella slowed almost to a stop, and Clay nervously jumped to the front stoop of the cottage. It was like jumping onto a boat, or maybe a bouncy house. Gravity was more of a "suggestion" here. Clay nearly sprang back up onto the dragon before righting himself and heading for the cottage door.

Just before entering, he looked back at Ariella. Was it his imagination, or was the dragon slipping away?

Good-bye, Ariella said.

"Aren't you going to wait!?"

I'll be there when you need me.

And then, to Clay's alarm, the dragon vanished altogether.

Forcing himself to remain calm, Clay walked into the cottage and found himself in a tiny wood-paneled room the size of a coat closet. What was so familiar about this room? It was like a room from a half-remembered dream.

A little brass sign on the paneling read:

Then he realized what the room reminded him of: the entry to the old magician Pietro's house. When Clay was little—when his brother was not much older than Clay was now—Max-Ernest would often tell Clay a bedtime story about his adventures with Cass. And the story would often begin in Pietro's strange underground house.

In Max-Ernest's telling, the entry to the house was an elevator, activated when the magic word was spoken, that word being *please*. Max-Ernest seemed to think this was hilarious, but Clay had never found it especially funny.

Funny or not, saying "please" didn't work. Perhaps this wasn't the same room after all. Well, of course it wasn't; he was on the Other Side. Nothing would be the same here.

Clay thought a moment; for him and his brother, there had never been magic words, only bad words. That is, *bad word* had been their preferred word (or phrase, actually) for magic word.

"Bad..." he said, and waited. When nothing happened, he added, "...word."

Sure enough, there was a jolt, and the room started to descend. Max-Ernest's story had morphed to suit Clay.

When the elevator door opened, Clay saw an old man with a bushy gray mustache and twinkling eyes. He was wearing a black suit and a top hat, and he appeared to be floating a few feet in the air, like a man in a Magritte painting.*

---

* René Magritte was a twentieth-century surrealist painter whose work celebrated the absurd with wit and bowler hats. See especially the painting *Golconda*, which depicts dozens of men in coats and hats, floating over a suburban streetscape. Another famous Magritte work, which certain magicians,

"Paul-Clay, if I do not make a mistake? Welcome, my young *amico*—"

He beckoned to Clay, who hesitantly stepped out of the elevator and into—what? Not a cloud. More like blankness. He found he was able to walk, but the sensation was a bit like swimming.

"You look a little like your brother, but I do not remember him wearing a helmet. Or carrying a sword."

The man's voice was warm and crusty, like bread out of the oven, and he had an Italian accent. Clay felt immediately that he could trust him.

"Do you know who I am?" the man asked.

"Pietro?" Clay guessed. "My brother—he used to tell stories about you."

"*Sì*," Pietro said with a warm smile. "Tell me, why have you come to the Other Side? You are chasing after a chicken?"

"A chicken?"

"Oh, just a little joke." Pietro waved his hand

AUTHORS, AND SECRET-SOCIETY MEMBERS MIGHT APPRECIATE, IS *THE TREACHERY OF IMAGES*: A PAINTING OF A PIPE ABOVE THE PHRASE *CECI N'EST PAS UNE PIPE*. IF YOU DON'T SPEAK FRENCH, IT'S JUST AS BEWILDERING IN ENGLISH. TRANSLATION: "THIS IS NOT A PIPE." SOMETIMES, ADDITIONAL INFORMATION BELOW A WORK OF ART CAN CREATE GREATER CONFUSION, BUT I DIGRESS.

dismissively. "You know, why did the chicken cross the road?"

"To get to the other side?"

"Right. But then the next one to cross the road, he is chasing after the chicken, no?"

"Okay," said Clay, still not exactly sure what Pietro was getting at, but already seeing why he and Max-Ernest had gotten along so well.

"But speak truly," said Pietro. "Why are you here? You are so young. I hope you have not come to stay!"

"No, I'm here on a...chase, I guess you could say. But not chasing chickens. Chasing dragons."

"Ah, dragons, yes." Pietro beamed. "We must all face our dragons. Our darkest fears. Our secret hopes. Those monsters we vanquish to find our true selves..."

Clay shook his head. "Um, that's not what I—"

"Now, your brother, he had many dragons. Do you want to know what was one of the most important?"

"The Midnight Sun?"

"Well, yes, of course. But I was thinking of one closer to home.... You."

"Me?" Clay blinked.

Pietro nodded genially. "You are surprised? Like many older brothers, when you were born, Max-Ernest, he was a little jealous. He felt he was being replaced in his parents' hearts. But then what happens? Your parents, they were so lost in their own world that he had to take care of you himself, did he not?"

"Yeah, maybe, for a while, but he didn't stick with it for that long," said Clay, unable to keep the bitterness out of his voice.

"Perhaps not, but it is a big challenge for a teenage boy, to be not just a brother but a father. To put another life first before his own."

"Right. Well, anyway," said Clay, "that's not the kind of dragon I'm talking about. I mean real dragons. *Dragon* dragons."

Pietro frowned, disappointed. "*Dragon* dragons. Hmph. I do not think I can help you with *dragon* dragons." He looked around as if to show that there were no dragons easily available.

"Oh, that's okay," said Clay, disappointed. "Do you know who can?"

"I have no idea," said Pietro, bemused. "Are there dragon specialists? Is that a branch of zoology I'm not aware of?"

"There are Dragon Tamers," said Clay.

"Well, there you are," said Pietro contentedly. "Then a Dragon Tamer you shall find."

"But I don't know how to find a Dragon Tamer, either." Clay sighed. At least he had Ariella's word for it that there were dragons on the Other Side; he had no evidence that there were also Dragon Tamers here.

"Maybe you should try calling for one. In the real world, this might not work, of course. But here..." Pietro shrugged.

"You mean just, like, call out loud...or on the phone?" asked Clay, confused.

"Either. It matters not. But if it makes you happy, you can use this—" He held up a white-tipped black stick.

"Your magic wand?"

"Oh, sorry, I meant this—"

Pietro tapped the air with the wand, and the wand turned into an old-fashioned black telephone receiver with white ear- and mouthpieces. A cord dangled uselessly; the main body of the phone was missing.*

"Um, that's okay," said Clay. "Maybe I'll just try shouting."

"Have it your way," said Pietro amiably. "Before you go, I have a message for your brother." He removed the hat from his head and turned it over,

---

* In the olden days, before phones were things that you put in your pocket, a telephone had two major parts: the main body of the telephone, on which you found the telephone dial; and the receiver, which had a mouthpiece and an earpiece so that primitive peoples could speak to each other—even without the ability to text. The receiver was connected to the rest of the phone with a curling cord, like the one dangling in the paragraph above.

showing Clay the inside. "Tell Max-Ernest to look under the lining. I've left one last surprise for him."

With that, Pietro put the top hat back on and started to walk away.

"Hey, don't you want to give the hat to my brother?" Clay called after him, confused.

"Oh, no," Pietro chuckled, disappearing from sight. "He already has it."

Clay thought of the old top hat that Max-Ernest wore during his magic shows; it did look very similar, come to think of it. Max-Ernest had had the hat for as long as Clay could remember. Along with that rabbit of his, with the silly name. Quiche. Whenever he wanted to make Clay laugh, Max-Ernest would pretend Quiche could talk. The way Max-Ernest described it, Quiche was always mad at him and always demanding more carrots.

It was funny, thinking back to that time. Maybe Quiche really could talk. Clay had seen stranger things by now—including a few talking animals.

Clay turned, thinking he would get back in the elevator, but the elevator was gone. He was all alone in the nothingness.

Trying not to panic, he took a breath. There was no reason not to take Pietro's suggestion and call for a Dragon Tamer. Which Dragon Tamer? The author of the memoirs, presumably. Clay didn't know his name, but maybe that didn't matter any more than whether or not he used a telephone.

"I am looking for the last Dragon Tamer! The author of the memoirs!" Feeling extremely foolish, Clay shouted as loudly as he could, but his voice did not seem to carry very far in this nowhere land. "I am a follower of the Occulta Draco!"

He waited, not knowing what to expect or what he would do if there was no response.

The wait was not long. As soon as he started to yawn, a stone archway appeared where the elevator had been. Behind it was a narrow stairway leading upward.

Full of trepidation, Clay mounted the stairway. It was long and steep, with hundreds of steps. He climbed, huffing and puffing, until he had to stop to take a breath.

A voice cried out from above:

"Keep going! Are you afraid of a few measly steps? A Dragon Tamer must have strong legs!"

A few measly steps. Right. Clay's legs burned from climbing all those stairs with the added weight of his shield and sword, but eventually he reached the top.

A man stood in front of a heavy wooden door that glowed around the jambs. He wore an old leather vest, had long dark hair swept back, and met Clay's eyes with an intense gaze.

"Hello," Clay said.

"Hmph," the man said. "Do you know why I'm here?"

Because I called for you, Clay thought, but he didn't say so.

"I'm here to judge whether you're worthy to meet with the dragons. So far I'm not impressed."

"How did you know that's why I came?"

"The dragons told me."

"How do they know?"

"Because the dragons have a different experience of time. In a sense, you've already met them. They live forward and backward at once."

"Well, why can't I just meet them, then? You're making me jump through hoops for no reason."

"It doesn't work like that."

"I need to ask them for help," Clay said.

"Don't. They will see no reason for a dragon to help a human."

"Should I try to ally with them first?"

"No! That would be worse. These dragons are very proud. If you try to do favors for them, or start singing..." The Dragon Tamer's eyes strayed to the sword in Clay's hand. His expression darkened. "Your sword—is that the one they call DragonSlayer?"

Clay nodded.

"That is an evil thing. It is no sword for a Dragon

Tamer. Be gone with it. If the dragons see that, they will burn you alive."

"But—but your poem said to bring an enemy's sword," Clay stammered.

"That's just an old saying, and I can't imagine that whoever first said it was thinking of Dragon-Slayer! But perhaps . . ." The Dragon Tamer furrowed his brow. "Perhaps the sword may be of use after all. I shall send you to the dragons, if you like. But I warn you: It may not end well."

"Thanks," said Clay, wondering what not ending well meant. Could you be killed on the Other Side? Or did you just get stuck there?

"They will ask you three questions."

"What questions?"

The Dragon Tamer shrugged. "The questions don't matter. It is how you answer them."

"How should I answer them?"

"The only advice I can give is to take your time about it. Years, if you like."

"I don't have years!"

"Dragons like to talk sideways, around a problem. To them, a quick answer is a careless answer."

"Okay. So I answer slowly. Then what? If they like my answer, I ask if they'll help me?"

"No. They already know why you're here. Tell them you have a gift for them."

"But I don't have a gift."

"The sword. They may not like it, but they will be glad to know it can never be used against a dragon again."

Clay nodded. "And the Midnight Sun won't be able to use the blood on it to make any more little dragon clones. . . ."

"What?" The all-knowing Dragon Tamer was mystified.

"Never mind," said Clay. "I don't totally understand how they do it, either."

"Here, wrap the sword in this." The Dragon Tamer handed Clay a tattered piece of cloth.

"How do I find them?" Clay asked.

"The dragons? Well, don't go looking for them. That's always a mistake."

"Call to them, then? Like I did for you?"

"Like a child or a pet? Never! They would be very insulted."

"What, then?"

"Close your eyes. Let them find you."

"Okay, um, thanks." He started to close his eyes, then opened them again. "You aren't going to leave, are you?"

"No. You are."

When Clay opened his eyes, he understood what the Dragon Tamer had meant. Clay was on the other side of the door now, in some sort of canyon.

It was daytime. No, that wasn't right. It was day where he was, the sky a bright blue; but in the distance it was night, the sky a dark purple, with twinkling stars. As though he were looking into a different time zone. Or as though in this place all time zones were one.

Immediately in front of him was a gray, hulking rock formation. Farther into the canyon, there were a few trees scattered about, but mostly there were more rock formations. Hundreds and hundreds of them. Jagged and craggy and menacing. A white mist swirled around them, like a stream.

"Hello?" Clay said tentatively.

He turned around. There were no signs of life. Not so much as a fly to be seen, never mind a dragon.

He turned around again. By the time he'd made a full rotation, the closest rock formation was gone and an enormous dragon was staring at him—a dragon that would have made even Ariella look small, and would have made Bluebeard look like a puppy.

Behind the dragon, other rock formations were shaking, as if in an earthquake. Gradually, Clay could make out hunched shoulders, folded wings, curled tails; the rocks were dragons.

The dragon in front of him looked old in the way a mountain looks old: like it had taken millions of years to grow and would take millions more to crumble back into the earth. The dragon breathed, and its scales rippled, sending silvery shimmers across its massive body.

Hello, human.

"Um—hello . . ." Clay stammered.

Hello what? Hello, dragon? Hello, Mr. Dragon? Mrs. Dragon? No, dragons were neither male nor female.

You may call me Old One, said the dragon, as if it had heard Clay's thoughts (which it probably had).

We have three questions for you, human. If you answer properly, we will consider your request.

Answer properly, Clay thought. Is that the same thing as correctly?

"Right," said Clay. "Fire away." As soon as the words *fire away* were out of his mouth, he regretted them: Not only was the phrase slangy in a way a dragon might not appreciate, but also there was the possibility that the dragon would take the words literally and fire away at him.

Thankfully, Old One didn't appear to notice.

Here is your first question, human, said the dragon. *What is the worst mistake a dragon can make?*

Clay felt an immediate sense of relief: He knew the answer to this question from reading the *Occulta Draco*. But he remembered the Dragon Tamer's advice about not answering too quickly, so he bent his head and pretended to think it over.

"A dragon cannot make a mistake," he said

slowly. "Whatever a dragon does, it has already done. So it's not right or wrong; it just is."

Yes. It just is. The dragon nodded, though it did not seem especially pleased by Clay's answer.

Clay waited for what seemed to him a very long time, which was probably only a blink for a dragon.

Finally, the dragon spoke again:

What is the worst mistake a human can make?

This question was trickier. To kill a dragon, perhaps? No. Too risky. A dragon would be insulted by the very idea of a person killing a dragon.

He thought for another moment. Probably a dragon would think anything a human did was a mistake.

"To think he is like a dragon—that he cannot make mistakes. That is the worst mistake a human can make."

The dragon looked at Clay without indicating approval or disapproval. Clay's hands were sweating. Had he answered too quickly? He had meant to take his time, but nerves had gotten the better of him.

What is the greatest mistake you have made?

Clay thought of all the mistakes he'd made in his lifetime. Which was the worst? And did he really want to share it with Old One? If the mistake was truly terrible, would the dragon think him unworthy of help?

Then again, maybe his worst mistake was one he

didn't yet know he'd made. For instance, coming to the Other Side might have been his worst mistake. Or maybe it wasn't a mistake at all. There was no way of knowing.

He wished his brother were there to help him with the riddle. *But it isn't a riddle*, his brother would say. *It's just a question!*

Yeah, yeah, I know, answered Clay in his head. *Do you always have to be so logical?*

"The worst mistake I've made is not forgiving the mistakes of others," he said finally. Maybe it was time to forgive Max-Ernest. That was what Pietro had been trying to tell him, wasn't it?

You are uncertain.

"Well, how can you be certain of something like that? I mean..."

Yes.

There was a long silence. Clay wasn't sure whether or when he was supposed to speak.

"I have a gift for you," he said, unable to bear the silence any longer. He unwrapped the sword and laid it down in front of the dragon.

The dragon glared at him.

"Its name is DragonSlayer," said Clay nervously.

I know what its name is, human, the dragon roared. *You dare call this a gift? This thing that has murdered so many of our kind.*

"I was going to get rid of it, but I thought you'd

want to do that," said Clay, trying not to cower. "You know, to make sure it was done right."

Have you used this sword yourself? Have you drawn blood from a dragon?

"No, never!" declared Clay truthfully. Silently, he thanked Ariella for forbidding him to use the sword.

There was another long and uncomfortable silence. Uncomfortable for Clay, that is, not for the dragon.

Very well, said the dragon at last. *You have done right to bring us the sword. We will help you, and we will save our young if they can be saved—but when we are done, we will come back here and we will shut the door behind us. We dragons are finished with your world, and you are finished with ours.*

Clay wanted to say what a terrible idea this was, how much he loved and admired dragons, more even than skateboarding and graffiti art and animals and magic and all the other things he loved (well, dragons pretty much *were* magic, but still...), and how he wished there would always be dragons in the world, and what a sad and boring world it would be without them, but all he said was,

"Thank you."

CHAPTER TWENTY-FOUR

THE RAID ON THE LABORATORY

Later that afternoon

Satya wasn't afraid anymore. Not of Ms. Mauvais. Not of the dragons. Not of being stranded in the middle of a jungle in the middle of a crater in the middle of a desert. She figured she'd seen the worst of all of those things already, and she'd survived.

Survived. Like Cass. The survivalist. Satya's new role model. Cass wasn't afraid of anything.*

Still.

* I know this not to be true; Cass was afraid of plenty of things. Dehydration. Certain extinction-level events. Plastic bags. I am merely trying to convey Satya's state of mind.

Not being afraid was no reason not to be careful.

She had Hero with her, of course. Her spy, bodyguard, and secret weapon. But Hero was unpredictable when it came to dragons. To say the least.

She looked at the laboratory building, trying to study it analytically.

Getting in wasn't going to be a problem. She still had Gyorg's keys. It was the getting out that would be tricky. Most staff members were occupied with salvaging materials from the castle and building temporary shelters. Nonetheless, it was more than possible that one or more guards might be chasing her. They might even go after her with a helicopter.

And then there was Bluebeard, still out there somewhere. Waiting to get revenge. Snowflake and Rover were back under the dome, but so far Bluebeard had evaded capture. The dragon had either found a way to deactivate its collar or flown so far afield that the collar no longer worked. All Midnight Sun staff were under orders to shoot the one-eyed menace on sight.

Satya had watched Dr. Paru exit the laboratory. Then she waited a full five minutes to make sure the scientist wasn't coming back. (If Satya had hoped to find an ally in Dr. Paru, she'd given up; Dr. Paru was too married to her science, or too afraid of Ms. Mauvais, or simply too well paid, to question what the Midnight Sun was doing.) And now it was time.

Satya unlocked the laboratory door and walked swiftly toward the nurseries. Hero was tense, even shaking a little bit, but the falcon seemed to understand that she was supposed to remain silent.

The little dragons, in contrast, were shrieking noisily. The last time they'd seen Hero, she'd really riled them up, and it appeared that they remembered. Satya wasn't sure whether they regarded the falcon as friend or foe or food, but whatever the case, they didn't find Hero's presence soothing.

One by one, she released them from their cages. First the four babies, whom she called Louis, Percy, Sarah, and Garby (all named after former pets of Satya's). Then Houdini and Bodhi, whose hoods and jesses she carefully removed. Usually so mellow, Bodhi wasn't very mellow now. None of them were. There was total chaos in the room. Talons scratching walls. Bottles crashing to the floor.

Attempting to convey a sense of calm authority, she carried a cooler full of meat in front of her—the only thing that would focus the dragons' attention—and walked out of the room. The little dragons followed her, fighting for the positions closest to the meat. They didn't make a line so much as a writhing black ball. Hero circled the dragons, trying to keep them all going in the same direction, like a dog shepherding a flock of sheep.

Amazingly, the motley group made it outside

without interruption. They appeared to be alone. Satya allowed herself a small sigh of relief as she marched her crew steadily forward.

Her father, she felt sure, would help her when the time came. They were to leave that afternoon, one way or another. He'd sworn it, and she intended to hold him to his promise. But they simply couldn't leave knowing that all these baby dragons were still in captivity, property of the Midnight Sun.

So they would take the dragons. How? Vaguely, she imagined that she and her father would put all six dragons and Hero in a helicopter and then escape to parts unknown. An island, maybe. Or somewhere in the Arctic.

Realistic? Probably not. The dragons wouldn't like being confined in the helicopter. How long before they revolted? And even if she and her father successfully relocated the dragons, what would they do when the dragons got bigger? But what other options were there?

One step at a time, she told herself. Or one flap of the wing, in the case of the dragons.

She noticed the silence first.

The chattering and the screeching, the flying and the fighting—suddenly, it had all stopped.

She looked down. There were no more little talons or teeth scratching and snapping at the cooler.

She turned around. Where were all the dragons?

A large fern drew her attention; a pair of yellow eyes stared out from the shadows beneath it.

Satya spotted the little dragons, one after another, peering out from the foliage. They were quiet but alert, quivering. She smiled uncertainly. Were they hiding from her? Was it some kind of game? No, they didn't seem the least bit interested in her. It was something else. Something they feared.

Hero hissed in her ear.

Slowly, Satya raised her eyes to the sky.

Bluebeard.

CHAPTER TWENTY-FIVE

THE THUNDER OF DRAGONS

"...and then Old One yawns, this huge, huge dragon yawn, with the big bumpy tongue and the big broken teeth, rows and rows of them, and everything, and suddenly it's like the biggest windstorm ever, a really hot and smelly windstorm, and it sends me flying, and I guess I hit my head and get knocked out, or maybe there's like some kind of sleeping gas in the dragon's breath, and then I guess Ariella finds me and takes me home, because I wake up here in Puke Yurt with a splitting headache and you guys staring at me like my face peeled off or something, and..." Clay faltered, nervous. "Wait, it didn't *actually* peel off, did it? I mean, I look normal, right?"

Leira and Brett peered down at him.

"Define *normal*," said Leira.

Brett nodded judiciously. "Yeah, it's hard to say without knowing what the bar for normal is."

"You guys are always so reassuring."

Clay sat up and surveyed the round room, filled with mysterious medicinal herbs and ointments.

"So, they're not here... are they?" he asked, looking out the window. All that was visible were trees.

"Who?" asked Leira.

"Old One. And the other dragons."

"Here at camp? Should they be?"

"Well, yeah," said Clay. "I mean, if they aren't, then it was all for nothing, wasn't it—the whole trip?"

"Why do you say that?" asked Brett. "It sounds sort of amazing, if you ask me. You got to go where nobody ever gets to go, or at least where, er, nobody ever gets to go back from."

"Did I? How do I know it wasn't a dream?" Agitated, Clay threw off his blanket. "I'm not even sure the dragons were real."

Before Clay's friends could respond, the yurt's flap door was thrown back and Jonah stuck his head in. "Um, hey, guys?" he said, hesitant. "You might want to come look at this."

Rubbing his eyes, Clay climbed out of bed, and they all peeked out of the yurt. Jonah pointed his thumb over his shoulder, toward the clouds.

The horizon was filled with undulating black shapes.

Dragons—hundreds of them—were sweeping across the sky, headed right for Earth Ranch.

And now it's time to answer a question that (if you're anything like me) has been eating away at you for the last few chapters:

What do you call a group of dragons? In other words, what is the correct collective noun? Is it a *herd* of dragons? A *school*? A *flock*? A *pride*?

Short answer: There are several answers.

While a group of dragon eggs may be referred to as a *clutch*, a group of very young dragons is a *brood*, and a group of grown dragons is most often known as a *weyr*. But that's only if they're on the ground. A group of aquatic dragons may be referred to as a *lagoon*. A group of dragons soaring through the sky is a *flight*, though some insist on calling it a *stampede* or a *thunder*.

If you'd found yourself among the dragons arriving en masse over the crater, I think you would have gone with that last word, *thunder*. With so many wings flapping at once, it was like being inside a hurricane; and if that wasn't enough, their roaring and flame-spitting created a raging firestorm that was indeed thunderous.

Alas, Clay was the lone human to experience this firestorm. Leira and Brett had wanted to come, too, of course—all of Clay's friends had—but Clay had insisted that it wasn't necessary. (In fact, he'd asked Old One about bringing his friends along, only

to be treated to an angry lecture about how dragons weren't pack animals.) If a full thunder of dragons—a *fleet*?—couldn't handle the job, what difference would a few kids make? As a compromise, Clay had agreed to wear the ski hat again, this time under the skateboard helmet. His head was hotter and itchier than ever, but he was grateful for the extra protection, especially with all the balls of fire streaking past him.

As the dragons descended on the Keep, their wings drew closer together, darkening the sky like a great cloak. Peering over Ariella's neck, Clay had to strain his eyes to see what was happening down below. It had been less than twenty-four hours since he'd left the Keep, but in that time enormous progress had been made. The remaining walls of the old castle had been knocked down, and the frame for a new building was already being erected. Most of the rubble had been carefully stacked in piles or already removed.

"*Howzit look down there?*" Leira asked in his ear.

"All I can say is the Midnight Sun works really fast."

At this rate, the Keep would be back in business in a few days. But Clay didn't intend to let that happen. And neither did the hundreds of dragons flying with him. The plan was very straightforward: All humans and dragons were to be removed from the crater—forcibly if necessary. The lab was to be destroyed. The Midnight Sun would have to move on.

Alighting on the crater's rim, the majority of the dragons took positions around the sides of the crater. They sat like enormous gargoyles, guarding the pathways out into the desert.

Ariella, meanwhile, led a smaller group of dragons down toward the bottom of the crater to begin a sweep.

Where in the darkness below was Satya? Clay wondered. Had she and her father already escaped? For her sake, he hoped they had. And yet he wanted nothing more than to see her again.

First things first, Ariella chided him. *The hatchlings. Where are they?*

From over the tents, Clay steered Ariella toward the laboratory. The long building was dark, and no one was outside.

"That's where the baby dragons are," he said to Ariella, pointing at the lab.

Ariella headed toward the entrance, then abruptly pulled up before landing. *Are you certain? I don't feel them in there.*

"I dunno, actually," said Clay, peering down at the building. "I feel like something's wrong, too."

They circled the laboratory a few times, each time making a wider loop. Clay started to feel apprehensive.

Then he heard a familiar squawk. Not too far from the laboratory building, Hero was perched on a tree branch that hung over a jungle path. Beneath her, six little dragons were frantically hopping up and down in distress. And lying between them...

"We need to get down there now!"

Ariella landed, and Clay jumped to the ground.

"Satya!"

As Clay approached, the little dragons hissed, but Ariella silenced them with a stern growl.

"Clay?"

"I told you I'd come back."

Satya sat up shakily and propped herself against the meat cooler. She looked pale and frazzled but unharmed.

"What's with the helmet?" she asked, peering at the graffiti lettering. "Just feeling sort of *radical?*"

Clay blushed. "Long story. Are you okay?"

"Yeah, I fell, but I'm fine.... I was just catching my breath. Bluebeard was about to pounce on us, and then the next second the sky was filled with dragons, and Bluebeard split." She gestured to the little dragons. "These guys were pretty freaked."

"They don't look so freaked now," Clay observed.

While they were speaking, Ariella had started speaking in a low rumble with the smaller dragons. They yelped and whined but sat still, their eyes fixed on the older dragon. Even Houdini and Bodhi.

"Guess Ariella is talking some sense into them." Satya smiled. "So, that army of dragons up there—did you bring them?"

Clay shrugged, nonchalant. "Those guys? It's only a few hundred dragons. Whatever." He smiled.

Satya nodded. "Yeah, right. No big deal."

They both laughed.

"You ready to climb onto Ariella's back with me?"

Satya's eyes shone with excitement. "Wait—I get to fly with you?"

Clay grinned. "What do you think I'm here for? I mean, that's okay, right, Ariella?" he asked, backpedaling.

The dragon snorted in a way that seemed to say, *Now you ask?*

"What about these little guys?" asked Satya.

The little dragons were all standing at attention now, like dragon Cub Scouts. In unison, they bowed to Ariella and made a strange humming sound deep in their throats.

"Well, how about it?" Clay asked Ariella. "Are they Lost Ones?"

Not anymore, said Ariella, with a hint of pride.

It was a brief flight, about a quarter of a mile. For Satya, nonetheless, it was memorable; it was the first time she'd flown on a dragon. For Clay, it was memorable, too, but for a different reason; it was the first time Satya had put her arms around him, even if it was only to keep herself from falling off.

The four youngest dragons were also riding on Ariella's back—or, more precisely, on Ariella's wings. They seemed to think it was a lot of fun getting flung up and down, over and over.

The two slightly older dragons, Houdini and Bodhi, flew behind, repeatedly turning their heads to either side; they'd been given instructions to keep looking in all directions and were avidly following their orders to the letter.

The guest tents, whatever remained of them, had been rolled up, and Clay and Satya didn't see any signs of life until they neared the castle courtyard.

The two bronze dragons in the center of the courtyard fountain had fallen over, and a crane was parked nearby, ready to lift them back up. As Ariella glided to the ground beside the fountain, one of the Land Rovers nearly collided with them, then sideswiped the bottom of the crane.

Charles leaned out the driver's-side window. "Austin, I must say, you know how to make an entrance!"

He smiled at Clay, apparently untroubled by the dozens of fire-spitting dragons flying directly above him. "I'd stay for a chat, but Reginald and Minerva here have a game waiting for them in Palm Beach.

And frankly, all these dragons are beginning to be a bit of a bore...." The Wandsworths were sitting stiffly in the backseat, looking directly ahead, with piles of expensive-looking luggage behind them.

"Until we meet again!" said Charles. With a casual wave, he stepped on the gas and headed out of the Keep.

"Now, that's what I call blasé," said Clay to himself.

As the one Land Rover disappeared, the other stopped in front of them, and Vicente jumped out.

"Satya! There you are!"

Vicente looked up at his daughter and Clay, obviously somewhat amazed to see them sitting on Ariella's back. But all he said was "Glad you're not alone.... Can you guys fly out of here on that thing?"

"This thing's name is Ariella," said Clay. "But, yeah, we can."

"Good. I'll meet you on the landing strip in half an hour."

"But how are you going to get there?" his daughter asked, anxious.

"In the car. I have to help shuttle a few more employees out of here." He pointed his thumb backward; the Land Rover was full to capacity. Blowing her a kiss, he hopped back in and drove away.

"Okay if we don't leave quite yet?" Clay asked Satya. "I want to make sure this thing is finished."

She nodded, and they both slid to the ground.

A long, gleaming trailer, the kind used by movie stars on location, was parked in front of the dismantled castle. CONSTRUCTION OFFICE, read a sign on the door.

As more dragons flew overhead, sending the occasional fireball into the courtyard, the trailer door slammed open and various people started spilling out, some looking terrified, other just annoyed. Last to join the commotion was Ms. Mauvais, accompanied by Amber and Gyorg. Just as they'd stepped out of the trailer, another dragon made a pass over the courtyard, and a second later the trailer erupted in flames.

Amber clutched her arms over her head, nearly bowling over Ms. Mauvais in her haste to get away from the fire.

"Clumsy girl!" chastised Ms. Mauvais. "Panicking because it's a little warm."

When Ms. Mauvais regained her balance, she saw Clay standing before her. Behind him was Satya, standing by Ariella.

"Oh, it's you," Ms. Mauvais said, showing no reaction. (Charles might be blasé; she was a block of ice.) "Welcome... back."

"I figured out who he is!" said Amber excitedly. "He's Max-Ernest's little brother. That man who brought him here before—he wasn't his father; he was a spy!"

"Pity your epiphany didn't come a day or two

earlier," said Ms. Mauvais in a tone notable precisely for its lack of pity. She studied Clay as if he were a specimen in a museum. "But now that you mention it, I do see a bit of a resemblance. Of course, Max-Ernest was always so..."

"What? So much cleverer than I am?" said Clay, with just a touch of bitterness.

"So much shorter, I was about to say."

"Didn't stop him from beating you, though, did it? Him and Cass?" said Clay defensively. "And they're beating you again—*we* are, I mean."

Ms. Mauvais gave him a mocking smile. "Oh, we are, are we?"

Gyorg had walked up and was standing stiffly beside her, ready to protect her if necessary.

"Yep," said Clay, willing himself not to be scared. He had Ariella on his side, after all. "I'm here to tell you you're done. You, this place, and your dragons."

"Says the boy of what—twelve?" hissed Ms. Mauvais. "No one tells me when I'm done. *I* say when I'm done. And when I do, you will be a distant memory."

A sustained **ROARRRRRRRRR** cut into the moment.

Clay turned to see an enormous dragon approaching. The biggest one of all. Old One. The dragon landed next to Ariella, taking up half the courtyard.

On Old One's back was a young man. He laughed as Clay stared at him.

"Who's that?" Satya whispered.

"His name is Flint," said Clay through gritted teeth.

Flint grinned down at him. "Surprised?"

Clay shook his head.

Flint on a dragon's back? In fact, no sight could have surprised Clay more. Surprised him and infuriated him.

"How'd you do it?" Clay asked, struggling to contain his temper.

"The *Occulta Draco*—what else?" said Flint. "You should never have let it out of your hands."

"You used a spell?" Clay was dubious.

"I made a trade," said Flint.

Clay understood immediately; it was just what he'd done with DragonSlayer. Old One would have hated the idea of a book that might teach a human to control a dragon. Far better to take the book out of human hands, even if it meant having to give Flint a ride.

Behind him, a rumble came from deep inside Ariella's chest. Old One gave an answering rumble. Clay wasn't certain, but he thought Old One was saying something like *Hold your fire*.

Ms. Mauvais stepped toward Flint, clapping.

"Bravo, darling," she said in her most seductive voice. "I, for one, am very impressed. And very glad to see you again."

Flint stood up straighter and frowned. "You are?"

"Why not? Things have changed." Ms. Mauvais lifted her arms to the sky. "As you see, we have a veritable army of dragons now."

"They aren't yours."

"With your help they might be...." She met the young man's gaze and held it. Until, with an effort, he turned away.

Clay glanced at the dragons. He knew they would be insulted by the notion that dragons could be made into an army under human control, but they showed no reaction. Yet.

"You just want to go to the Other Side to become immortal," said Flint.

"Yes, but with the dragons at our command, why, we could do so much more," said Ms. Mauvais. "That would be just the beginning."

Flint looked around as if weighing the possibilities. "What do you want?"

"To start? Take me away from here."

"What about me?" Amber protested.

"You?" said Ms. Mauvais, as if only just noticing her. "Stay here and await my return. If something comes up, do whatever your instincts tell you *not* to do. I'm sure that will be the safest course. Gyorg will assist you."

Standing nearby, Gyorg coughed but said nothing. Neither he nor Amber was very happy about this plan.

"You and I will be a team," said Ms. Mauvais, returning to Flint. "All we need is one dragon to start. If others follow, fantastic. If not, we make more. A drop of blood is all it takes."

Clay watched to see what Flint would do, and what Old One would do in response. What game was the wily old dragon playing? Did Old One perhaps want something that the Midnight Sun had? If Old One went back on the deal with Clay, all the other dragons would likely follow suit, and there was nothing Clay could do about it. A bead of sweat dripped down from his forehead to his nose.

"Really? Just one drop of blood?" said Flint at last, his feverish excitement evident in his face. "And with it we could—*ahhhhhhh!*"

Flint fell off Old One's back as the dragon let out a roar that literally made the ground shake.

You dare speak of dragon blood? raged Old One. *I promised to take you here, but I said nothing about taking you back. I am done.*

Like a huge Viking ship setting sail, the dragon

spread its creaky wings and lurched into the air, while Flint watched aghast.

Clay's smile of satisfaction lasted only a second. Next to him, Ariella growled, ready for battle.

Another dragon had swooped into the courtyard. The last dragon anybody wanted to see. Bluebeard.

Clay could feel Satya tensing. What was the one-eyed monster after this time?

Landing in the fountain, Bluebeard perched on top of the fallen bronze dragons as if they were a recent kill and Bluebeard was protecting them from predators.

As the dragon's head swiveled back and forth, its good eye caught sight of Satya and Hero, and blinked. Or was it winked? *I'll deal with you later*, Bluebeard seemed to say.

"Let's wait and see what Bluebeard does," Clay whispered to Ariella, knowing that Ariella still had not fully recovered from the first encounter with Bluebeard. A second fight was to be avoided if possible. Ariella, he sensed, felt the same way.

But Bluebeard appeared not to be interested in them. Instead, the dragon focused on Ms. Mauvais, the woman who more than anyone else was responsible for this place and for the dragons' captivity. She, it seemed, was the reason for Bluebeard's visit. The dragon dropped back down on all fours and advanced on her.

Ms. Mauvais maintained her perfectly calm expression as Bluebeard pushed her back toward the trailer. "Gyorg, Flint, somebody, do something," she said, with only the barest hint of urgency.

Just as the dragon was about to reach her, its huge mouth open, Ms. Mauvais finally lost her composure. She shrieked and shoved Gyorg in the dragon's path.

Gyorg had no time to register his employer's betrayal before Bluebeard's great sharp jaws grabbed the muscleman around the middle and tossed him aside. As though nothing had happened, Bluebeard resumed its advance on Ms. Mauvais, its single eye glistening.

"Stop, dragon!"

It was Flint, intervening at the last second—perhaps to save Ms. Mauvais, perhaps to show off. Clay couldn't tell.

With his eyes locked on Bluebeard, Flint touched his lips to his fist. In a flash, his fist was on fire. Raising it in the air like a torch, he waved it back and forth in front of Bluebeard's good eye.

"Get down!" said Flint, as if he were speaking to a dog.

Then, shocking Clay and probably everyone else present, human or dragon, Bluebeard knelt down. Not bowing out of politeness or respect, as Ariella had done, but in submission, as a weaker creature kneels before a more powerful one.

"That's right, there's a good boy," said Flint, smiling victoriously.

Clay could feel waves of anger coming from Ariella; it was unbearable to see a dragon humiliated by a human in this way.

It matters not, said Ariella spitefully. *The dragon is a Lost One.*

When the debased dragon had almost flattened itself to the ground, Flint offered a cocky a little wave to the people watching, then climbed onto Bluebeard's back. "Bye-bye, fools!"

Flint kicked into the dragon's sides. Bluebeard reared slightly, then rounded on the trailer, giving it one final blast of fire.

Then, with Flint astride, Bluebeard rose up and took off into the night sky.

"Good riddance," said Satya.

Clay watched for a moment, stunned. He thought he knew what he'd just witnessed: a kind of black magic that was described in the *Occulta Draco*, the magic of the Fire Breathers. But where Flint was heading now, Clay had no idea. Wherever it was, it wasn't far enough.

In Bluebeard's place, other dragons began swirling around the smoldering remains of the trailer. Clay caught Ms. Mauvais staring at them, with something almost like fear on her frozen face.

"You want to come with us instead of being

stuck with those guys?" said Clay. "You'd have to be tied up, of course. And if you tried to hurt anyone, Ariella would probably kill you. . . ."

"And be the prisoner of the Terces Society?" said the leader of the Midnight Sun, with all the haughtiness at her command. "I'd rather die."

Clay looked up at the thickening mass of dragons circling directly above. "Okay, if that's what you want."

He turned to Satya. "Let's get the heck out of here."

Using Ariella's leg as a ladder, they climbed onto the dragon's back.

A moment later, they were lifting off into the night. It was like swimming against a current; around them, dozens of dragons were diving toward a single goal.

Looking over his shoulder for a last time, Clay saw a pair of gloved hands, unmistakably Ms. Mauvais's, waving in the air. There was a scream of pain that sounded strangely like a cry of joy. Then the hands disappeared and she was lost in the vortex of roaring, screeching dragons bearing down on her.

CHAPTER TWENTY-SIX

THE OTHER SIDE OF THE COIN

Now that they had recovered from the fear of attack, the littlest dragons had left Ariella's back and were flying behind with Houdini and Bodhi.

Unlike Satya, Ariella was somehow able to make the unruly young dragons stay in a single line, although a straight line admittedly it was not.

No, they did not look anything like ducklings (not even ugly ducklings). And few people would call them cute or cuddly. Nonetheless, the people watching them couldn't help smiling.

With the little dragons trailing behind, Clay guided Ariella out of the crater, to the landing strip just on the other side of the crater's rim. They coasted down to the asphalt stretch, just before the second helicopter that belonged to the Midnight Sun, and parked by a row of Cessnas.

Behind Ariella, dark figures were erupting over the side of the crater, flying up into the starry night. The dragons—they were leaving.

"I think the dragons are almost as happy to get out of there as I am," said Clay, watching. "What about you?"

Satya looked up at him with her dark eyes hinting at a smile. "There are some things I'll miss."

Clay felt himself turning red. "So," he said, looking down at the scaly dragon back beneath them. "About that kiss. Would you maybe want to try again—even if we're not about to die?"

"*Smooth line,*" said Brett.

"*Yeah, real classy,*" said Leira.

Clay's ears were burning pink.

Satya laughed. "Sure," she said. "But no gum chewing this time. And don't you want to take off your helmet?"

Quickly, Clay removed the helmet.

"And maybe the ski hat, too, while you're at it?"

"Wait, no, don't ruin our fun!"

Clay emphatically pulled off his hat. His hair was messier than ever.

Satya looked at him critically. "That's better, although I have to say I'm curious to see what you look like with your hair brushed."

"The truth? I look exactly the same."

"Well, then I guess there's no reason to wait any longer, is there?"

She closed her eyes and Clay leaned in. Now that he wasn't chewing, he could appreciate how soft her lips were and how nice she smelled. After a moment, Hero started squawking and scratching.

Satya sat back, beaming. "Darn bird," she complained.

Clay felt like he might float away.

Except that he could still hear the sounds of Leira and Brett laughing and cheering coming from the ski hat bunched up in his hand.

Ariella made a noise that was suspiciously like a human cough.

Isn't it time for you two to disembark?

In the not-too-far distance, a Land Rover was heading toward them from the crater, leaving a wake of dust and sand behind. The vehicle was packed with employees, or former employees, of the Keep. They looked like refugees.

Vicente waved from the window. Satya waved back.

"Me too?" Clay asked Ariella. "Aren't you taking me home?"

That wasn't part of the bargain. Besides, I have to take these little creatures home. Ariella nodded fondly in the direction of the young dragons frolicking on the tarmac.

"You mean you're taking them to the Other Side...."

Of course, he'd known it all along, but the reality suddenly hit Clay: When he'd agreed to let the dragons shut off access to the Other Side, permanently, he was saying good-bye to all of them. Including Ariella.

"I guess you could come with us," said Satya as they climbed down from the dragon. "But it looks like it's going to be a tight squeeze."

As the Land Rover pulled up beside them, a sound came from above. They covered their eyes to peer out into the night sky.

Something with blinking lights was approaching, flying in the opposite direction from all the dragons.

"That's not your dad's seaplane, is it?" asked Vicente, hopping out of the Land Rover.

Hardly daring to hope, Clay stared at the plane as it came to a rest about fifty yards down the tarmac.

"I don't seem to remember that thing having such big wheels," Vicente said.

Although, as you know, it didn't actually belong to Clay's dad, it was the seaplane, all right. But there was something different about it. Where before there had been long skis attached to the bottom of the plane, to keep it afloat in water, there were now four almost absurdly large wheels that looked like they had been pulled from a tractor.

"Well, now that your ride is here, we'd all better get going. I'll give you two a minute to say good-bye." Vicente shook Clay's hand, then started walking back to the Land Rover.

"Where will you guys go?"

"To another animal park, probably," Satya said. "But, you know, with animals."

"Yeah, I guess that might work out better," said Clay.

She gave Clay a quick squeeze. Then she and Hero went off to join her father.

Clay watched them go. Then he walked toward the weirdly repaired seaplane.

Owen met him with a hug. "I'm guessing the fact that you're alive means you were successful?"

"Mostly," said Clay, thinking about Flint and a few other loose ends.

"Mostly is usually as good as it gets."

Clay nodded at the truth of this. "So you got your plane out of the lava."

"Mostly..." He grinned, gesturing at the big wheels that had replaced the seaplane's skis. "And that's not the only surprise...."

I think I've had enough surprises, Clay thought. "Yeah, what else?" he asked warily.

Clay heard him before he saw him, sneezing and grumbling to himself as he stepped out of the plane: "It's all those dragons....I must be allergic! Can you be allergic to dragons? What's the collective noun for dragons, anyway? Not a flock. Maybe a herd..."

"Max-Ernest?"

Max-Ernest smiled sheepishly at his little brother. "Guilty as charged."

As they followed Owen back into the plane, Clay thought about how angry he'd been at Max-Ernest. For abandoning him for so many years, then avoiding him and not talking to him when they were finally reunited. For being so overprotective one minute, and then the next minute sending Clay on a crazy mission into the nest of the Midnight Sun. For so many things.

But he was too tired to confront his brother. Besides, there would be plenty of time to yell at Max-Ernest later, and Max-Ernest would have to grin and bear it; they'd be stuck in the plane for hours.

"Sorry it took me so long to get to you," said his brother when they were seated: Max-Ernest in the copilot's seat, Clay crouched behind. "As soon as I heard you were out here alone—I mean the first time you were here—I started looking for a ride to Earth Ranch. Only it's pretty hard to find any ships going anywhere near Price Island. So I had to settle for sitting in the hold of a Japanese fishing ship. Then rowing five miles..."

"You rowed five miles?" asked Clay skeptically.

"Well, one of the fishermen did," Max-Ernest admitted.

Clay wrinkled his nose. "Did you even shower afterward? You smell like crap."

"Not *crap*... *carp*. Which is an—"

"Anagram," Clay finished. "I remember."

Max-Ernest smiled. "Well, I taught you something, at least."

Clay laughed.

"So... I met Pietro," he said after a while.

Max-Ernest looked at him askance. "Pietro? But he's..."

"On the Other Side. Uh-huh. He told me he left you something in the lining of your hat. When you get home, you should look."

Max-Ernest eyed Clay, trying to ascertain whether his younger brother was pulling his leg.

"Actually, the hat's right in here," said Max-Ernest. "I never travel without it, remember?" He unzipped a battered black leather valise that looked like an old doctor's bag, and pulled out what resembled a black Frisbee. He shook it once; it popped into a top hat. "How 'bout that?"

"Nice," said Clay admiringly. "I forgot it did that."

"Now, let's see what we've got here." Max-Ernest put the hat on his lap and started feeling around. "Seems a little odd that I wouldn't have found

something that Pietro left in the hat over twelve years ago, but you never know, I guess."

There were several hidden pockets in the hat, and Max-Ernest started pulling out one thing after another: three playing cards (an ace, a king, and a joker); a half dozen magician's "silks" (i.e., scarves); numerous chocolate-bar wrappers (Clay saw jokes scribbled on a few of them, as well as a set list of tricks); a wilted carrot top (left there by Quiche the rabbit, no doubt); and what was unmistakably a pair of underwear (always good to have a spare, right?). From the very bottom, Max-Ernest scooped out a handful of coins, which he was on the verge of pocketing, when he stopped and held a nickel up to the light.

He flipped it around between his fingers, frowning.

"Could this be what Pietro was talking about? I'm pretty sure it's not mine...."

"What is it?" Clay asked.

"A trick coin. Both sides are tails. See?" Max-Ernest handed it to Clay. "But why would he leave it for me? You can get them in any magic store in the country. They're a dime a dozen. Well, a nickel a dozen in this case."

Clay tried to hand the coin back, but Max-Ernest wouldn't take it. He was obviously disappointed.

"You know, he was like a second father to me, Pietro," he said, shaking his head. "Then one day, poof, he's gone. All he leaves is a note saying he's going to the Other Side, and I never see him again."

Yeah, that sucks when somebody leaves like that, thought Clay, but with none of his usual anger.

"And now he wants me to have this old trick coin?" Max-Ernest complained. "Is that supposed to make me feel better? Remember him fondly?"

"Maybe it was like a good-luck charm for him?" Clay guessed.

"Maybe..." Max-Ernest shook off his grim mood and smiled. "Anyway, you keep it. If it gives you good luck, that's enough good luck for me."

"Okay, um, thanks," said Clay, pocketing the coin.

"You know the real reason I've been avoiding you, don't you?" said Max-Ernest suddenly.

"Uh, not really," said Clay, startled by the sudden turn of the conversation.

"Because I feel guilty for abandoning you."

Clay raised his eyebrows. "So basically you're saying you abandoned me because you abandoned me?"

"Makes a lot of sense, I know." Max-Ernest made the embarrassed half-laughing sound he made sometimes. *Hmghh.* "I won't do it again."

"Good... You know, you didn't really have to take care of me when you were a kid, but you did," Clay added after a moment. "So there's that."

"Sure I had to," Max-Ernest protested. "You're my brother!"

Clay shrugged, smiling. "Okay, fine. You had to. I guess that means you still have to."

Owen, who'd kept silent while the two brothers talked, now pointed out the window. "Look—"

Clay peered out the glass and saw a flock of birds flying in perfect formation back in the direction of the crater.

Earth Ranch might have been a magic camp, but it wasn't often that people performed magic in Big Yurt. Not stage magic, anyway.

When you could really read minds, seeing somebody pick your card out of a deck wasn't all that impressive. When you could levitate somebody with a spell, levitating someone with strings seemed a little pointless. As for the two-tailed coin, that hardly counted as a magic trick at all.

Nonetheless, the campers were charmed by Clay and Max-Ernest's show. They laughed a lot, anyway—sometimes *at* the two brothers, sometimes *with* them, and sometimes both.

For Max-Ernest, the performance was bittersweet, reminding him of the shows he had put on with Clay when Clay was five or six, and Max-Ernest not much older than Clay was now; but also, he was reminded of Pietro and *his* childhood performances with his brother, Luciano, the story of which had helped inspire Max-Ernest's own magic career, such as it was.

For Clay, it was bittersweet also. Sure, it had been fun, but he had the sense that it was the last time he would perform onstage. That was his brother's thing, not his. If there was magic in Clay's future, it wasn't the sort you did for an audience.

Afterward, Clay took Como for a walk up Nose Peak. With Como sitting on the ground beside him, Clay sat on the rock, watching the sun set, much as he'd watched the sun rise on so many mornings. And then, as before, the ever-sharp llama nudged him: In the far distance, in the middle of a pink cloud, there was a tiny speck. Clay could just make out the shape of wings, and for a second he thought it might be Ariella. But of course it wasn't; it was Owen. Owen had delivered Clay and Max-Ernest to camp more than a week ago and then left the next day on a supply run. Now it was time for him to take Cass and Max-Ernest away for good.

As he watched the plane grow bigger and bigger, Clay idly flipped Pietro's coin in the air over and over, letting it land in his open palm.

Tails.

Tails.

Tails.

Always the same side.

Suddenly, he closed his fist around the coin.

"That's it!" he exclaimed. "There's no other side!"

The llama looked blankly at him. Clay shook his head—"Never mind, *no importa*, it's a human thing"—but his mind buzzed with excitement.

He had figured out Pietro's message; he was sure of it.

Sometimes trying to get to the Other Side would get you nowhere; sometimes you had to bet on the side you were already on.

Clay jumped off the rock. He couldn't wait to tell Max-Ernest about his discovery.

With the irritated llama trotting behind, Clay ran down the hill, then jumped onto his newly repaired garbage-lid sled. As fast as he could, he slid down the scree-covered slope. But he slowed a little when he got near the bottom, allowing himself to enjoy the end of the ride.

There was no need to rush, he told himself. Max-Ernest would never leave again without saying good-bye.

APPENDIX

ENTOMOPHAGY: THE EATING OF INSECTS

Insects can be a great source of protein on the fly, so to speak. To get a significant amount of nutrition from most bugs, however, it's vital to eat more than one. *A lot* more. The nutrition facts below are based on a 100-gram (3.5-ounce) serving. Since ants can weigh as little as 1 milligram, a proper serving might be as many as 100,000. Of course, if you cover those ants in chocolate, as people do in many parts of the world, you won't have to eat nearly as many, and I think you'll agree they taste much better.

ANTS (RED ANT)

Nutrition Facts

Serving Size 100g

Amount Per Serving

	% Daily Value*
Fat 3.5g	5%
Carbohydrates 2.9	.01%
Protein 13.9g	28%

*Percent Daily Values are based on a 2,000-calorie diet. Your daily values may be higher or lower depending on your calorie needs.

Iron 5.7g

Calcium 47.8mg

BEETLES (GIANT WATER)*

Nutrition Facts	
Serving Size 100g	
Amount Per Serving	
	% Daily Value*
Fat 8.3g	13%
Carbohydrates 2.1g	.01%
Protein 19.8g	40%
*Percent Daily Values are based on a 2,000-calorie diet. Your daily values may be higher or lower depending on your calorie needs.	
Iron 13.6g	
Calcium 43.5mg	

* We may extrapolate that the nutritional value of Namib Desert Beetles would be similar.

TARANTULA (LARGE)*

Nutrition Facts	
Serving Size 100g	
Amount Per Serving	
	% Daily Value*
Fat 10g	15%
Carbohydrates 2g	0.1%
Protein 63g	126%

*Percent Daily Values are based on a 2,000-calorie diet. Your daily values may be higher or lower depending on your calorie needs.

* Technically, of course, tarantulas are not insects; they are arachnids. Nevertheless, they are reputedly delicious.

BAD WORDS

When Clay was a little boy, he and his brother used to call magic words *bad words*. To eliminate any lingering confusion, I am supplying a list of actual bad words. Use sparingly. For actual magic words you'll have to consult someone else.

XXXX

XXXX

XXXXXX

XXXX

XXXXX

DEADLINE

XXXXXX

EDITOR

XXXXXX

EMPTY (when applied to box of chocolates or chocolate wrapper)

XXXX

XXXXXXXXX

XXXXXXXX

GLOVE (white color assumed)

XXXXXX

MIDNIGHT SUN

MS. MAUVAIS

XXXXXXXX

XXXXXX

SHARE

XXXXX

XXXXX

THAT SOUND QUICHE MAKES WHEN HE'S OUT OF CARROTS

THAT WORSE SOUND PB MAKES WHEN HE'S OUT OF CHOCOLATE

XXXXXXX

VANILLA

WORK

XXXXXX

&^@!#%#$!*

* An unpronounceable but unmistakable dragon curse.

DRAGONS OF THE WORLD: A MAGIC TRICK

As you know, most dragons left our planet long ago. But I, Pseudonymous Bosch, sometimes known as the Great Boschini, have secretly implanted a dragon in your brain, and I have hidden it among the names of dragons from all over the world.*

To find this dragon rose among dragon thorns, carefully follow these instructions:

First, choose a two-digit number.

Add the two digits together.

Then subtract the sum from your original number.

(In other words, if your original number was 24, you add 2 and 4, then take the sum of those numbers—i.e., 6—and subtract it from 24.)

Last, take the number you end up with and find the corresponding dragon.

---

* These dragons include *Dreq* (Albanian dragon), *Ryū* (Japanese dragon associated with water and granting wishes), *Neak* (Khmer dragon with characteristics of a cobra), *Imoogi* (Korean ocean dragon), *Gyo* (Korean mountain dragon), *lindworm* (Scandinavian serpentine dragon), *wyvern* (a two-legged dragon most often seen in medieval heraldry), *Zilant* (the legendary dragon that symbolized the power of the Kazan Tartars), and *Slibinas* (Lithuanian hydra-headed, i.e. multiheaded, dragon).

0. Dreq	1. Ryū	2. Neak	3. Dreq	4. Imoogi
5. Gyo	6. Neak	7. Lindworm	8. Neak	9. Ariella
10. Lindworm	11. Wyvern	12. Imoogi	13. Zilant	14. Imoogi
15. Slibinas	16. Wyvern	17. Ryū	18. Ariella	19. Dreq
20. Wyvern	21. Zilant	22. Gyo	23. Ryū	24. Wyvern
25. Dreq	26. Lindworm	27. Ariella	28. Wyvern	29. Zilant
30. Slibinas	31. Neak	32. Wyvern	33. Ryū	34. Zilant
35. Imoogi	36. Ariella	37. Lindworm	38. Imoogi	39. Wyvern
40. Ryū	41. Zilant	42. Dreq	43. Slibinas	44. Ryū
45. Ariella	46. Imoogi	47. Ryū	48. Lindworm	49. Dreq
50. Zilant	51. Ryū	52. Gyo	53. Slibinas	54. Ariella
55. Slibinas	56. Ryū	57. Lindworm	58. Gyo	59. Neak
60. Ryū	61. Neak	62. Dreq	63. Ariella	64. Lindworm
65. Ryū	66. Imoogi	67. Ryū	68. Wyvern	69. Gyo
70. Slibinas	71. Ryū	72. Ariella	73. Dreq	74. Zilant
75. Ryū	76. Zilant	77. Wyvern	78. Ryū	79. Wyvern
80. Dreq	81. Ariella	82. Wyvern	83. Gyo	84. Dreq
85. Neak	86. Zilant	87. Lindworm	88. Wyvern	89. Lindworm
90. Ariella	91. Imoogi	92. Ryū	93. Zilant	94. Dreq
95. Slibinas	96. Dreq	97. Zilant	98. Neak	99. Zilant

Now turn the page to reveal the hidden dragon.

Et voilà! The dragon you wound up with was ARIELLA.

How can I control your mind all the way from my secret hideaway? A good magician never reveals his tricks. But I am not a good magician, so I will give you this hint: Flip back two pages and follow the instructions a second time, choosing a different number, and see what result you get.

Better yet, go back to the beginning of the book.

ACKNOWLEDGMENTS

One of the ~~best~~ **worst** things about writing anonymously, pseudonymously, and surreptitiously, as I do, is that I ~~get to~~ **have to** pretend that I write my books entirely by myself. As much as I might *want* to give credit where it's due, it is far safer for me to stay quiet. Any name I might mention is one more way for my enemies to try to track me down.

Nonetheless, after nine books, it is perhaps time to say a word or two on behalf of those who have supported me on the road to literary greatness. Or so the rabbit typing these words for me very strongly suggests. Who has been there, year after year, slaving away by your side, Quiche asks, always ready to lend a hand, or foot, or paw?

Well, Quiche, I hate to admit it, but you're right. It would be shameful not to acknowledge the hard work and dedication of the people who make the chocolate that sustains me as I—

Tussle—Quiche abandons typewriter—Pseudonymous takes over.

It seems that I have offended my rabbit somehow. Evidently, Quiche was *not* saying I should thank the chocolatiers of the world. Perhaps he meant the carrot farmers? What's that, Quiche—I should be thinking of something furry that lives in a top hat? Hmm. Do you mean I should be checking my hat for mold? It *does* need cleaning. . . .

If not chocolatiers, I suppose there are a few others I should thank. True, I'd rather not reveal their names, but perhaps I could put them at the bottom of the page. In very small type.

It seems fitting that I end this book with a footnote.*

---

* *Warning: This footnote is going to be very long. I have ten years' worth of thank-yous to cover. If that sounds daunting, or if you happen be part of a sinister secret society with the initials MS, please turn away.*

Pseudonymous Bosch was born not with a book but with a series of letters that I wrote to a fourth grader named May, as part of her school's adult volunteer program, Writing Partners. At the time, I had no idea that my musings about secrets, chocolate, and the pleasures and pitfalls of procrastination would lead to a novel called *The Name of This Book Is Secret*, let alone to The Secret Series or The Bad Books. If anyone had an inkling, it was May's mother, my friend Margaret Stohl, who'd forced me to volunteer at her daughter's school in the first place. In the years since, Margie has always been the one to push me kicking and screaming over the finish line whenever a book is due. Thus my books can truly be said to begin and end with her. At the risk of breaking an unspoken rule, thank you, Margie. You are the best friend a neurotic writer, or anyone, could have.

Many other generous friends have helped in the effort to push, and in some cases pull, my books along over the years, propping me up, tearing me down, and even reading drafts as the situation demanded. To name just a few of these long-suffering souls, I am grateful to: Michael Ravitch, Roxana Tynan, Nicole de Leon, Cara Tapper, Tania Katan, Melissa de la Cruz, Jennifer Lehr, and the best literary cheerleader in the world, Hilary Reyl. I have Hilary to thank for introducing me to my agent, Sarah Burnes, who took me on when Pseudonymous Bosch was barely a glimmer in my inner eye. Sarah has great taste (obviously!), manages to be optimistic and realistic at once, is tough when she needs to be, and is a good friend always. Thank you, Sarah, for helping turn a few half-formed pages into nine full-fledged books, each with its very own bar code.

When it came time to find a publisher, Sarah escorted me into an office tower, where we were greeted by a roomful of people in white gloves. As readers of my books can imagine, the gloves gave me quite a scare. I am glad to report that the people wearing them were not members of the Midnight Sun, but rather the enthusiastic, dedicated, and very talented staff of Little, Brown Books for Young Readers, who had decided to host a surprise party for us, replete with costumes and props for a flea circus–sized production of *The Name of This Book Is Secret.*

That was the day I met the editor of The Secret Series, Jennifer Hunt. A legend among her writers, Jennifer has unerring editorial instincts and a great smile. For years, her reactions served as a compass for me, telling me when I was on course or off. She was also my taskmaster, forcing me to write five books in five years when on my own I might not have written two. Thank you for cracking the whip, Jennifer. It was more than worth it.

Happily, when Jennifer left Little, Brown, I was not left adrift. Editor in Chief Alvina Ling has made sure that my books are well taken care of. The delightful and clever Connie Hsu edited the (intentionally) unfinished *Write This Book* and the first Bad Book, *Bad Magic,* helping make sense of my scattershot storytelling—a horrendously difficult task in which she was aided by Leslie Shumate. In the writing of the subsequent Bad Books, *Bad Luck* and *Bad News,* I have had the pleasure of working with a model editor and human being, Lisa Yoskowitz. I can think of no higher compliment than to say that I do everything she tells me to do; there are very few people, least of all editors, of whom I can say that. I'm not quite sure how she manages it, unless it is by knowing exactly how and when to soften me up with the perfect morsel of praise. Also, she's usually right. Lisa, I am putty in your hands.

I'm not suggesting that every single book of mine has been turned in months past deadline, but if that *were* the case, and if my books had nonetheless made it all the way to the bookstore in one piece, it would have been thanks to the infinite patience and expert juggling of LBYR's managing editorial team: Andy Ball, Jen Graham, Christine Cuccio Radlmann, and Amanda Hong. Here I must also mention a certain copy editor who is as generous with her time as she is exacting with her pen. Pseudonymous Bosch may be a grammar snob, but even he is prone to making the occasional grievously embarrassing ~~error~~ typo. Thank you, Barbara Bakowski, and please remember that any grammatical mistakes I may or may not make are to be kept strictly between you and I—er, *me*.

Over the years many young readers have told me how much they like the look of my books. I do, too. I feel very lucky to have worked with such inspired designers as Kirk Benshoff, Gail Doobinin, Maggie Edkins, Karina Granda, Sasha Illingworth, Alison Impey, and Tracy Shaw, not to mention creative director Dave Caplan. Readers also often compliment me on the artwork they see in the books. *Do you do the illustrations?* they ask. I shrug vaguely and change the subject. In fact, as much as I'd like to take credit, the illustrations in The Secret Series, and also in *Bad Magic*, are by the multitalented Gilbert Ford. From the very beginning I have marveled at how well Gilbert's quirky sensibility complements PB's. In a way, we have been collaborators in creating the world of The Secret Series and The Bad Books together. For the last two books, the interior art has been beautifully rendered by Juan Manuel Moreno. It is exciting to see the characters of The Bad Books take on this new life.

As of this writing, The Secret Series has sold well over two million copies in the United States alone, and both *Bad Magic* and *Bad Luck* have become *New York Times* bestsellers—a record that can fairly be called neither secret nor bad. For this success I place the blame squarely on Melanie Chang's team at Little, Brown. If I may be permitted to publicize my publicists, please applaud Lisa Moraleda and her colleagues Jennifer Corcoran and Jessica Shoffel. Lisa is one of the few people to have worked with me on every book I've written, escorting me from one coast to the other and sending me from school to bookstore to festival and back. Thank you, Lisa, for your unflagging efforts and for making the odd moment of tour downtime so much more enjoyable.

On the other side of the marketing and publicity equation are LBYR's crack marketeers Jenny Choy, Ann Dye, Nellie Kurtzman, Jennifer McClelland-Smith, Tina McIntyre, Stephanie O'Cain, Alice Morley, Adrian Palacios, Emilie Polster, and my fiercest competitor in sunglasses-wearing, Victoria Stapleton. Thanks, all of you, for spreading PB's secrets hither and yon and everywhere else. Thanks also to the sales team: Dave Epstein, Shawn Foster, and Chris Murphy. And production: Renée Gelman, Virginia Lawther, and Rebecca Westall. I know I am forgetting a few names; if yours is one, please forgive me. It's heartening, though a little hard to believe, that so many people are involved in what often feels like a solitary enterprise.

Of course, in the end, we all serve at the pleasure of Little, Brown's big brass: the publishers. Andrew Smith and, most of all, Megan Tingley, thank you from the bottom of the heart-shaped box of chocolates in my chest for all the support you have given me over the years. I am humbled—well, honored, anyway—by the trust you have placed in me and my books. After ten years, I consider you my friends and LBYR my home.

That almost wraps it up, except for a few thank-yous closer to my writing desk. Quiche may be the wind behind my typewriter, but my rabbit assistant has had human assistants of his own: Pablo Valencia and Shane Pangburn, or as I call them, Quiche I and Quiche II. Thanks, guys, for keeping PB up to date and up to snuff in his correspondence and online. Even with the help of specially trained penguins, we could not do it without you. Just try not to be quite so funny in the future. It's disconcerting.

I explained how PB's life began, but my own life as a writer began much earlier, inspired (against their advice) by my parents, both writers themselves. One of my very first jobs was writing a screenplay with my father, Roger L. Simon. Thank you, Pop, for an experience that taught me a lot about plot and character and, more important for a working writer, how to survive getting script notes from an angry employer. My mother, Dyanne Asimow, I cannot thank enough, so I won't. Suffice it to say she started helping me write stories before I could write them down myself, and she's never stopped helping me. She wouldn't even if I'd let her. Which I never would. I love you, Mom.

Finally, always waiting impatiently for me to finish, is my own family. We are two dads and two daughters, and I wouldn't want it any other way. Phillip, India, and Natalia, you are the best reason I can think of to start writing in the morning, and the best reason to stop at the end of the day. My love for you is in every word and in the spaces in between.

—Raphael Simon